WITHDRAWN

THE SOWER WENT FORTH

Book IV in the Leicestershire Chronicles–
Emily, now with a career, is married to Rory
and living in London, but theirs is a
tempestuous marriage, with the old
attraction between Adam and Emily still
simmering in the background. Adam
himself is in love with Emily, but has
fathered twins with the scheming Hattie in
Leicester. When Jed dies, leaving Rachel
unable to run her business without Emily's
help, the future course of events seems
inevitable...

THE SOWER WENT FORTH

THE SOWER WENT FORTH

by

Audrey Willsher

Magna Large Print Books
Long Preston, North Yorkshire,
BD23 4ND, England.

British Library Cataloguing in Publication Data.

Willsher, Audrey
    The sower went forth.

    A catalogue record of this book is
    available from the British Library

    ISBN   0-7505-1570-8

First published in Great Britain by
Severn House Publishers Ltd., 1999

Copyright © 1999 by Audrey Willsher

Cover illustration © Len Thurston by arrangement with
P. W. A. International Ltd.

The moral right of the author has been asserted

Published in Large Print 2000 by arrangement with
Severn House Publishers Ltd.

Magna Large Print is an imprint of Library Magna Books Ltd.

Printed and bound in Great Britain by
T.J. (International) Ltd., Cornwall, PL28 8RW

*With thanks to the Staff of Oadby Library
and the Leicestershire Record Office.*

1848

One

An April sun filtered through the smoke of a thousand London chimneys, was doing its level best to shine and Emily, her bonnet defiantly trimmed with the Chartist colours of red, white and green, and looking as if she meant business, linked arms with Rory, and watched her father do a quick head count. 'Well, how many do you reckon have turned up?' she asked.

'At a rough guess about two hundred, a decent enough number. Less and we'd have looked a bit foolish marching through the streets. We're bound to pick up more on the way, too.'

'That'll worry the old Duke. He thought we'd be so cowed by his threats of troops and guns, no one would put a foot outside their front door.'

'Well if I had my way, *you* wouldn't be here,' Rory put in.

Emily unthreaded her arm from her husband's and her mouth tightened. 'We've been all through that, and I'm marching. Like you, Rory, I have a constitutional right.'

'Get that look off your face, Emily, you know I'm talking sense. I don't suppose the military will be considering your rights when they have their pistols aimed at your head.'

Once a woman became a wife, she was expected to obey her husband, Emily was perfectly aware of that, but she was too independent by nature and she'd gone into married life determined to make her own voice heard, even at the risk of argument. 'I'm in no more danger than you and Papa,' she pointed out.

'She's right, you know.' Jed gazed at Emily with fatherly pride. 'Let her be, Rory. She's a chip off the old block, and you'll not change her now.'

'I'm coming to see that. But she might be killed.'

'In a good cause, though,' Emily shot back, determined to have the last word.

After only a day in their company, it was apparent to Jed that Rory and his daughter had a somewhat confrontational marriage, and he knew that this argument could go back and forth like a tennis ball over a net. But of course, two strong characters living under the same roof was always going to be a combustible mix. He just hoped there was enough love between them to stop it exploding into rancour. 'Come on,' he cajoled, in an attempt to dampen the rising tension, 'don't let's fall out. This is a day to show a united front. Wellington's a wily old devil and he's using the revolution on the Continent to put the fear of God into people with his talk of civil war.'

Rory's face darkened. 'And there could be yet if the military turn their guns on us.'

'I doubt they'll do that. The English are a tolerant race, and they can work out for themselves that we're fighting for their rights.'

Remembering the cruelty and oppression inflicted upon his people by the so-called tolerant English, Rory was about to explode this myth in his normal forceful manner when raised voices distracted him. For a while now the police and Chartist Executive Committee had been huddled together in discussion. Suddenly, however, Feargus O'Connor, who was the MP for Nottingham, broke free from the group and marched off in the direction of two waiting wagons.

Rory didn't have a high opinion of O'Connor, considering him a man full of bombast and bluster, but it was impossible not to admire his brave stand as the MP turned to the police and thundered, 'I'm leading this march to Kennington Common with or without your permission. Shoot me if you like, but if you do, I promise you my death will be avenged.'

The marchers waited, their glances moving from the police to the MP, while the horses, unaware of the tense situation, rattled their harnesses impatiently. But good sense prevailed and O'Connor and the other delegates were permitted to climb into the waiting wagons unmolested. It was a minor victory against the forces of oppression and O'Connor, the hero of the hour, was given a tremendous cheer of support. The MP acknowledged the crowds with a regal wave, then the horses, their manes and tails also braided with the Chartist colours and with their coats buffed to shining perfection, moved off and immediately the foot soldiers fell in behind them. To the steady rhythm of four hundred marching feet and singing the Chartist hymn, they wound their way out of Fitzroy Square, their banners, inscribed with the six points of the Charter, bringing a splash of colour to the dull streets.

'Universal Suffrage, Secret Ballot, Annual Parliaments, Payment of Members,' Emily recited. 'Are we demanding too much, Papa?' she asked, experiencing a brief lapse of faith. 'Have we really got much chance of achieving any of our aims today?'

'Don't be such a Doubting Thomas, of course we will. Although I'm not so sure about, "More Pigs and Less Parsons", I wonder who thought that up,' Jed laughed, pointing to one of the more bizarre banners. 'Some wag I suppose. Mind you, he's got a point. Getting rid of a few parsons would do this country of power of good and I've no doubt there's many a pig could deliver a far more interesting sermon than your average man of the cloth.'

But Emily also noticed more unsettling signs; closed shops and shuttered windows, which meant Wellington was well on the way to achieving his aims and turning the Chartists into terrifying bogeymen. The Duke still behaved like a soldier and she suspected he was spoiling for a fight, for he'd made it clear to the people of London that they were entitled to place themselves under arms to protect their property and families against the rampaging hordes. He'd also ordered government buildings to be defended by guns, as if we have the wherewithal to storm them, Emily mocked. But a twitchy finger on a trigger was a dangerous thing, so in the marchers' minds there lurked the knowledge that their lives could be cut short by a bullet today.

With an air of bravado but keeping their eyes skimmed, the procession turned into Tottenham Court Road to find it lined with Special Constables. Immediately the marching lost its rhythm and the singing tailed off. But when their sharp eyes saw that the Specials wielded nothing more deadly than truncheons, the marchers' confidence returned, along with some well chosen insults. 'Arse-lickers! Turncoats! D'you think yer armbands makes you important?' they jeered and waved their slogans provocatively under the enemy's noses.

The atmosphere was obviously still too threatening for some, however, and nudging her father, Emily muttered, 'We've got deserters,' and watched the ranks thin as several of the more cowardly slunk off into the crowds. But the gaps were soon filled: first some trade unions fell in behind and they were followed by a contingent of French Republicans singing the *Marseillaise*. Although few knew the words, the tune was catchy and they were soon whistling along with them. At the next corner they were joined by a dozen or so Irish rebels, whom Rory insisted on shaking by the hand. It was all good-natured, the onlookers seemed to find it a welcome diversion, and some of the dafter slogans brought a smile to their lips. Then suddenly, several youths charged round a corner. Yelling, 'Scum! Traitors!' they began hurling stones and cabbage stumps. Missiles rained down on them, hats were knocked to the ground, foreheads grazed but the marchers trod gamely on. Until a stone caught Rory hard on the temple, drawing blood.

14

Rory staggered back and clutched his head, but his reactions were quick and shouting in fury, 'I'll get you, you buggers!' He went to make after his assailants, who'd melted into the backstreets.

Just in time Emily managed to grab his jacket and pull him back. 'Don't play into their hands Rory, they've probably been planted by the authorities.'

But Rory's hackles were up. Dabbing the wound, he held out the bloodstained handkerchief for Emily's inspection. 'If I could find the culprit I'd wring his scraggy little neck. They could have killed me, you know.'

Although Emily thought this a slight exaggeration, she wisely didn't say so. 'Can't you see it's what they want, trouble, so that they can blame us?'

'I suppose you're right,' he admitted reluctantly, but the attack had made everyone more edgy and, gazing at upstairs windows, Emily was a aware of figures drifting out of the shadows to stare down at them, some with expressions of blank fear, others with hatred. Her instinct was to try and make herself invisible, but she held her head high and waved to the ghostly figures behind the curtains, determined to reach out and reassure them that the Chartists had no plans to torch their houses or murder them in their beds.

The two wagons had now come to a halt

outside the Chartist Land Company and they broke rank to watch Feargus O'Connor, walking with the bearing of a man aware of his place in history, disappear inside the building. When he reappeared he was accompanied by several men carrying five large bundles that looked like bales of tattered cotton.

Emily knew better, though, knew that these unimpressive bundles were the National Petition – yard upon yard of paper, which they would escort to the House of Commons – and their reason for being here. Some of the marchers pressed forward to touch the bundles reverently and glancing at her father, Emily could see he was having trouble keeping his emotions under control. 'Imagine,' he said, clearing his throat, 'over five million signatures, and forty-three thousand of them from Leicestershire. That's a real achievement and we should feel proud.'

'Yes, those fossilised specimens in Parliament are in for a surprise if they think they can ignore the will of the people for much longer,' Rory answered and forgetting their earlier spat, he gave Emily a jubilant hug then kissed her soundly.

'Right, it's a long way to Kennington Common, so I suggest we get moving,' O'Connor called to his troops, and they were lining themselves into some semblance of order when Emily realised her father was missing. 'Where's Papa?' she asked, looking around.

'Over there.' Rory pointed to where Jed was sitting on a wall. 'Today's been a long time coming and I think he's feeling a bit emotional. He probably wants a few moments on his own.'

But Emily didn't like the way her father's shoulders were slumped forward and as she approached him, she noticed that his lips had a pinched look. 'Papa, are you all right?'

Seeing no need to mention the bad pain in his arm, Jed gave his forehead a quick dab and leapt to his feet. 'I'm right as rain. It's a bit warm so I was having a breather before the next lap.'

'There's no law says you have to walk all the way if you don't feel up to it, you know?' Emily studied his face with some concern. He looked pale and was sweating heavily.

'My dear girl, this is an historic day. Democracy is within our grasp. Do you think I would forgo the chance to be part of it? I also owe it to the people of Leicester.' Jed took his daughter's hand. 'Now, come on or they'll go without us.'

Spectators continued to pour in from all over London and people were crammed tight as salt herrings in a barrel along the footways. En route they had collected a young musician and he skipped along at their head playing a penny whistle and collecting coppers in his cap. What with the flags and crowds, the procession had taken on the air of a jousting tournament. No longer fearful that her own nemesis might be round the next corner, Emily relaxed. The dramatic changes in her life, when she paused to think about it, still astonished her. She'd married Rory, moved to London, made new friends, found an interesting job, all in the space of a year. This perpetual round of activity helped to keep thoughts of Adam at bay, but occasionally a small incident, or perhaps a stranger in the street, would trigger a memory of him and sadness and regret would catch at her heart, leaving her drained and depressed. But then she would give herself a severe talking to, tick off in her mind the many times Adam had betrayed her, and thank heaven she had Rory for a husband.

'We're nearly at Blackfriars Bridge,' Emily heard her father announce, and shaking herself out of her introspection, saw masts and rigging ahead. Although she'd been careful to wear her most comfortable boots, by now Emily could feel every cobble and stone through the soles and when she reached the bridge, she was grateful that a five-minute rest was announced. Leaning on the parapet she gazed down at the murky surface of the river. The Pool of London was

18

crowded with vessels; many of them, taking advantage of high tide, were moving slowly down river towards the sea. A lighterman guiding his barge under the bridge, shouted up, 'Good luck,' and as he disappeared from view, Emily leaned rather precariously over the parapet and called back, 'Thank you!'

'Emily, for heaven's sake, do you want to fall in?' Rory's voice was in her ear and his hand was grabbing her shoulder and pulling her down.

Shaking him off she answered, 'There wasn't the slightest chance of me falling in.'

But Rory had other matters on his mind. 'Look, Emily, there's trouble ahead, like I predicted, and I want you to turn back now, while you still can.'

'Rory, stop treating me like a child.'

'I'm not, but I am thinking of your safety. There are two dozen mounted police stationed on the Surrey side of the river armed with cutlasses and pistols.'

'I can't see anything.'

'You must take my word for it. If they do decide to attack, there'll be serious injuries, limbs hacked off, stomachs split open, and they won't stop to ask what sex you are first.'

Emily imagined the feel of steel slicing her flesh, and battled with nausea. She also noticed that the crowd was growing fidgety. The patriotic songs had ceased and the

19

young musician had put away his pipe and moved off, as if already sensing that they were a defeated army. Life was good and she had no wish for martyrdom, but neither did she wish to become a widow nor lose a beloved parent. 'I'll go home on one condition.' She bargained.

'What's that?'

'You and Papa come with me.'

Rory's small reserve of patience was wearing thin. 'You know we can't, Emily.' As he spoke, he very firmly turned her round so that she was facing the City side of the river, then gave her a small shove. 'Do as I say, woman, and go home.'

'Let her be, Rory,' Jed intervened. 'We've done nothing to provoke an attack and there's a huge crowd to act as witnesses. We also have Feargus O'Connor. The police would be wary of injuring a member of her Majesty's Government.'

Rory's face darkened. 'Why do you always side with Emily? Well, if she gets killed it will be your responsibility. I'm washing my hands of her.'

A conspiratoria glance between father and daughter further in furiated Rory and he stomped off towards the head of the march. Emily could smell the sour odour of sweat as the nervous tension rose, knew the marchers didn't want to be seen as cowards, but guessed they were probably weighing up the pros and cons. It had all been good fun so far, but was the Charter a cause worth losing a limb or a life for? they might be asking. Their problem was resolved when Rory returned. 'The police are letting us through,' he shouted over the heads of the crowd and the disquiet eased. Whether it was through his intervention or merely coincidence, Emily never discovered, but a short while later they were permitted to cross the river. Edging their way past the silent but challenging mounted police, the marchers eyed their cutlasses and pistols nervously. Once past them they struck out confidently again, and finally reached their destination at about half-past eleven.

Two

By the time the marchers reached Kennington Common the excitement was like a bomb waiting to explode. A triumphal arch of flags and banners greeted them, brass bands thumped out tunes and the cheering of the crowds was so intense, Emily feared for her hearing at one point.

Gratified at the public's open support, Rory's humour had returned. 'Well, Parliament will find it hard to ignore this reception,' he commented, when the parade finally came to a halt.

'And all achieved without any violence, in spite of their predictions,' Jed replied.

But after this it all seemed a bit of an anticlimax. Various delegates stood up to speak, but the noise was so intense they might as well have saved their breath. Then a rumour began to circulate that O'Connor had been arrested. Immediately the mood darkened and ripple of unrest ran through the crowd. Emily was beginning to fear that the day might indeed end in strife when the MP himself appeared on the podium. But it soon became clear that he'd come to an arrangement with the police, when he disclosed that only he would be permitted to accompany the Petition to the House of Commons.

'Traitor!' several dissenting voices shouted, then a bunch of young men moved towards O'Connor in a threatening manner. But he had faced more dangerous situations than this and he stood his ground.

'This is the last thing we want, war within the ranks,' Jed exclaimed, for the atmosphere was extremely volatile; blowing hot and cold by the minute. Then suddenly and blessedly there was small cloud-burst. Jed held his palms upwards to receive the rain. 'Thank heaven, this will cool their passions,' he said, and laughed as he watched the young thugs, defeated by the vagaries of the English weather, run for cover. The rain broke the meeting up, the crowds dispersed and the only violence was a bit of elbowing in the rush for cabs.

'Come on Papa, let's find some shelter, or we'll be soaked,' Emily urged and the three of them ran, heads down against the driving rain, towards a large plane tree. But several people had beaten them to it and they were not going to budge for anyone.

Rory, however, had other ideas. 'Excuse me, please,' he said and, making good use of his shoulders, he forced a way through for them. But the tree wasn't in full leaf, so there was little protection and they stood there with the rain dripping coldly down their necks. 'I'm going to see if I can find a cab to get us home,' Rory said at last and disappeared across the Common. When, after ten minutes, he still hadn't returned, Emily began to grow concerned for her father, who was wet through and shivering with the cold.

'Where on earth can Rory have got to?' she complained, peering out at the rain-sodden landscape.

As if in answer to her question, a voice called, 'Emily, over here,' and she saw Rory beckoning from a cab.

'Coming,' she shouted back, grabbed her father's arm and guided him towards the cab.

'Not so fast, Emily,' Jed protested and paused to get his breath. 'You forget, I'm not as young as you.'

'Sorry, Papa,' she answered contritely, and slowed her pace.

'Come on, up you get,' Rory ordered, when they reached him and, stepping down, he assisted them into the blessedly warm and dry cab. Jed sank back against the cushions and closed his eyes, Rory gave the driver the address of their rooms in Soho and off the horse trotted.

'Well, it's been quite a day,' Jed observed, opening his eyes again.

'And a tiring one,' Emily replied,

searching her father's face. He still looked drawn and she could imagine her mother's anger if she sent him back to Leicester with a chill. Rachel had never shown much enthusiasm for Jed's political activities but she was becoming increasingly set against it and she'd made it quite clear that at 'his age' her husband should no longer be gallivanting off to London on some wild scheme that would probably come to nothing. With this in mind, Emily was concerned to get her father back to their lodgings and out of his wet clothes. Rubbing the steam off the cab window, she peered out. 'We're in the Strand, so not far now. As soon as we're home I'll light the fire and make us something to eat.'

'That sounds nice, because without exaggeration, I could eat a horse,' said Rory.

'I'm afraid you'll have to settle for a pig, dear, rashers to be exact,' his wife replied as they drew up outside Number 10, Franklin Street.

Their lodgings – or more precisely, two rooms – were located on the first floor and while Rory paid the fare then went to buy some beer, Emily hurried her father up the stairs. The living-room was large, the furniture shabby, the carpets well-worn, but their windows looked down into the hub of Soho: its sleaziness, its wickedness but also its sheer vibrating life, which continued night and day without ceasing.

Emily's first priority was to get her father warm, so she sent him into their bedroom to change while she lit the fire. By the time he emerged from the bedroom, she'd got it going and Jed extended his hands towards the flames gratefully. 'My, that's good to see,' he said, and Emily was relieved that his face had regained some of its colour.

'There'll be something to eat as well in a minute, so sit yourself down,' she said as she placed rashers of bacon in the frying pan and they began to sizzle.

Rory came in with the beer and stood sniffing appreciatively. 'Mmm, that smells good,' he remarked, then finding two tankards, he poured beer for Jed and himself and sat down. The rain rattled against the window, the coals glowed brightly in the grate and the two men sat supping their ale companionably and discussing the day. Emily turned the rashers with a fork until they reached a crispy perfection, then placed them between slices of bread. She was handing the plates round when there was a bang on the door and a male voice called,

'Anyone at home?'

'Oh no!' Emily exclaimed, as she saw their quiet domestic evening receding.

Without waiting to be asked, a face appeared round the door and Rory called jovially, 'Come in, Edmund, come in.'

Behind Edmund was his young lady, Prudence, who was anything but prudent, in Emily's opinion, and she had little time for either of them. They had rooms above them and Edmund called himself an artist. To Emily, his canvases appeared to be nothing but crude daubs, a view not shared by the painter himself, who was convinced of his own genius: an unrecognised one as yet, because so far he hadn't made one sale. Edmund lived on a small allowance from his father, which he topped up by scrounging off his friends and he had an amazing ability to smell a free dinner. He always arrived empty-handed but, mystifyingly, Rory appeared to find his company congenial.

Edmund advanced to the fire sniffing like a hound. 'Is that bacon I smell?'

'It is,' Emily replied and bit quickly into her sandwich.

'Sorry we can't offer you any, old chap,' Rory apologised through a mouthful of bread, 'but we haven't eaten all day. Emily will make you some toast, though, won't you my dear?'

'No I will not,' Emily snapped back. 'I'm hungry, too, you know.'

Rory's eyebrows rose at his wife's lack of hospitality and a touch ashamed, Emily thrust the toasting fork at Prudence. 'Here, if you want some you can do it yourself.'

'Ta.' Quick to make herself at home, Prudence cut thick slices of bread and speared one on the end of the toasting fork. She burnt the first piece, slung it aside and giggled, 'Silly me.'

When she reduced the second slice to cinder as well, Emily, growing agitated at the waste, snatched the fork back from her. 'Let me do it,' she said and wondered what they ate at home. When she first met them, Emily had been shocked to discover that Prudence was not only one of Edmund's models but also his mistress, and living with him openly. However, there were frequent fights, mainly due to Edmund's infidelity. 'Listen, they're at it again,' Rory would remark as thumps and screams were followed by the sound of crockery bouncing off the wall. As the fight grew in intensity the ornaments on their mantelpiece would have little convulsions. This was a signal to Rory and Emily to cast their gaze upwards, and they'd watch as the crack in their ceiling slowly lengthened another inch and a sprinkling of plaster like a light snowfall descended, covering everything. And the swearing! Words so crude, they'd make a sailor blush.

'You watch, Prudence will storm out in a minute,' Rory would prophesy, and sure enough, a short while later a door would slam then Prudence would make off down the stairs shrieking, 'And don't think I'm coming back!'

She always did, though, much to Emily's disgust. 'Why does she stay with that pig when he treats her so appallingly?' she would fume.

'Because the alternative is the streets,' Rory would point out.

'Well, it's not fair!'

'It's an unjust world, Emily.'

'Yes, especially for women,' she would snap back and, remembering Adam and his treatment of her, Emily wondered if men were ever capable of being faithful to one woman.

She looked across at her husband now. Was he? Ashamed of her doubts, she turned away. Of course he was. Rory loved her, she loved him, there was no reason for him to look elsewhere and only a fool would risk putting a happy marriage in jeopardy.

But for a girl like Prudence, without the protection of marriage, the world must seem a hostile place at times and Emily felt a sudden rush of feminine sympathy for her. Regretting her earlier churlish manner, Emily handed Prudence a perfectly toasted piece of bread along with a kindly smile. Edmund's toast she cooked with considerably less care. 'There you are.' She thrust the toasting fork at him.

'Prudence, butter it for me,' he ordered

indolently, and Emily's mouth tightened as the girl jumped to his bidding. What she saw in Edmund was a complete mystery to her, for he was thin and pale as a lily with oversized feet and pink, crusty eyelids which looked as if he hadn't bothered to wash the sleep out of them. But then, she had to concede, Prudence was no beauty either. Her figure was good, but she had frizzy black hair, heavy eyebrows which met across the bridge of her nose and an unfashionably large mouth. However, in spite of these handicaps men appeared to find her attractive.

'Well, how did the day go?' asked Edmund. He bit into his toast, then stretched his long legs towards the fire, effectively cutting off the heat to everyone else.

'If you'd come and given your support, like you promised, you'd have found out,' said Rory.

'We meant to but I'm 'fraid we overslept,' answered Prudence.

'Well, to start with it was pretty tense. We were half expecting someone to take a pot-shot at us from a window, but it all passed off peaceably in the end. And O'Connor was presenting the Petition to the House this afternoon. After that it's only a question of time before the Charter is the law of the land,' said Rory in a confident tone.

'Does that mean I'll be able to vote soon?'

asked Prudence with a bright smile.

'Women? Vote? You must be joking,' Edmund sneered. 'They haven't the brains for it.'

'I consider my brain power equal to yours, Edmund,' Emily said coldly. 'So don't insult me, particularly when you've just accepted my hospitality.'

The colour shot up Edmund's neck at this reprimand. 'Sorry Emily,' he mumbled, 'I didn't mean to offend you.'

'But Prudence is fair game, is that it?'

'Well you've got to admit it,' he drawled, talking as if Prudence weren't in the room, 'she is a bit of a dunderhead. England would go to the dogs if girls like Prue were ever allowed to vote.'

Edmund took a perverse delight in insulting his mistress and watching the girl's shoulders slump dejectedly. Emily knew it was her duty to speak up on her behalf. 'This Charter might only give men the vote, but take it from me, women won't be far behind in their demands. And I don't want to frighten you too much, Edmund, but one day they'll even be standing for Parliament, won't they Papa?'

'Yes, dear, of course,' Jed agreed, while trying to suppress a yawn.

'You're tired, aren't you, Papa?' Emily studied her father with concern.

'A little,' Jed admitted, 'but then we did

walk a fair old distance today.'

Seizing the opportunity, Emily went to a drawer and pulled out blankets and a pillow. 'I'm sorry, I'll have to ask you to go, Edmund. My father's exhausted, and the sofa you're sitting on is his bed.'

Edmund stood and stretched. 'Pity, I was just getting comfortable. And that's a good fire.'

'Haven't you got one?'

'What with gettin' up late and everythin', I never got round to lighting it,' Prudence confessed. 'Still, we've got our love to keep us warm, ain't we?' She wound her arms round Edmund. 'Come along me darlin'.'

'Hold on a minute,' said Rory and stepped out on to the landing with them and pulled the door to. While she made up her father's bed, Emily could hear a discussion going on between the three of them and a moment later Rory's head reappeared. 'The night is still young so I'm going for a drink with Edmund, if that's all right with you, Emily?'

Emily punched the pillow hard but didn't look round. 'Perfectly.'

'Why can't Emily come too?' Jed called after his son-in-law.

'Hush, Papa, I don't want to spend an evening in Edmund's company. I'd far rather stay and talk to you.'

'If I can keep my eyes open long enough,' Jed answered, eyeing the lumpy sofa. Still, only two more nights of loose springs jamming into my ribs, he thought to himself, then I'll be back in my own bed. And with my darling Rachel's comforting warmth beside me, perhaps this wretched pain in my shoulder and arm will ease.

'Go and get ready for bed, then, and I'll warm some milk up for you,' Emily said, concerned that she had allowed her father to overdo it today, and would therefore get a ticking-off from her mother. She didn't want her father to go back to Leicester with tales of Rory, either, so to show how little his desertion bothered her, she hummed a little tune while she heated the milk, poured it into a cup and grated nutmeg over the frothy surface in exactly the same way as her mother did.

'Here you are, Papa,' Emily said, turned to give the drink to him, only to find that he was stretched out full length on the sofa, fast asleep. Well, she thought, no point in wasting it. Stirring up the embers of the fire, Emily sat down and slowly slipped the milk. It tasted of childhood ailments, and of lying in bed being pampered by her mother. Emily yawned over its warm spiciness. It had been a long day. But a successful one? Well, that remained to be seen. All she knew was that right now bed and sleep were calling. Finishing the milk, Emily stood up, kissed her father, made sure the blankets were well tucked in, whispered, 'Goodnight, Papa,' then tiptoed into her own bedroom.

It was cold away from the fire so she undressed, climbed into bed and immediately felt wide awake again. I'll read for a while, Emily decided and picked up a book. But it was hopeless. A deep resentment against Rory was building up inside her, and she found it impossible to concentrate. Why had Rory gone off like that, with those two worthless characters? she fumed. Was he bored with her after only a year of marriage? Did he find them more entertaining companions, or what? She turned these questions over and over in her mind, but reached no satisfactory conclusion. The church clock struck ten, cab wheels clattered over cobbles in the street below, and when someone called goodnight, Emily eased herself up expectantly in the bed. But Rory didn't walk through the door and his side of the bed remained empty. *Oh, go to hell,* Emily muttered, blew out the candle and pulled up the bedclothes round her ears to cut out sound. But the darkness fuelled her imagination, unease replaced anger and she was no longer a neglected wife but a widow. In gruesome detail she saw Rory sprawled under the wheels of a cab, his handsome features smashed to a bloody pulp of bone and flesh by the hooves of a horse. In great distress she shot up in bed and screamed, 'No!' into the darkness.

'Emily? Are you all right?' her father called in a sleepy voice from the other room.

'Fine,' Emily reassured him, 'It was a nightmare, go back to sleep.' Telling herself she was a fool to worry, she fell back on to the pillow and eventually drifted off, and by the time Rory slid in beside her smelling like a whisky still, Emily had already been asleep for several hours.

Instead of relief, when Emily awoke the following morning and found Rory asleep beside her, she was consumed by a deep resentment at the unnecessary worry he had subjected her to. But the last thing she wanted was her father returning to Leicester with tales of matrimonial disharmony, so she curbed her tongue until she had given him his breakfast and he'd left to visit her brother Ben and his wife Maggie in Lambeth. She watched from the window until he was out of sight and, ready now to give Rory a piece of her mind, she went to wake him. 'And where exactly did you get to last night?' she asked, shaking him vigorously. 'I was worried half out of my mind.'

'Go 'way,' Rory slurred.

'A hangover, I might have guessed. But what can you expect when you spend your evening with that fly-by-night, Edmund?

And let me guess who paid.' Emily bent and picked up Rory's trousers, which were lying on the floor, and shook them. A couple of coppers fell out and rolled away to the other side of the bedroom. Incensed, she bent her lips to his ear and, exaggerating each syllable, hissed, 'How are we to live if you spend all your money on scrounging friends?'

Rory groaned and disappeared further under the blankets, but Emily showed no pity. Slamming out of the bedroom, she called over her shoulder, 'You'll be late for work, but see if I care.' Which was what she had no intention of being, so after swallowing a cup of tea, she tied on her bonnet and set off for her place of work.

Rory hadn't shown much enthusiasm when she'd first ventured the idea of looking for employment, obviously feeling it would reflect badly on his ability to support a wife. But Rory had a vast circle of friends, many of whom seemed to find their way to their rooms most evenings. Rory was also generous to anyone down on their luck. In fact it often alarmed Emily how little she had left in her purse at the end of the week. It would have helped, she often thought, if the loans were sometimes repaid. However, when she voiced her concerns, Rory had a ready answer. 'They helped me out when I was without work, I'm just repaying their kindness, Emily.'

Knowing that to disagree with this would have made her look mean spirited, Emily had let the matter drop. Anyway, her main reason for seeking employment was boredom. The novelty of being a wife, of shopping, cleaning and cooking, soon wore off. Domesticity, Emily decided, did nothing to stretch the brain. Of course a baby would have kept her occupied, but nothing had so far happened. When, after a few months of marriage, she'd expressed her disappointment at their childless state, Rory had surprised her by saying, 'Don't fret, my dear. I'm in no hurry to hear the patter of tiny feet. Children cost money, they also curb your freedom, so let's enjoy it while we can,' and with that, he'd whisked her off to the theatre.

Leicester folk weren't the sort to flaunt their wealth, so when she first arrived in London, Emily had been dazzled by its brightly lit streets, the large emporiums full of every describable luxury, fine carriages and fashionably dressed crowds. She'd tramped the streets gorging herself on culture and visited the National Gallery and British Museum so many times, she felt she knew every painting and artefact these great buildings possessed. But it was also on these journeys that she first glimpsed the dark underbelly of London and quickly concluded that London was an elegant façade hiding misery and corruption. She was taking a risk, she knew, poking around in such dangerous areas as St Giles and the Fleet Ditch but it opened her eyes, for the squalor outclassed even the worst slums in Leicester. Emily's compassionate nature was also moved by the plight of the hundreds of prostitutes who hung around Soho. Many of the women were old but others had hardly reached maturity, and in their knowing young faces Emily saw the ghost of Mary Todd. Although Mary's death had been an act of God, it remained a rebuke to Emily. She and Rory had a good relationship – well, most of the time, she reminded herself – and sex with a loving partner was a joyous experience, but to her mind, to surrender one's body several times a night in some dark alley for a handful of coins must be like a small death. With a shudder, Emily turned her thoughts to more pleasant matters. Her New Situation.

As soon as she'd made the decision to seek employment, Emily had started scanning the advertisement columns of *The Times*. She was beginning to despair of finding something which matched her capabilities when one morning she saw what looked like the ideal job. 'Wanted', the advertisement read, 'young woman of sound character and education to assist lady. Must write a good hand. Testimonials will be required. Apply in writing to Mrs Montague Haig, 2 Broadwick Street'.

Emily had sat down right away, got out pen, ink and paper and in her neatest script, gave a good account of herself; explaining how she was the daughter of a bookseller, with an education that had continued until she was past fourteen. She had then walked round to the house and pushed the letter through the door, noticing as she did so that it was a well maintained house, and obviously occupied by only one family.

Emily had prepared herself for a long wait, so she was surprised when a reply came from Mrs Haig the next day, inviting her to an interview at three o'clock on the following Wednesday afternoon.

Determined to make a good impression, Emily had immediately taken herself off to the china baths. Fashions in London were way ahead of Leicester and she had felt quite dowdy when she first arrived in the capital. But setting off to Broadwick Street in a new gown that was lined and stiffened with cotton, so that the skirt swung as she walked, Emily considered she was a match for any London girl. She had also taken the precaution of using the services of a crossing sweeper before risking her kid pumps to the hazards of horse droppings and rotting vegetables. Even so, they were a little less pristine than she would have wished when she finally reached her destination. She gave the door a rat-tat-a-tat with the fine brass knocker shaped like a dolphin, then stood back, smoothing her gloves nervously. A maidservant appeared, Emily gave her name and was shown into a room that was obviously used as an office, for it was cluttered with books, journals and papers.

'How do you do, Mrs Aherne.' Emily, who was trying to read the titles on the spines of some of the books, swung round, somewhat startled by the stentorian tones and saw that Mrs Haig was almost six foot. 'Please take a seat,' the lady invited.

'Thank you.' Emily looked around in vain for somewhere to sit.

'So sorry, Mrs Aherne.' Mrs Haig scooped up a pile of books and dropped them on the floor. 'As you can see, I'm in dire need of help. I have trouble throwing things away, but I never find the time to sort stuff out and the maids are forbidden to touch as much as pencil shaving.'

Trying to maintain an air of calm, Emily had sat down on the edge of one of the chairs and watched Mrs Haig go behind her desk and pick up a bundle of letters. 'These are the applications I've had.' She waved them in the air. 'Unfortunately some of them could barely spell, so I was particularly impressed with your credentials, Mrs Aherne and your handwriting is excellent.'

Emily had then relaxed slightly and eased herself back in the chair. 'Thank you, Mrs Haig.'

'You see, I'm a novelist, and I do need someone with a degree of competence. With your father owning a bookshop, you might have heard of me. I write under the *nom-de-plume* of Loveday Morell.'

'I certainly have.' Emily had just about managed to mask her astonishment because the name had always conjured up a delicate young creature with a penchant for pink silk and lace, not a woman with the shoulders of a prize fighter. 'Your books are extremely popular, particularly with young women. In fact our circulating library can barely keep up with the demand.'

Flattered as Emily intended she should be, Mrs Haig had beamed. 'Oh, that is gratifying to hear.'

By now Emily had sensed the job might be hers, so she was perturbed when Mrs Haig then handed her a sheet of paper and a pencil. 'I'd just like you to take some dictation,' she'd said. Since she'd never done anything like this in her life before, Emily was resigned to making an absolute hash of it, and as Mrs Haig proceeded to rattle off a page from one of her own novels, Emily's palms began to sweat. The pencil slipped, but sheer determination had kept her going. She was not going to lose this job. The lady halted at last and Emily had stared in dismay at her indecipherable scribble, wondering what Mrs Haig would make of it. However, she had only asked Emily to read it back and there her good memory came to her rescue and she managed it without too many glaring errors.

'I have one or two more applicants to see, Mrs Aherne, but of course I shall let you know as soon as possible,' Mrs Haig had said, before she was shown out. She was like a cat on hot bricks for the next few days, then at last the letter Emily had prayed for arrived, offering her the position of secretary at a salary of ten whole shillings a week, which seemed like a fortune, and she had danced around her room with delight imagining all the little luxuries she would now be able to afford to buy for her and Rory.

Emily had now been with Mrs Haig for three months. Rory allowed her to keep her wages and she loved the independence this gave her, although she made sure that not a penny of it found its way into the pockets of Rory's friends. Stepping out into the street this morning, she shook off the last vestiges of resentment towards her husband and paused to watch Soho going about its business. It was as if yesterday's march had never happened. Shops had reopened, costermongers cajoled and berated possible customers, and the little barefooted match-girl stood at her usual spot.

'Buy some lucifers, lady,' the small girl pleaded, and out of pity Emily put her hand in her pocket, although she already had quite a store of them at home. It wasn't the most salubrious of areas and Soho's dark alleys housed misery, poverty and crime. But Emily loved its diversity and the way different cultures managed to live cheek by jowl, without animosity. If only nations could be like that, she ruminated, the world would be a more peaceful place.

The previous night's rain had cleared away some of the more disgusting odours and the air seemed almost fresh. Emily inhaled the smell of freshly ground coffee, then called, 'Good-morning, Mr Mantelli.'

Mr Mantelli, who was standing in his shop doorway, kissed the tips of his fingers dramatically. 'My beautiful signora, gooda morning.'

Emily laughed and walked on, but the compliment made her hold her head a little higher, even if Mr Mantelli was on the elderly side.

Mrs Haig was already at her desk writing when Emily arrived. She knew better than to interrupt her employer when the muse was upon her, so without a word, she took the pages of manuscript from the extended hand, then sat down and started to make a fair copy of Mrs Haig's untidy scrawl. When she had finished, Mrs Haig would deface the pages with alterations and Emily would rewrite it: again and again, until her wrists ached and Mrs Haig was satisfied that her prose was polished enough to be set aside, ready for the manuscript to go to her publisher.

Mrs Haig wrote spectacularly lurid Gothic romances for which the public seemed to have an insatiable appetite. Emily guessed she must make a reasonable living because she supported three children and her husband, Monty, who had some unspecified ailment which prevented him from having a job, but somehow allowed him to indulge in his favourite pastime of horse-racing.

At eleven o'clock Mrs Haig laid down her pen, rubbed her neck and fingers tiredly and bid Emily good morning as if she had, at that minute, arrived.

'I had the most splendid idea for a plot which I had to get down, but now we can relax for a while and enjoy our coffee,' she said, smiling at Monty as he came through the door bearing a tray. This was a daily task, and hardly onerous, but Mrs Haig doted on her husband and when he'd placed the tray on the desk, (he didn't over exert himself by pouring it, too) she cooed, 'Oh, you are a good boy, come here my little pet and let Mummy reward you,' and flinging her arms around his neck she kissed him soundly on the lips.

Emily, who had long since stopped being embarrassed by this display of affection, poured the coffee and handed it round. As she sipped hers, Mrs Haig asked, 'Now, what are you going to do with yourself today, dearest?'

While he considered this question, Monty bit into a piece of cake. 'I thought I'd pay a visit to my tailor, then I might pop round to my club, sweet one.'

Mrs Haig beamed. 'Good. Go and enjoy yourself and I'll see you at dinner.' Then, picking up her pen, she said to Emily in a more businesslike tone, 'Now, shall we continue?'

Walking home later, Emily mused on their strange relationship. Mrs Haig toiled while her husband played. She earned while he squandered. It didn't seem right somehow. But then all marriages were unique, she supposed. Look at her and Rory. During the course of the day she had decided that she had behaved vilely towards her husband and she would now go home and make it up to him. After all, what had Rory done that was so terrible? He'd gone out with friends, drunk more than was good for him and arrived home late and with a hangover. It was what men did every day of their lives, and therefore hardly worth falling out over. Deciding that as a peace offering she would buy him something tasty for supper, Emily stopped off at the baker's for a loaf of freshly baked bread, found a stall selling whelks and jellied eels and finally popped into Mr Mantelli's, where she purchased a selection of cheeses.

She was surprised to see her father already back from Ben's and asleep on the sofa. He didn't stir, and gazing down at him she realised, with a tug of her heart, that he was looking older these days. He'd always been so vigorous, so deeply involved with life, it was almost impossible for her to accept that he was mortal like everyone else. But the idea of her father dying didn't bear thinking about. Stop being so morbid, Emily rebuked herself, he's not sixty yet and still hail and hearty. He'll be around for years, making trouble, getting up the noses of those in authority, doing his level best to improve the lives of people unable to speak up for themselves. She smiled to herself and put the kettle on, and the familiar ritual of tea-making, the clink of teaspoons, the sound of water being poured into the pot, woke Jed. He opened his eyes, stretched and sat up. 'A cuppa, just what I need.'

'How has your day been, Papa?' Emily

asked, as she handed him a cup and sat down beside him.

'Very enjoyable.'

'And Ben and Maggie, how are they?'

'Ben seems to be doing well with his printing business, I'm glad to say and Maggie is blooming. They both send their love. It was such a pleasant day I decided to walk back from their place and of course, it was a little further than I imagined, so when I sat down I was out like a light.'

'It's been a busy few days altogether.'

'Indeed it has. In fact I've decided to return home tomorrow, if that's all right with you?'

'But I've arranged for Ben and Maggie to come over for supper tomorrow evening.'

'Well ... er ... they send their apologies but they won't be able to make it.'

'Why ever not?' Emily jumped to her feet, poured herself more tea, then swung round to face her father. 'Go on, tell me, what's their excuse this time?'

'Maggie is near her time and doesn't want to move far from home.'

'What rubbish! The baby isn't due for another two months.'

'Well, they did say they'd be very pleased to see you and Rory one evening.'

'Hypocrites. The truth is they don't like our arty friends and that sister-in-law of mine has turned my brother into as big a prig as herself!'

'Come on now, be a little charitable,' Jed remonstrated.

Emily shrugged. 'Well, I don't really care about them, but after all the work you've put into it, I thought you'd at least stay and see the outcome of the National Petition.'

'I feel I've left your mother to cope in the shop on her own for long enough and it's not fair.'

'Natalie's there, she's old enough to help,' Emily pointed out although, sensibly, she knew she shouldn't be trying to delay her father. He was tired and it was natural he should want to go home.

But this debate was interrupted by Rory. Hurling himself into the room he flung himself down in a chair and Emily's first thought was that, as she'd predicted, he'd lost his job. Her mind began to leap around in panic. Destitution loomed. What would they live on if he became unemployed? Her wages would barely pay the rent.

Bracing herself, she waited to hear the worst but Rory's silence finally forced her to speak. 'Rory, what on earth's the matter?'

Rory slowly lifted his head as if it were too heavy for him. 'I've been talking to O'Connor. It seems the Petition was treated as a great joke in the House, particularly when our demands were read out by the Clerk.'

'Is there to be no debate?' Asked Jed.

'Yes, but not until Friday. And laying it on the table, O'Connor isn't hopeful. All he got was jeers and laughter when he asked if there was any hope of the extension of the vote. That's how seriously those cretins in Parliament take it.'

Emily, who had listened without speaking, was ashamed of the relief she felt that it was the Petition rather than Rory's job that was in jeopardy. 'We mustn't give up hope,' she said lamely.

'Hope? What good is hope?' Rory snapped. 'A few barrels of gunpowder up their arses, that's what they need.'

'Hush, Rory.' It was treasonable language and Emily glanced round the room as if a spy might materialise from the shadows.

'Well, Russell won't be Prime Minister for much longer if he ignores five million signatures,' Jed put in robustly, for if the Petition failed, all the years of hard work by dedicated Chartists like himself would have been in vain, and this was something he found impossible to contemplate.

'Don't bank on it. These aristocrats cling on to power.'

They talked on like this, going over old ground, until Emily grew tired of it and went to prepare their supper. She tried to keep up a lighthearted conversation as they ate, but it was a waste of time. Rory remained glum and she sensed he was none too pleased when Jed told him he was going home the next day.

Her job prevented her from seeing Jed off at Euston, and the next morning, Emily found herself struggling not to become tearful as she kissed him and helped him into the cab that would take him to the station. 'Give Mama and Natalie my love and we'll come up for a few days just as soon as we can arrange something,' she promised, then stood feeling unaccountably desolate as her father's hand emerged to give a final wave before the cab disappeared round a corner. Her sadness stayed with her until she reached her place of employment, where she bumped into Mr Haig on his way out. He lifted his hat, bade her good morning and Emily noticed that overnight, his greying locks had been transmogrified into a raven black. Emily returned his greeting, managed to hide her astonishment, but as she stumbled into the house, she was quite unable to hide her mirth at Mr Haig's astounding vanity.

However, there was little else to lighten her mood in the following days. Rory remained resolutely downcast. He railed against the Government, Lord John Russell, Wellington; went to the debate in the House of Commons on the Friday and came home in a foul temper, which was not helped by his excessive drinking. 'They laughed the Petition out of the House, said that many of the signatures were bogus. They're liars, of course. I ask you, who with any sense, would forge Queen Victoria's name, or Robert Peel's or Mr Punch's? It's my bet it's that lot who planted them.'

Emily wondered sometimes if she was failing Rory by not responding sufficiently to his misery. But then she'd tell herself that her own sense of frustration at the injustice of the present political system was equal to Rory's, but *she* didn't react by throwing even more ale down her throat. What she did know was that they mustn't be defeatist and let the Chartist dream die, and she shared her father's philosophy that they had to go on petitioning Parliament and fight, fight, fight until the bitter end. However, when she expressed these views to Rory, they were not well received. Particularly when she added, 'And as far as I can see, Rory, continually getting drunk creates, rather than solves problems.'

Standing up, he pushed the chair back with his foot and glared at her. 'Oh, who says so? Anyway, I'm not staying here to be nagged at.'

Rory had never spoken to her so disrespectfully before and she was struck dumb with disbelief. But worse was to come, and when the man who professed to love her ran upstairs and called loudly to Edmund, 'Come on auld fella let's really upset my disapproving little wife and go out and get soused as herrings,' to protect her pride, she had to tell herself it was the drink talking. Once he came out of his depression it would be the old Rory again, fired with enthusiasm, planning speeches, writing pamphlets and they'd regain that sense of comradeship that had always been such an important part of their marriage. But as the days passed and neither Rory's rage, nor drinking showed any sign of abating, Emily decided enough was enough. She was ready for a showdown when the letter came from her mother that was to act as a catalyst. '...*I pleaded with your father not to go to London and I was right because since returning home he's been utterly exhausted. In fact, he spent two whole days in bed, which is unheard of, but the stubborn man wouldn't allow me to call the doctor, saying I was making a fuss about nothing...*'

There was a strong tone of rebuke in her mother's letter and Emily felt a lurch of guilt. She suspected that the march had been rather too much for her father, but he was a proud man who refused to accept the ageing process, so if he had taken to his bed he must have been feeling pretty bad. A sudden cold feeling caught at Emily's heart. But exactly how ill was he? Well, there was only one way of finding out, she decided, and that was to go and see him. With a sudden urgency she started stuffing clothes into a bag. It was Saturday, she needed her mind putting at rest and Rory was, as usual these days, out. If she left now, she could be in Leicester in about five hours and back in about the same time on Sunday. It was such a brief visit, she would hardly be missed by Rory – even supposing he returned home tonight.

Emily counted the coins she kept hidden away in her drawer for such emergencies into her stocking purse, and it wasn't until after she'd purchased her ticket and was about to board the train at Euston that she remembered she hadn't left a note for Rory.

Three

Trains couldn't always be relied upon to get passengers to their destination in time but, by a stroke of good fortune, even the change at Rugby went smoothly and Emily was in Leicester by the middle of the afternoon. She took one look at the line of people waiting for cabs, decided it would be quicker to walk, and set off at a brisk pace down Granby Street. This being Saturday, wagons and carts jostled for space as families, dressed to the nines, drove in from outlying hamlets and villages; the wives to shop, the men to do a bit of business and the children to spend their pennies on tooth-rotting sweetmeats. Although the town was busy, after a year in London, Emily was struck by the leisurely pace of everything. People had time to stop and pass the time of day, several acquaintances greeted her with a warm, 'Nice to see you, me dook,' and the Midlands dialect, familiar and reassuring, reminded Emily that she was back among her own kind. She remembered too her first contact with the alien cockney accent, and how it was weeks before her ears became attuned to the harsh vowel sounds.

'Emily!' It was a voice she recognised calling to her and Emily looked up to see Clare dashing across the street. Delighted to meet up so unexpectedly the two young women embraced then, standing back, regarded each other with real affection.

'Oh, it's lovely to see you,' said Emily.

'I thought my eyes were deceiving me for a moment. But you look splendid, and very fashionable,' Clare observed. 'Marriage obviously suits you. But what are you doing in dull old Leicester?'

'I've come to see my father, he's poorly.'

'Oh, I am sorry. Nothing serious, I hope?'

'We had the big Chartist meeting in London, which you might have read about in the papers. Papa came down for it, over-exerted himself and I sense my mother is blaming me. So this visit is to make amends, although she's been married to my father long enough to know that he does exactly as he pleases and what I say doesn't have much influence.'

'Will I be able to see you while you're here?' Clare asked. 'We've got heaps to catch up on.'

Emily guessed that foremost in Clare's mind was Adam, and she probably imagined that she was eager for news of him. But she didn't want to hear his name mentioned in her company, ever. 'It will have to be another time, I'm afraid. You see I have a job now, so I have to return to London tomorrow.'

'In that case, I'll walk a little way with you.'

Determined to steer the conversation away from personal matters, Emily asked, 'So tell me, how is the school going?'

'Marvellously. It was the best idea Aunt Tilda ever had. Although of course, it couldn't possibly have succeeded without Christopher, who's a brilliant teacher. In fact we have so many pupils we're outgrowing the cottages, and the idea now is to try and raise funds to build a proper school. It's Christopher's ambition to teach every village child to read and write.'

'That would certainly be some achievement.'

'Yes, what we need is an altruistic gentleman of means to come along and endow the school. Since this is unlikely, Aunt Tilda has come up with various ideas for raising money and the first is to be a charity dinner at Trent Hall. Freddie's up at Oxford now, and the house seems empty without him but there's still no sign of any babies of our own, I'm afraid.' Clare gave a small disappointed shift of her shoulders. 'And there's Hattie Bonner with two.'

All the saliva dried up in Emily's mouth. 'Two?'

'Sorry, didn't you know? She had twins. Both boys, Luke and Aaron. She's like the goose that laid the golden egg. And I suppose she has in a way, with a nicely furnished cottage near us and nothing to do except look after her babies. Aunt Tilda swore blind she would have nothing to do with them, but that was before they were born. Also, Adam has vowed he will never marry again.' Here, Clare paused and gave Emily a sideways glance. When there was no reaction, she went on, 'So when my aunt realised they might be her only grand-children, she changed her tune and they are taken to visit her at the Dower House at least twice a week. Hattie, it goes without saying, has never been allowed set foot in the house, much to her chagrin. It annoys me that, putting all the blame on poor Hattie. Adam wasn't exactly an innocent lad, and after all those years in America he must have known how many beans make five. And he's as responsible for those little lives as Hattie. Besides, taking advantage of a serving girl shows pretty poor taste,' Clare ended snobbishly.

Yes, bedding her while vowing he loved me. But then, that is the way of men, Emily thought bitterly.

'But of course, Aunt Tilda has always been blind to her dear boy's faults,' Clare con-tinued.

'And no girl was good enough for him, either!' Emily shot back and immediately felt annoyed with herself. Her outburst could so easily be misinterpreted and the last thing she wanted was for Clare to think she still cared for Adam.

'Except Isabelle, which just shows you that my aunt isn't a very sound judge of character. I wonder what happened to her,' Clare mused. 'Do you think she is still in England?'

'No, she was quite an adventuress, but she wouldn't risk staying here, it would have meant prison. I imagine she's found fresh hunting grounds on the Continent.'

They were half way up the High Street and although Emily didn't want to hurt Clare, who was a dear friend, neither did she wish to prolong a conversation that was stirring up so many old hurts. It came as a barely disguised sense of relief then, when Clare paused and exclaimed, 'Oh, my Lord, I've just realised, I promised to get some linen in Sharpe's for Aunt Tilda. I'd better rush before it closes.' She pecked Emily on both cheeks, then gripping her hand said earnestly, 'We mustn't lose touch. Promise me you'll write and I'll keep you up to date with all the news?'

Emily gave a noncommittal smile. The less she knew of Halby and its inhabitants, the better she liked it, and the last thing she needed was reams and reams of Adam's, Hattie's and Matilda's doings. However, such bluntness would hurt Clare, so taking the coward's way out she answered, 'Rory and I are coming up to stay later on in the year. You must pay us a visit while we're here, then we can have a really long chat.'

'You'll let me know the exact date, won't you, because of the school?'

This was the easiest of promises for Emily to make, and after a final goodbye, she escaped into High Cross Street. Further along the road the sign, Jedediah Fairfax, Bookseller, creaked backwards and forwards in the breeze, and she hastened towards it, at the same time struggling with the grim reality of Adam's bastard sons. One was bad enough but *two?* It was illogical, Emily knew, but the fact that Adam's seed had produced twins made it seem like a double betrayal. But then there had been so many betrayals, what was one more? I hope they're ugly and grow up into horrible monsters, she thought spitefully, and immediately felt a stab of shame. What sort of person was she, casting her malign spell on poor innocent babes like some wicked godmother? But that was the trouble with coming back to Leicester; much as she fought against it, the past was always going to haunt her. And all that poppycock about Adam never marrying again. Emily gave a snort of disbelief. The gentry were a pragmatic lot and a man was judged by his acreage, not his morals. The odd bastard child was neither here nor there and would always be accommodated. The size of the estate was what counted and it wouldn't be long before Adam was snapped up by some sharp-eyed young woman.

Emily was about a hundred yards from the shop when the door opened and a young woman she might not have recognised if it hadn't been for her flame-bright hair, stepped out into the street. 'Natalie,' she called, and the girl turned with a puzzled expression. Then, realising who it was, she galloped up the road towards Emily, grinning with pleasure.

'I thought I was seeing things for a moment. What are you doing here? And where's Rory?' Natalie gazed over Emily's shoulder.

'He couldn't come, I'm afraid,' Emily lied and noticed Natalie's face fall. She and Rory had a particularly close relationship and, although she'd never visited Ireland, influenced by stories Rory told her of the hardship and the English repression, Natalie now identified strongly with its people. 'And I'm only stopping the night,' Emily went on. 'Mama's letter worried me, she said Papa hadn't been well and since I feel partly responsible, I had to come and see for myself.'

'He did have a bad chill, but he's up and about now.'

'I thought it was more serious than that?'

'Well, nothing to make you come all this way.'

'But he's been in bed?'

'Yes, but only for a couple of days.'

'Only? It's unheard of for Papa to take to his sickbed.'

'Yes, I suppose it is,' Natalie agreed then, the subject disposed of, she pressed her shoulder against Emily's and asked, 'Do you think I've grown?'

'You certainly have. Why you've nearly caught up with me and there you are, not even fourteen yet.'

'I soon will be.'

'Not until Christmas. And don't wish your life away Natalie. You'll be wondering where it's gone soon enough.'

'But I do so want to be grown up. And I hate school!'

'You'll probably look back on these years as the best of your life,' Emily prophesised.

'The most boring you mean. I want to be older so that I can do exciting things.'

'Such as?'

Natalie shrugged. 'Oh, you know, go to Balls. Visit you in London on my own. Or maybe I'll go and fight for the Republican cause in Ireland.'

Emily laughed. 'I should stick to Balls, they are much more fun.'

'I have to get away from Leicester.'

'Come on, it's not that bad,' Emily chided, the town's virtues having grown since she'd been away.

'Yes it is, it's dreary! And were your schooldays the best years of your life? Be honest now.'

Emily considered Natalie's question carefully. 'I enjoyed school and my only worries were childish ones, like not knowing my times table and being afraid of the dark. When you grow up everything becomes much more complicated.'

Natalie peered into her sister's face. 'In what way?'

But Emily was not prepared to share the secrets of her heart. Patting Natalie's cheek playfully, she answered, 'You ask too many questions, young lady,' then, to deflect further questioning, pushed open the shop door. The bell gave its familiar tinkle, she inhaled the slightly musty smell of old books and tooled leather and knew she was home.

Her mother, who was serving a customer, looked up and her eyes widened in surprise, then delight. 'Emily, what are you doing here?' Abandoning the customer, she rushed round the counter to embrace her daughter.

'I've come to see Papa. Your letter worried

62

me. But I can only stay the night.'

The gentleman her mother had been serving cleared his throat rather pointedly, and Rachel, with profuse apologies, went back to tying up the books he had purchased. 'My daughter,' she explained unnecessarily, then to Emily, 'Go on up and see your father, I'll be along in a bit.'

Emily was behind Natalie and when her sister opened the door, she was slightly reassured to see her father sitting by the fire with a blanket draped over his knees, reading.

'Look who's come to see you, Papa,' beamed Natalie then, quite the little mother, she went over and tucked the blanket more firmly around her father.

Jed lowered his book. 'Good heavens, where did you spring from?'

'Well, that's a fine welcome,' Emily laughed. Dropping her bag, she planted a kiss on her father's forehead.

'Did your mother write to you?'

'Yes, she did.'

Jed clicked his tongue in irritation. 'Well, I don't know what she's been telling you, but let's say you didn't have to come all this way on my account.'

'I felt responsible because she said you were exhausted after the march and had been in bed.'

'Piffle! You know your mother, she always

63

exaggerates. A few sneezes, that's all. And of course, the news from London has depressed me.'

'It's depressed us all.' *And Rory resolves it by drinking heavily,* Emily thought resentfully.

'But don't think a few ignorant men in Parliament will stop us here in Leicester. Midlanders are made of sterner stuff. Further meetings are already being arranged and O'Connor is paying us a visit in May.'

'Oh, that's good news. Perhaps I'll come up for that meeting and we'll go together?'

'If you go, it will be on your own,' Rachel interrupted from the door. 'Your father's health isn't up to it, and I'm finally putting my foot down. He's worn himself out in the cause of politics and I've also had to put up with his absences. Now it's time to call a halt.'

Emily glanced at her father, waiting for him to contradict his wife. There was no way he would agree to give it all up. Politics was his life's blood. Instead, to her astonishment, he said, 'Your mother is right, it's time for someone else to take up the reins. But come in May, just the same, because I'll want to hear about what O'Connor has to say for himself and you can report back to me.'

'Good, that's settled then,' said Rachel

and trying not to look smug at her victory, she began laying the table for tea.

If the journey from London to Leicester had been straightforward, returning was quite the opposite. There was an hour's wait for the connection at Rugby, and when they did get underway the train started and stopped so often Emily decided she could have walked the distance more quickly. Then there was the usual scramble to find a cab, and by the time Emily paid the driver and wearily climbed the stairs to their rooms, it was almost ten o'clock.

In her mind's eye, she'd seen herself returning to chilly, empty rooms, with a fire that had long since gone out, so she was rather taken aback when Rory leapt from a chair.

'Emily where on earth have you been? I've been half out of my mind.'

'Well, that's usually my privilege, so it makes a change.' Emily removed her bonnet and mantle and went over to the fire. She was hungry, travel weary and cold and in no mood for a confrontation with Rory. He'd let the fire burn low, so she banged it back into life with a poker, added a few sticks and some coal, waited for it to catch, then placed the kettle on the flames.

'Emily, I asked where you've been.' Rory's tone was hard-edged with anger.

'If you want to know, I went up to Leicester to see Papa. He hasn't been too well.'

'Why on earth didn't you leave a note?'

'It slipped my mind,' she answered casually.

'Slipped your mind? I've been sitting here imagining you dead or abducted. Did you give no thought to that?'

Emily turned and her tone was as chilly as her expression. 'Actually I didn't. No more than you consider me when you go off to carouse the night away with your friends.'

'That's different.'

'Oh, in what way?'

'Well, you know I'll come home.'

'I'm never that certain. But apart from my feelings, what about your job? The paper won't put up with your poor timekeeping forever.'

'It was this business with the failure of the Charter. It knocked me for six,' Rory retorted, failing to mention that he had already been given one warning by the editor, told to pull his socks up, or else. 'The Government treat the people of this country – and their demands – with such utter contempt, is it a wonder I drink?'

'It hardly solves the problem, though, does it Rory?'

'I'm turning over a new leaf, I promise.' Looking suitably contrite Rory moved closer, wound his arms round Emily and kissed her lightly. 'Am I forgiven?'

'I suppose so. But it had better not happen again,' Emily warned. 'I'm not very good at acting the understanding wife.' She rubbed her forehead wearily, but the sound of the kettle whistling on the hearth lifted her spirits.

Having survived the journey on bread and cheese packed by her mother, she was longing for a cup of tea.

But Rory had started unhooking her dress. 'You look tired. Shall we go to bed?'

'I'm dying of thirst, I must have some tea first,' Emily protested, knowing what was on his mind. But Rory was already pulling her towards the bedroom door. 'Tea can wait. I'm dying for something else.'

With a sigh Emily surrendered to his demands, thinking to herself, after all, what was a cup of tea compared with trying to mend the cracks so visibly appearing in their marriage?

Four

Her sons were her one great achievement. Hattie watched them punching their little fists in the air like boxers with a deep sense of maternal pride. She could see already that they'd go far – they had that fighting spirit – plus they'd been sired by the son of one of the best families in the county. And the bloodline was good, strong and pure like the best English ale. 'Mark my words, you'll grow up into fine handsome young men, just like your papa,' Hattie promised, then picking them up she smothered their plump little faces with kisses. They responded by grabbing at her hair and giving loud gurgles of delight. Totally immersed in their perfection, she swung back and forth in the rocking chair. 'Oh my little angels, your mummy does love you,' she cooed, and kissed them again, inhaling their soft, sweet milky smell with a sense of joy and wishing she could stop all the clocks in the world so they'd remain this age forever, dependent on her and without sin.

Although there had been some queer goings on with that Isabelle, what with her trying to poison Adam, then her being already married and everything, in a roundabout way it was her she had to thank for her present situation. And it could all have turned out so differently, Hattie mused, gazing round her cosy, shining cottage. She had no parents to support her and girls in her situation were usually disowned. Adam, typical man, had tried to wheedle his way out of his obligations and if it had been left to him, she'd be living in Birmingham now, isolated and among strangers.

At six months the boys were sturdy and Hattie's arms were soon aching from the combined weight of them. She laid them back down in their cradle, gave them their coral gum-sticks to suck then, to remind herself of her good fortune, she ran her hands along the waxed surface of the Welsh dresser, which she polished once a week with beeswax and turpentine, and pinged her forefinger and thumb against the blue and white crockery hanging from the hooks. The Windsor chairs had come from the big house, and she didn't have to put up with cold flagstones, oh no, because a large carpet covered the floor. Not the usual rag thing either, but a fine Turkish rug with an intricate design of flowers and trees.

Yes, Hattie thought a trifle smugly, I've fallen on my feet, no doubt about it. In fact, more than she could have dreamed of. Mrs

Bennett had provided a more than adequate layette for each infant, plus a weekly allowance to ensure that her grandchildren wanted for nothing. A piece of wisdom Hattie had often heard quoted, was that it was better to be born lucky than rich and she would agree, for she deemed herself extremely fortunate. But she still nursed ambitions, hadn't given up on the idea of a small shop in Leicester, wasn't improvident and managed to put a bit by each week. Her one regret was that her boys had been baptised and recorded in the Parish Register as Aaron and Luke Bonner, rather than in their rightful name of Bennett. Not that it was any secret who their father was, except that he never came near his sons, or her, and yet Adam had liked what she had to offer well enough in the past. Indeed, could still have, for he'd be very welcome to leave his boots under her bed. Except that he was a cold customer with, Hattie had long ago concluded, ice for a heart.

A small clock chiming two reminded Hattie that she should be on her way. 'Time to be thinking about your visit to Grandmama, my bonnies,' she informed her sons and put the smoothing iron on the fire. While she waited for it to heat, she took each child to her breast, changed their tailclouts and powdered their chubby bottoms. Hattie could imagine *her up there*, just looking to find fault, scrutinising every detail of their dress, so she made sure that she sent them up to the Dower House sweet-smelling and spotless. With their day caps and gowns ironed to perfection and looking the picture of gurgling baby innocence, Hattie placed them in the stick wagon and tucked several shawls well in to protect them against the hazards of too much fresh air.

Daffodils in cottage gardens, golden as sunshine, dazzled the eye, green leaves were unfurling from the sticky buds on the enormous horse chestnut tree on the Green and winter was behind them. Deciding there was little risk of the twins developing a chill, and to give as many villagers as possible the opportunity to share in her joy of them, Hattie took the longer route round the Green. Disappointingly, the only person to show the slightest interest in her boys was Mrs Dowse, recognised as being the source of all village gossip.

'My they're handsome young tikes,' the woman remarked, peering over her garden gate at them.

'Who do you think they favour, Mrs Dowse?'

'Why their papa, of course. And maybe someone a bit further down the line,' she added slyly.

'You mean their grandfather? The old

71

Squire?' Hattie asked, keen to emphasise her children's exalted position in the social structure of the village.

Mrs Dowse gave a knowing laugh. 'I well remember the day Mr Adam were born. Premature, they said.'

Hattie was all ears now.

'Hasty marriage it were, too. And a mystery why a pretty young thing like Miss Matilda should choose to tie herself to a drunken widower of fifty. We found out soon enough, though. Halby folk might not have a lot of larnin' but they can count up to nine.'

'Are you saying that the Squire wasn't Mr Adam's pa?'

'Could be.'

'Who is then?'

'I'll leave you to work that out but it shouldn't take long, for it were at the time of the great Battle of Waterloo. They think it's all forgotten, but I tell you it in't. The Pedleys, with all their airs and graces, came from nothing. There's lots more, too. Miss Clare that was, well her ma were a bit soft in the head, and Miss Matilda's brother took advantage of her. Nature's bin kind, not giving her any babbies of her own, 'cos more than likely they'd have come out monsters, fit for nothing but the circus.'

Hattie shuddered. She liked a bit of tittle-tattle, but this talk of monsters was gruesome. Terrified the woman's shadow might cast a malignant spell on her little innocents, she edged away. 'I'd better go,' she said and dragging the wagon after her, she made off up Blackthorn Lane, unsettled by this worrying news. The dynastic implications of Mrs Dowse's disclosure set Hattie's brain whirring like a spring on an over-wound clock. If Adam had been fathered by a nobody and the Pedleys weren't up to much, where did that leave her babies? As Hattie had discovered, it was amazing what dirt you could dig up by keeping your eyes and ears open, like she had with that whore she'd worked for – more than she could have imagined, in fact. If it hadn't been for her, Adam would be dead now, and yet he hadn't even had the decency to thank her. There was gratitude for you.

In her concern for her children's blood-line, Hattie had failed to notice the poor state of the lane, until a sudden jolt on her arm brought her to a halt. 'Blast it!' she cursed when she saw that the front wheels of the wagon had jammed themselves in a deep, hard rut. She yanked at the towing bar. But at six months the twins were no lightweights, and wheels wouldn't budge. Then the boys, taking exception to this rough treatment, began to scream. 'Hush,' she murmured and waved their rattle in

73

front of them. But they wouldn't be pacified. 'Why is it,' she asked, addressing her question to a nearby herd of cows, 'that when you need help, the world empties of the human race?'

One of the cows gave a sympathetic moo, then almost on cue, Adam came striding out of the drive into Blackthorn Lane. When he saw her, he paused and gazed about him in panic. Hattie knew exactly what was on his mind: he was planning to make a bolt for it, and this really riled her. She noticed, too, that he managed to avoid looking at his sons, even though they were screaming their heads off.

'Don't worry, you won't turn into a frog if you look at them,' Hattie taunted, infuriated by his indifference to his own flesh and blood. Adam coloured, but refused to be drawn and instead began to edge away. This was just too much for Hattie. Of late she'd been trying to improve her diction but that was forgotten and all the months of pent-up resentment poured forth 'Can't you see we're stuck, you self-centred bugger? Are you really goin' to leave me and the babbies here and not even try and help us? Huh, so much for your so-called breeding,' she snorted.

'I ... I'm sorry, I ... didn't realise,' Adam apologised and grabbed hold of the towing bar.

'No, there's a lot you don't realise, but one of these days...' Hattie didn't finish. She hadn't enough to go on and besides, what she had to say would have more impact when she had the full facts.

With one deft movement, Adam released the wheels from the rut, and the babies stopped crying. 'There you are.' He handed to towing bar to Hattie, then, his conscience obviously smiting him, he asked, 'Which is Aaron and which is Luke?'

'Well they're not identical. Luke's the dark one and he's got your eyes.'

Adam took a closer look. 'So he has.'

'You can come and seen them whenever you like. You'd be made very welcome,' Hattie said very pointedly.

'Well ... er ... umm...' Adam stammered, at the same time observing Hattie from the corner of his eye. She was less hefty round the hips than she used to be and she looked quite pretty in a pink-cheeked, country girl sort of way in the mulberry coloured wool dress she was wearing. Or perhaps in his lonely miserable state, he was endowing her with a beauty she didn't possess. A hayloft and an image of Hattie's soft accommodating body floated across Adam's vision. *Get a grip on yourself, for heaven's sake,* he admonished himself. Look where your urges landed you last time. A few moments pleasure for a lifetime of remorse, with the consequences right here in front of your eyes. He knew Hattie thought he was a cold-hearted devil with no feeling for his sons, but really it was shame. He'd fathered two children who would always carry the stigma of illegitimacy. It was unlikely Hattie would ever find a man willing to marry her and Emily must loathe him. Lord, what a trail of destruction. But he did recognise his responsibilities and he'd made generous provision for his sons in his will. Adam had never had much of a taste for whores and on the occasions he'd gone with one he'd always spent the following day despising himself. His mother was always hinting – well, more boldly stating – that with the estate needing an heir, he should be on the lookout for a wife, although after the fiasco with Isabelle, he had little interest in marriage. But sex was another matter, and he wasn't cut out for the celibate life, so why should he deny himself? He glanced again at Hattie. She was growing more comely by the minute. *No! No! for God's sake don't,* a residue of good sense warned somewhere in his head. In haste to remove himself from temptation, Adam lifted his hat. 'Good day to you, Miss Bonner,' he said, as if she were a mere acquaintance rather than the mother of his children, and strode off, his back stiff with resolution.

Hattie watched him with a complacent

smile. She knew Adam well enough to guess the general drift of his thoughts and his tussle with his conscience. But men were guided by that thing between their legs and if he wasn't getting it anywhere else, it was her betting that one dark night soon, there would be a tap at her door. Growing more ambitious, she thought, and why shouldn't he marry me even? As the idea took root, Hattie's eyes glazed over. Mrs Adam Bennett. Imagine. She had two lusty sons to take over the estate, was working hard at trying to talk properly and she'd always closely observed the ways of gentry, knew how to behave at the table, which knife and fork to use. And she was no whore, which was more than could be said for that so-called wife of his. And what did the family have to crow about when it came down to it? His mother was a jumped-up nobody who'd had to marry in a hurry. No better than her really, just luckier to find a willing cuckold. And to think, she had the nerve to forbid her to push her own children up to the House, as if her feet would contaminate the ground, whereas her darling boy was blameless, pure as the driven slush, thought Hattie cynically. 'Well, we'll soon see about that, won't we, my boys?'

'Come on Hattie, get a move on.' The young kitchen maid, Nell, whose task it was to escort the twins up to the Dower House, was standing in the middle of Blackthorn Lane, beckoning impatiently and no sooner had Hattie reached her than she began to complain in her whining voice. 'I've bin stood here ages and I'm perished.'

'I couldn't help it, I got held up.'

'Yeah, so I could see, havin' a good gab with the Master. Trying to lead 'im astray again are yer?' The girl gave a sly snigger.

Hattie grabbed the girl's collar, furious that she had hit the nail so accurately on the head. 'One more remark like that and I'll slap your stupid face. Is that clear?'

Nell nodded dumbly, seized the towing bar of the wagon and fled, bumping the babies unceremoniously over the rutted cart tracks. 'And see they are back here by five o'clock, on the dot,' Hattie threatened, 'or I'll come up to the Dower House and collect them, whether Madam likes it or not.'

'Don't tell me, Hattie Bonner, tell the missus.' Now that she was at a safe distance, Nell found the courage to answer back.

Hattie felt like pursuing the girl and shaking her hard, but her particular worry was that Nell would start blabbing to the other servants. And if Lady Muck got wind of her schemes she'd probably have Adam spirited away somewhere safe.

To fill in her time, Hattie continued on up Blackthorn Lane. Since she started work as a skivvy at Trent Hall when she was twelve

78

years old, Hattie's days had been spent occupied with work and the company, bickering and companionship that went with it. Now she was in a situation which was neither one thing or the other and she often felt lonely. Leisure didn't come easily to her and without the twins to occupy her, the rest of the afternoon stretched aridly ahead.

Even walking at a snail's pace, Hattie had soon reached Thatcher's Mount, where Blackthorn Lane petered out. She paused and stared at the house, remembering past inhabitants and how strongly disliked Joseph Pedley had been in the village. Although not as much as his son who, if Mrs Dowse was to be believed, had been as dangerous as a sackful of snakes. And how much of this bad blood coursed through her boys' veins? It didn't bear thinking about really, particularly when she remembered her own pa, whose one notable achievement was to have been rarely sober. Supposing all the bad on Adam's side of the family and all the bad in hers was mixed up in them? Thinking about it made her fear for her babies and their future. She did so want them to grow up into young men she could be proud of, not debauched ne'er-do-wells. But then, Hattie mused, we might have our failings, but neither Adam nor me is bad and it's upbringing that counts. If I'm a good mother and instil into them manners and morals and a consideration for other people, they'll probably turn out all right. Her mind a little more composed, Hattie was about to turn back when a small dog rushed up to the gate and, leaping up and down like a rubber ball, began to bark frantically.

Although small, it looked ferocious and Hattie was backing away nervously when a voice commanded, 'Jelly! Stop that noise immediately!' and Mrs Harcourt, who'd taught her to read, appeared from round the side of the house.

'Hello Hattie, sorry about my silly dog,' she apologised and grabbed Jelly's collar. 'Don't worry,' she added when she saw the girl's nervous expression, 'he's all noise but harmless.'

'Well ... if you're sure,' said Hattie, who was still gazing at the dog uncertainly.

'Anyway, I don't often see you up here.'

'The twins are visiting the Dower House, I was just killing time really.'

'Well, if you're at a loose end, why don't you come in for a cup of tea?' Clare invited, for she felt sorry for Hattie, whom she considered had been badly used by Adam. And being pleasant cost nothing, although she knew her aunt would disapprove of such familiarity, claiming it would encourage the girl to get ideas way above her station.

'That's very kind of you, Mrs Harcourt.' Deeply flattered at being treated as a social equal, and curious to see the inside of the house, Hattie quite forgot her fear of the dog, undid the latch on the gate and followed Clare down the path and into the house.

'Shall we go through to the drawing-room?' Clare suggested, after pausing by the kitchen to order afternoon tea.

Hattie had no intention of being intimidated by her surroundings, and when Clare said, 'Do have a seat,' she settled herself into the chair and gazed about her with bright-eyed interest. So this was where Madam was brought up. Well, it was no hovel, she decided, and the room was tastefully furnished. Nevertheless, moving to Trent Hall must have been a leg up socially.

When the maidservant brought in the tea she glared at Hattie resentfully, making it quite clear that the proper place for the likes of her was in the kitchen, and not taking tea with the lady of the house. To irritate the girl further, Hattie gave her a self-satisfied smirk and bit daintily into a small triangle of sandwich.

The old gossip's tittle-tattle about Mrs Harcourt's mother had niggled away at Hattie, so she studied Clare's placid features closely while she was pouring the tea, searching for signs of incipient madness.

81

Being Adam's cousin she was kin, and such things could be passed on – Hattie shuddered – maybe to the twins. To her relief, Clare's features had no sinister aspect. In fact she was as Hattie remembered her from her schooldays, fair-haired, extremely pretty and with kind brown eyes.

Unaware of the girl's scrutiny, Clare stirred her tea. 'Well, how are you getting on, Hattie?'

Since she knew it was bad manners to talk with her mouth full, Hattie swallowed before replying. 'I'm fine, except that I do get a bit lonely at times. Actually, I've been thinking about setting up a little business.'

'Oh, what sort of business?'

'Well, I'm quite good with my needle, so maybe dressmaking. I made this.' Hattie smoothed the skirt of her gown. 'I wouldn't have to go into Leicester for the material, I'd just order it from Sharpe's and it would come out on the carrier's cart. Buttons, ribbons, thread and suchlike I could buy from the pedlar when he comes to the village.'

Clare studied the dress with a keen eye. 'Well, I must say it looks very professional,' she commented. Then, because she didn't want Hattie to set her sights too high and fail, felt obliged to add, 'But do you think you'd get much in the way of business? A new dress is a luxury few of the village women could afford.'

'I'd do alterations as well, and there are better-off folk around. The miller's wife and the publican's wife. It would save them going into Leicester and I'd be a lot cheaper.'

'Tell you what, why don't you make me one?' Clare suggested. 'Then, if I'm satisfied I can give your name to friends.'

'That's very kind of you, Mrs Harcourt. Will you order the material?'

'I will. Right away. Something practical for school, that will see me through the summer.'

'You'll need a fitting. Would you mind coming to the cottage?' Growing excited, Hattie bit into a piece of Madeira cake. She was on her way. Already she could see her name in gold lettering above a shop in Leicester.

'Not at all, it's practically next door to the school.' And while I'm there, thought Clare, it will give me an excuse to cuddle the babies. For there was a terrible hunger at the centre of her being, a sense of loss that could temporarily be assuaged when she held a child in her arms.

'About this charity dinner in aid of the school building fund, Adam.' Matilda looked up from the list she was preparing.

'Yes, Mother?'

'If you don't mind, I'd like to have it here at Trent Hall. My little house won't seat twenty people, whereas your dining-room is enormous.'

'That is fine with me.' Adam, who'd been staring out of the window turned and sat down. Then he stood up again and went and leant against the fireplace.

'You are restless, what's wrong?'

'Nothing.'

'Have a look at the guest list. They've all agreed to pay a considerable sum, so I want the dinner to be a glittering occasion.'

Adam wasn't in the least interested in this dinner, or the people who would sit at his table. He knew it would be the same boring faces, with the same tedious conversation, that turned up at any function in the county. Out of politeness, however, Adam took the list from his mother and quickly scanned it. He was right, on it were the names of families he'd known since childhood. One name, however, was unfamiliar to him. 'Who's this? Mr and Mrs Philip Bellamy and Miss Grace Bellamy.'

'Oh, they've recently returned from India, and are most eager to meet the right people.'

'What was this Bellamy's line of business?'

'I believe he was in the East India Company. Anyway, it's provided him with enough money to buy Chenies Manor and a few hundred acres. Apparently they've brought an Indian servant back with them. Rather exotic, don't you think?'

'Pretentious is the word that comes to my mind. But I'm warning you now, Mother, don't try and pair me off with Miss Bellamy at this dinner. I'm not interested.'

Matilda's mouth tightened in exasperation. 'Where shall I seat you then?'

Adam ran his finger down the page. 'Next to Judith. I see she's coming with her father, and she's always a jolly good sport.'

'Adam, while we are on the subject, you are thirty-two now. How long do you intend to remain single?'

'Perhaps forever.'

'But you can't! What will happen to the estate? I slaved for years on my own to make this debt-ridden place solvent and it wasn't easy. But I made a promise to you when you were barely six weeks old that one day it would be yours, and I kept to it. It's your duty now to see that there is a new generation to carry on.'

Adam's eyes glinted with anger. 'Don't blame me, Mother. I know who I love: Emily, and I always will. If I'd been allowed to marry her, you'd probably have umpteen grandchildren by now.'

'Don't keep harking back, Adam. It's done and finished with. And you want her because she belongs to someone else.'

'No, you're wrong. But I made one ghastly mistake with Isabelle, so I don't intend to marry for convenience's sake again. I would only make some wretched woman as miserable as I am. Anyway, there are Aaron and Luke, if you're so bothered.'

Matilda shuddered visibly. 'That Hattie Bonner won't get her greedy hands on an acre of this land.'

Adam studied his mother. 'Why did you never remarry? You might have had more children of your own, if you had.'

'When I was in debt, no man was interested. Of course, once the estate began to make a healthy profit, I had several offers, but I had no intention of losing control of what I'd worked so hard for. As you know, once a woman marries, her property becomes her husband's.'

'That's unfair.'

'My dear boy, life is exceedingly unfair on women.'

Adam shifted uncomfortably, wondering to whom she was referring. Emily? Hattie? Isabelle? No, never Isabelle. Meeting her had been the worst day's work of his life, for from it stemmed all his subsequent problems. What a gullible, trusting fool he'd been, although she'd probably found a few more since, wherever she was. But before Isabelle's malign influence spoilt everything, life had been good in America. In

86

fact, looking back, it was the last time he could remember being truly happy. Perhaps if he returned he would recapture some of his lost, carefree youth. Just pack a bag one day and leave. It would be so easy to disappear into its vastness, to leave all his problems behind and start a new life. But that was the coward's way out. Still, Adam thought, a new start on the other side of the herring pond did have its attractions and was worth bearing in mind if life here became unbearable. Except, Adam glanced at Matilda, it would kill his mother. Hemmed in by his responsibilities, Adam made for the door. 'I must go. I want to check that all the Spring sowing has been done.'

'I can start making arrangements for the dinner with Mrs White then?' Matilda called to him. 'I want to use the silver and the best glass.'

'You have my permission, Mother, to do exactly as you please.'

Five

'I've lost my job.' Rory stood in the door-way, his manner a mixture of defiance and bluster.

Emily turned round from the fire with the frying pan in her hand. 'You've what?'

Rory raised both hands and advanced into the room. 'Lost my job,' he repeated. 'But before you start, it wasn't about time keeping, it was that idiot of an editor. The man's a fool!'

Aware that hot fat was slopping all over the floor, Emily placed the frying pan in the hearth and wiped her hands. In spite of instant penury staring her in the face, she tried to speak calmly. 'Now, tell me slowly and truthfully. What happened?'

'We fell out over an anti-monarchist piece I'd written, which he'd refused to print. He's a man frightened to tell the truth. But I'm not.' Rory paused and his broad shoulders expanded across the width of the door with manly pride. 'I told him that if he didn't print it, I would leave as a matter of principle, whereupon he replied, "You don't have to leave because I'm sacking you."'

'Oh Rory, how could you? What are we to live on?'

'Well, your wages will tide us over but you don't have to worry, because I've already been offered another job.'

Emily let out a gasp of relief. 'Thank heaven for that! When do you start and what paper is it?'

'Well, you won't believe this because it was such a coincidence, but I stopped off at the Red Lion on my way home and I bumped into a very old friend from my Dublin days by the name of Patrick Quinn. I told him of my misfortune and incredibly, he's on his way to New York to start a radical newspaper and there and then, over a pot of ale, he offered me the post of editor. I've got a good reputation, you see.'

'New York! Don't be silly, Rory, you can't go to New York.'

'Yes I can.'

Stunned, Emily could only wail, 'But what about me?'

'Don't worry, immediately I'm settled I'll send for you. Can't you see? Emily, it's a chance to make a new life for ourselves. England is done for. America is the place to be. People have rights, it's a fairer society, more democratic and not under the thumb of the church and crown. And there's none of this stifling class thing that holds people back. No bowing and scraping to your so-called betters. Everyone has the same chance and if they're prepared to work, the sky's the limit.'

'When are you going?' Not only were Emily's hands trembling but her legs too and she found it necessary to sit down.

'I'm sailing a week today.'

'I can't believe this. You say that in a week's time you will just walk out of my life? You seem to forget, Rory, that I'm your wife and you have responsibilities towards me,' Emily protested.

'I'm not walking out on you. As I've already explained, I'll send for you as soon as I've saved the fare and found somewhere to live.'

'You should have consulted me first. It's an enormous step to take, leaving your country and family.' Emily hid her hurt in anger.

'Quinn wanted a decision there and then. And I needed a job. If I stay in London I could be out of work for months. I thought you'd congratulate me on my enterprising spirit, not nag.'

'I'm not nagging. But I'm entitled to say what I feel. It's called free speech, Rory, remember? Something you are supposed to believe in. Anyway, you can't go, you haven't the money for your fare.'

'Patrick is buying me a ticket. He's a man of considerable means.'

'So you've really made up your mind?'

Rory nodded.

'It appears there is nothing more to say then?'

'You could try wishing me luck.'

Emily was bereft after Rory left. Because she couldn't bear the thought of him arriving in New York without a penny to his name, she plundered her small cache of savings and gave it to him. He refused the money at first, but she pushed the money into his pocket, insisting that it was her gift of love to him. As she packed his clothes, she held each garment against her wet cheeks, trying to store in her memory the familiar essence of him. Never had she loved him as much as in those last few days together and in their lovemaking they recaptured some of the tenderness and intensity of the early days of their marriage. Not wanting to prolong the agony of parting, she refused to go with him to Liverpool and when she returned from the station, she went and lay on the bed, where she remained for the rest of the day.

In his own way, Emily knew that Rory loved her, but by nature he was a rolling stone, restless, unable to put down roots, and she wondered if this trip, like so many other ventures that had started so promisingly, would also fail in the end. Emily dozed, woke to find the room in darkness, but she couldn't find the will to rise and light the lamp. A while later her door was thumped, then Edmund's voice demanded, 'Emily, are you there?' Knowing an evening in the company of Edmund and Prudence would only make her feel even more wretched, Emily didn't reply. She heard them debating about whether they ought to look in to check that she was all right, and when the handle was tried, she thanked heaven she'd had the foresight to lock the door. Still arguing they moved off down the stairs, a door slammed, and she was left to sink back into a state of introspective misery. That is, until the sounds of the Soho night began to infringe. A German band thumped its way along the pavement, two drunken woman shrieked obscenities at each other, weird shapes shadow-danced across the walls.

Eventually Emily was forced to get out of bed and pull the heavy curtains across the windows. Deciding she needed to use the privy, she went downstairs and when she returned she realised she'd had nothing to drink or eat since breakfast. Unable to summon up the energy to make tea, Emily made do with the last of the milk. It tasted sour as she gulped it down and the bread she stuffed into her mouth was stale, but Emily hardly cared. However, she retained enough self-respect to undress and wash her face before crawling between the sheets. The bed smelt of their lovemaking and she could taste Rory on her lips. Aching with loss, Emily rolled over to Rory's side of the bed, buried her face in the pillow that still bore the indent of his head, and wept. Gradually her tears subsided and the worries began to crowd in. The rent for these rooms, where was she to find it? She'd have to move to a single room, and even then it would be a struggle on her wages. And what about her parents? How would she break the news to them that Rory had gone off to a new life in America and that she would soon be joining him? But perhaps it would be best to spare them that for a while, particularly with her father not being in the best of health. And at least there was one consolation in being childless, Emily decided, before she finally rolled over and went to sleep; there were no extra mouths to feed, because if there were, it was doubtful if she would have coped, even for a few weeks.

With the help of Prudence, a week later Emily moved her belongings across the landing to a single room which had become vacant. She hung her clothes in a small cupboard and looked about her. The rooms she'd just vacated seemed luxurious in comparison and the single carpet was in such tatters it hardly seemed worthy of the name. Lifting the soot-streaked window, she stared down at a sunless yard. It overflowed with wooden crates and broken bottles. 'Lord, what a depressing sight.'

'Yeah,' Prudence sniffed, 'there's a definite smell of cats' pee. And you're right above the jakes.'

'Thanks for cheering me up, Prudence.' Emily quickly slammed down the window. 'I shall really miss our small home,' she sighed. 'We were happy there, you know.' Emily felt she had to emphasise this point to Prudence.

'Of course you were, ducky. Like pigs in clover. But once you've got a few of yer own bits and pieces around you and a couple of pictures on the wall, this room'll be just as cosy. And yer missing Rory, too. It's understandable.'

'And it won't be long,' Emily said brightly. 'As soon as he's settled, he'll send for me.'

'Course he will.' Prudence gave Emily an awkward hug. 'Look, why don't you come upstairs and have a bite to eat wiv us? I bought some chitterlings and a loaf of bread earlier on and there's enough to go round.'

'Won't Edmund mind?'

'Why should 'e? The bugger's had a few free meals off you.'

That was true enough, but Emily wavered. However, weighed against an evening alone in one poky room, putting up with Edmund seemed a small price to pay.

'You comin' then?'

Emily nodded and followed Prudence up the stairs to their room on the top floor. Flinging open the door, Prudence announced grandly, 'We 'ave a guest.'

Their room was large, with a window that reached from floor to ceiling and let in a cold north light. Paint was splattered over every surface and Prudence's lack of house-wifely skills were evident in the unmade bed, dirty crockery and almost extinct fire. Edmund, who was at his easel dabbing away at a canvas, turned when the two young women entered.

'I've brought Emily up for some supper, Edmund,' Prudence explained, then went and gave the fire a push with the toe of her boot. A feeble flame shot up the chimney and quickly died away. 'Dratted thing.' Prudence gave it a more ruthless dig with the poker but it failed to respond. 'Why didn't you keep an eye on, it Edmund?' she demanded.

Edmund gave Prudence a haughty stare. 'I'm an artist. I don't keep a dog and bark myself. However, you frequently appear to forget this, and looking at the mess the room is in, I do wonder why I remain charitably disposed towards you.' Edmund swept his dripping paintbrush round the room to emphasise his point, adding a few more daubs to those already there.

Incensed by his rudeness, Emily silently urged Prudence to retaliate. But although her bottom lip trembled at this public humiliation, she just hung her head mutely. Concerned for her, Emily moved to the girl's side. 'Here, let me,' she said, rolled up some newspaper, then laid a few sticks and coal on top. Prudence handed her a lucifer, and when the kindling caught, Emily held a sheet of newspaper in front of the fire to help it draw. In no time the coals were glowing.

'Ooh you are clever,' Prudence exclaimed, as if Emily had performed some Herculean task. And it was Emily who went on to cook the chitterlings while Prudence cleared enough dirty crockery from the table for them to have plates to eat off and a space to sit down.

'Mmm, this is good,' Edmund exclaimed, spearing a piece of chitterling with a fork. 'You can move up here any time, Emily.'

Emily put her knife and fork down noisily and glared at him. How could Prudence put up with this pig. For two pins she would get up and leave.

Realising that perhaps he'd overstepped the mark, Edmund patted Prudence's hand. 'Just joking. But seriously, Emily, Rory was an idiot to trot off like that and leave you here on your own.'

'Rory hasn't left me,' Emily explained in a tight voice. 'In a short while I shall be following him. He just has to get the money for my fare together. It was all so sudden you see, with him losing his job.'

Edmund swung back on his rickety chair and took a sup of ale. 'He told me he was planning to leave England well over a month ago, long before he was sacked.'

Emily's stomach gave a sickening jolt and when Prudence leapt up and yelled, 'Why can't you keep yer bloody mouth shut, Edmund?' she felt she might spew up her supper.

'He ... to–told you a month ago?'

'Sorry, have I put my foot in it?' Edmund bared his teeth with wolfish pleasure.

Clutching the table, Emily dragged herself to her feet. 'I ... must go.' As she stumbled to the door, she heard Prudence scream some insult at Edmund then follow her. At the back of her mind there had always lurked a niggling doubt that Rory's departure hadn't been as quite as spontaneous as he'd made out. And to tell others, but not her, to make her the laughing stock ... well that was utterly contemptible.

Back in the dingy room, Prudence addressed Emily drooping shoulders. 'I could ring that stupid sod's neck.'

Emily swung round. 'So you knew, too?'

Prudence shifted uneasily. 'He 'ad mentioned it, but I didn't take much notice. You know Rory, 'e was always a talker, a bloke wiv ideas and a touch of the blarney. You 'ad to take a lot of what 'e said wiv a pinch of salt. But it don't mean 'e's deserted you, Emily. I could see 'e loved you and I always envied you that.'

Emily snorted. 'Some love! If he thought so much of me, why did he run off?'

Prudence shrugged. 'I dunno. But then I'll never understand blokes. Leastways, he always treated you nice and not as if you was a lump of dog poo on the sole of his boot, like Edmund does me. No, I can't see Rory lettin' you down and I bet by this time next year you and he'll be settled in America and you'll have forgotten all this.'

Emily tried to find comfort in Prudence's prediction and to hold on to it during a sleepless night. But daylight forced her to regard her marriage with a more detached eye, and on her way to work she came to the painful conclusion that Rory had felt so shackled by marriage that this supposed job in America was a way of casting off his chains. So much for love. But perhaps she was to blame in some measure for spurning the solid, dependable qualities of a man like the Reverend William Jackson in favour of an Irish charmer who'd abandoned her without a second's thought? Never again, she vowed, would she allow passion to cloud her judgement; there'd be no more listening to lies and believing them. Instead she would pawn her wedding ring, revert to her maiden name and then, apart from a small legal matter, she could consider her marriage over.

But of course she wouldn't and she must guard against bitterness, remain anchored to life and hang on to her self-esteem. There would be days when things looked grim, but the trick was to think positively. For instance, she was young, that was a big plus, and she was healthy. Intelligent? Emily wasn't vain so she thought carefully about this. Yes, definitely yes, and most important of all she had work, even if her wages weren't enough to live on. Her belief in herself returning, Emily began to notice the world about her, realised for the first time that she'd stepped out into a beautiful morning, saw how the sun gave Soho a smoky luminance that disguised the squalor and crime. And *I can, will* survive without a man, she repeated to herself then, fixing a brave smile on her face, she continued on her way to work.

But the effort made her jaw ache and by the time she reached Broadwick Street, the smile had vanished along with the early confidence. 'My dear, you look absolutely ghastly,' Mrs Haig exclaimed, bluntly but honestly, as she came through to the hall where the maidservant was relieving Emily of her outdoor clothes.

Emily glanced in the mirror, pretending to smooth her hair and straighten her collar, but she saw what her employer meant. Her skin looked pasty, her eyes lifeless as a dead fish. 'I am a trifle under the weather,' she admitted, turning to face Mrs Haig, 'but it won't affect my work, I promise.'

'Go home if you are feeling unwell,' Mrs Haig urged, 'I can manage on my own for today.'

Emily thought of the room she was already beginning to detest. 'No, *The Tribulations of Theodora* has to be finished, it's due at the publishers at the end of the week.'

'That's true. But I'm not a slavedriver and I wouldn't dream of keeping you at your desk if you are ill, my dear.'

'If I could perhaps have a cup of coffee...' Emily was hesitant about taking advantage of her employer's kindness, but she'd had no breakfast, her food cupboard was empty and she had a shilling to last her until the end of the week. And to think she'd handed over her savings to Rory. Oh, what a trusting fool she'd been!

Mrs Haig disappeared into the kitchen, while Emily went into the office. Sitting down at her desk, she pulled the manuscript towards her and commenced copying out the last chapter of her employer's novel in her neat, copperplate handwriting. It was reaching an exciting climax with the heroine, Theodora Cavendish, heiress to a large fortune, imprisoned in a tower by her dastardly uncle, who stood to inherit his niece's money if she should happen to depart this world prematurely. And the burning question is: will the hero, tall, dark and quiveringly handsome Lord Nicholas Stacey reach her in time to avoid her being murdered and thrown into the moat? Totally caught up in the drama, Emily's pen flew over the paper. If only she could meet a man like Lord Nicholas. She paused and gave a pensive sigh. Having followed him through three hundred pages, he was almost flesh and blood to her and she knew his character intimately. Honourable to his toenails, caring while being a little gruff, and given to saying, 'You silly little goose', as a form of endearment. The predicable plot ran its course and by the time uncle had leapt from the tower to a messy death and the hero and heroine had fallen into each other's arms, Mrs Haig had returned. Reluctantly Emily left the lovers to their happy fate and watched the maid follow her mistress in. She was bearing on a tray a jug of coffee, several slices of bread and butter, and a small dish of honey. At the sight of food, Emily's stomach began to rumble and she laid her pen aside.

'Just in case you're a bit peckish,' said Mrs Haig. She didn't want to dent Emily's pride by seeming to be handing out charity, but as she watched the plate empty, it occurred to her that with that husband of hers gone, unless he'd left her provided for – which she very much doubted – Emily was probably living in rather reduced circumstances. But what on earth had induced the man to leave such a charming girl and go off like that? It was so thoughtless. Unless the marriage was in trouble, although Emily had never given any indication that it might be. Quite the opposite, in fact, and she had always spoken warmly of her husband. With an unpleasant jolt it suddenly occurred to Mrs Haig that if things got really tough, Emily would probably return home to Leicester and, selfishly, she had no wish to lose such a treasure. There was a solution, of course, and one which would incur no loss of pride; a wage increase, and one generous enough for her to no longer to live in penury.

Six

Adam had to admit it, his mother knew how to rise to the occasion and the dining-room table looked splendid. Silver candelabra he'd forgotten they even possessed held tall slim candles; cut glass sent out little prisms of light. But looking at the arrangements of hothouse flowers and the dishes of fruit not native to England, Adam did some mental arithmetic and began to wonder if his mother was actually going to make any profit for her school project. Well, the guests were enjoying themselves and that was the main thing. She might not have managed to woo the Duke of Rutland to her table, as she'd hoped, but his mother hadn't allowed it to depress her and the food and wine were excellent, her guests relaxed. The conversation proceeded along its normal uncontroversial tracks: politics, the state of agriculture, hunting, shooting, with a bit of local gossip thrown in from time to time. Their opinions were set in stone like the Ten Commandments, and Adam found them as uninspiring now as he did the first time he had heard them. If only someone would challenge them, question their values. He thought of Emily and smiled to himself. If she were sitting here, with her radical views, she would surely upset the apple-cart. Certainly there was no one else here who would dream of being contradictory.

He glanced in the direction of the Bellamys. What about them? Surely being well-travelled, they would have some opinions that hadn't been chewed over a thousand times before. But one look told him they were the sort of people who would hesitate to even pass a view on the weather in case it was construed as provocative. Maintaining the status quo and fitting in was their only concern. Mr Bellamy's red veined, bulbous nose spoke of too many chota pegs, and from the jaundiced colour of his wife's skin and her reptilian neck rising from a low-cut gown, it was apparent that she hadn't fared well in the Indian climate. Except that she was younger, all Mrs Bellamy's features were replicated in the daughter, a thin young woman with a withdrawn expression, who seemed as unimpressed by her fellow guests as Adam. Because they were new to the area, his mother had honoured the husband and wife by placing them on either side of her. Not one to give up easily on her plans, his mother had tried to cajole him into escorting the girl into dinner, but Adam stubbornly refused. In the end the dubious honour had gone to Harry, who'd struggled throughout dinner to engage her in conversation. Adam smiled, watching Harry practise his middle-aged charms and failing, possibly for the first time in his life. The girl might have been a mute, and she sat staring at the tablecloth, obviously unimpressed by the grandness of the occasion.

Thankful to have Judith as his dinner companion and not the dull Miss Bellamy, Adam decided he could afford to give Harry a helping hand. Framing a question he knew she would have to reply to, he leaned across Judith. 'And how are you enjoying being back in England, Miss Bellamy?'

After her previous passivity, the force of her reply startled Adam. 'I loathe it!'

'Oh. What is it you dislike about this country?' he asked.

'It is cold, damp and dull.'

Which would just about describe you, thought Adam a little uncharitably.

'India's my home, it is where I was born.' She glared at her parents. 'But I have two brothers still there, so I shall go back,' she added defiantly.

Entertained by her sudden directness, Adam began to study the girl with more interest. Here, at least, was someone not frightened of speaking her mind. 'Tell me what it is about India that you prefer,' said Judith kindly.

'Absolutely everything. The heat, the

colour, the landscape, but most of all the people. England is devoid of colour.'

'It is quite green,' Judith pointed out. 'And at this time of the year when the May blossom is out and the meadows are full of wild flowers, it would be hard to find a more beautiful spot on earth. You must come riding with Adam and me and we'll show you.'

Although Mrs Bellamy had given every indication that she was deep in conversation with Matilda, she turned when she heard Judith's invitation. 'You would like that, wouldn't you, Grace?' But her daughter disdained to reply and with a glued-on smile, Mrs Bellamy went on, 'I'm afraid Grace has this romantic idea of India and glosses over its imperfections.'

Grace reddened. 'I do not.'

Mrs Bellamy's eyes flashed and she opened her mouth as if to contradict her daughter. But, in time, she remembered where she was and turned back to Matilda and less contentious subjects.

The brief animation on the girl's face subsided and she retreated into a sullen silence. Adam, who'd already nicknamed her Miss Graceless, smothered a yawn, but knowing the misery of being an outsider, Judith pressed on. 'I've lived in Paris for several years, but it's in a state of revolution at the moment and when Louis Philippe

106

was overthrown in February, lots of foreigners fled. I stayed on, but then my father came over and insisted I return home with him. So like an obedient daughter I did, although I shall go back as soon as the troubles die down,' she confided. Out of common courtesy, Judith had expected some response, instead Grace showed her indifference, by making a design of the crumbs on her plate and ignoring her. Astounded at such deliberate rudeness, Judith thought, well, two can play at that game and turned her back on the girl.

'Given up on Miss Graceless, have you?' Adam smiled.

'Totally. By the way, talking of Paris,' Judith lowered her voice and glanced up and down the table. 'Isabelle's living there.'

Adam, who had a glass of wine half way to his lips, very carefully placed it down on the table. 'Are you sure?'

'Absolutely. I saw her at the Opera, with an elderly gentleman.'

'That sounds like Isabelle. She prefers doddery old fools, they're more gullible. And she speaks French, so we always suspected she would make her way there.'

'Even so, you would expect her to lie low for a bit and not show herself off in public quite so brazenly.'

'Perhaps she was with her husband. He went looking for her.'

'No, the man was definitely French.'

'She was probably plying her trade then, it's the only profession she knows.'

'I imagine so, but as a courtesan rather than a common whore. And very successfully, if the splendid jewels she was wearing were anything to go by. When the troubles die down why don't you come over to Paris? I have friends so finding her wouldn't be much of a problem. And imagine Isabelle's face!'

'Take my word for it, Isabelle has the instinct of a rat, and at the first sign of a sinking ship she'd be off, before a shot was fired. Anyway, she was so unredeemingly evil I never want to set eyes on her again.' Adam shuddered. 'It makes my flesh creep just talking about her. It's as if she still has the power to harm me.'

'Now you're acting all superstitious, like one of the village folk,' Judith laughed. 'Do you think she spends her evenings sticking pins in a wax likeness of you?'

'Isabelle is capable of anything. She has no sense of right or wrong and that is very dangerous for other people. Here, feel my hands.' He pressed his fingers against Judith's bare forearm.

'Good Lord, they're freezing!'

'Yes, that's the effect she has on me. Do you understand now why I don't want to see her?'

'You're letting a criminal get off scot-free.'

'Although I know darn well she was trying to poison me, according to the police, it couldn't be proved. It would be hard to bring her to trial now.'

'She's committed bigamy, as well,' Judith pointed out.

'Her deeds won't go unpunished. Hard as it is to imagine, there are even wickeder people than Isabelle out there. One day, she'll get her comeuppance.'

'How?'

To allay his fears, Adam began to describe various unpleasant ends he'd often imagined for Isabelle until he was interrupted by Matilda rising to her feet. Knowing it was time to depart and leave the men to their port, cigars and risqué jokes, Judith rose and followed the other ladies into the drawing-room.

Although he couldn't be blamed for *all* the misfortunes that had befallen him, Adam's life was in rather a mess and Judith felt sorry for him. What he needed was a wife, she decided, then smiled to herself remembering how well-intentioned acquaintances were always trying to palm her off with a husband and how she resented it. She didn't desire men and never would and the life she led now in Paris, where sexual attitudes were more relaxed, suited her perfectly. Judith was stirring her coffee and thinking that it was fortunate she was going to be around for a while to keep an eye on Adam, when she heard Mrs Bellamy hiss, 'You are behaving shamefully, now *mix*.' Since there was only one person the lady could be addressing, and that was her intractable daughter, Judith glanced in their direction. The air pulsed with animosity. Those two don't get on, she thought, and remembered her own mother. She'd known from an early age that Olivia was the favoured one and it had been a painful truth to swallow. Again she began to feel a certain sympathy for Grace. Mrs Bellamy said something else which obviously displeased her daughter because the moment her mother turned away, Grace extended her tongue like a petulant child. Judith suppressed the urge to giggle and thanked the Lord she'd been spared having children. Grace was now sidling towards her but Judith considered that she had done more than her fair share of trying to humour the girl, so she studied her fingernails and prayed she would move away.

But Grace wasn't deterred. Dumping herself down in a chair next to Judith, she said, 'I'll come out riding with you and Mr Bennett tomorrow, if you like.'

'Don't feel obliged to come on my account, Miss Bellamy.'

'I know I was beastly earlier but it's my

110

mother, she treats me as if I haven't got a mind of my own. I want to come, really.'

Wondering how Adam would react to having Miss Graceless as a riding companion, Judith answered, 'All right, where shall we meet?'

'Well, you know the area better than I do, so could you come up to our place?'

'Certainly. How would seven-thirty suit you?'

The previous owner of Chenies Manor had ruined himself with rash investments in overseas markets and it was rumoured that the Bellamys had acquired the house at a knock-down price. And they'd certainly been fortunate, Judith decided as she and Adam rode up the drive, for it was a fine property of mellow brick, gabled at each end and legend had it that Charles I had once spent the night there.

Grace was already waiting for them in the stableyard, dressed in a dark blue riding habit. There wasn't a trace of the sullen girl of the night before, and she greeted them with a cheerful smile. Beside her stood the young Indian servant there had been so much talk about and Judith wondered if he – her one link with her beloved India – was responsible for her change of mood. 'This is Anil, he will come with us,' Grace announced imperiously.

The young man pressed his hands together and gave a slight bow. 'Good-morning Mr Bennett, good-morning, Miss Bennett.' He enunciated each syllable with well-rehearsed care.

'Good-morning,' Judith and Adam answered, a little flummoxed by this exotic creature.

'Tell me where you're taking me,' Grace called over her shoulder as she moved over to the mounting block and Anil steadied the horse for her.

'I want to show you Bluebell Wood,' Adam answered. 'It's one of my favourite places at this time of the year.'

Grace said something to Anil in his own tongue, he nodded, then he went and leapt on his own horse with such amazing agility, his feet barely touched the stirrups. Halby was close-knit, ignorant to a large degree of the outside world and newcomers were treated with a certain suspicion. So the arrival of the Bellamys with a dark-skinned servant wearing strange clothes had given rise to much speculation. In the end it was decided that, with plenty of servants available for hire in Leicester, they were 'just showing off', or 'trying to go one better than their neighbours'.

Although it was unlikely they would have found one half as handsome, Judith decided, as the four of them rode out of the yard. Sleek and watchful as a leopard, with enviously long eyelashes, Anil remained at a respectful distance behind them, although Judith did wonder how he felt about being dumped down in an alien culture and separated from family or friends. Obviously it wasn't a question Grace or her parents had given much thought to, or they wouldn't have brought him all this way. And there was no going back; he was a prisoner here now, doomed to live in England until his dying day. If Grace hated it, how must it be for him, Judith wondered, although his opinion was probably never sought.

With Adam leading the way they came out of the drive, then trotted along between hedgerows starred with milky white blossom enclosing deeply ridged fields, both evidence of the lost open field system. When they came to a five-barred gate, Adam slipped from his horse and went to unlatch it. It opened on to a meadow golden with buttercups. Pointing to the farthest corner he said, 'That's where we're headed, Blue-bell Wood. You'll see why it's called that when we reach it.'

'Right.' Grace clicked her tongue. 'Go on Pegasus, go!' she ordered. At the command, the horse did seem to literally fly and they were away with Anil barely a footfall behind. Soon he had caught up and they were no longer servant and mistress, but competitors, racing neck and neck.

As Grace's laughter carried back to them, Adam's competitive spirit swung into action and he leapt up on to Whitesocks, a chestnut gelding. 'An odd relationship,' he commented, adding, 'come on, let's see if we can overtake them,' and he and Judith went thundering after the younger couple. But although their horsemanship couldn't be faulted, they failed to catch up and Grace and Anil were waiting for them when they reached the other side of the field.

'Where did you learn to ride like that?' asked Judith admiringly, when she'd got her breath back.

'Anil taught me.' No longer the pale, monosyllabic creature of the night before, Grace acknowledged the servant with a sideways glance.

'You must ride out with us when hunting starts again in the autumn, Miss Bellamy,' Adam invited, revising his opinion of the girl in the light of her horseriding skills.

'Thank you, Mr Bennett, but I don't care for foxhunting. It's barbaric.'

'Oh!' Rather put out at having his generous offer turned down, Adam reverted to his earlier opinion of the girl. 'Right, I think we'll leave the horses here and walk, in single file, I don't want the bluebells trodden down.'

Leading the way, Adam set off, taking a

narrow path through the woods and soon they were ankle deep in slim-stemmed blue-bells. Primroses, violets and wood anemone nestled against banks and spreading his arms expansively, Adam grew poetic. 'God's certainly in his heaven this morning,' he observed, proud that he owned this small piece of England, that he practised good husbandry, and his workers were well cared for. Turning to Grace, he said, 'I bet there's nothing to compare with this on the dusty plains of India.'

'Not all India is dusty,' Grace retorted in her plain-speaking way. 'The hills are beautiful. As green as anything you'll find here, is that not so, Anil?'

'Yes, memsahib.' The young man answered obediently. They had paused and three of them, assured in their slightly arrogant upper-class way, were leaning casually against the trunk of a fallen tree. Anil, however, knowing his place, stood a little apart, reserved, patient, tactful; the ideal servant.

Most young women – particularly plain, single ones – would have agreed with every utterance that issued from the mouth of a man of Adam's standing, so it amused Judith to see the slightly vexed expression on his proud, handsome face. It was refreshing, too, to find a young woman who wasn't afraid of being contentious. Gossip travelled with the speed of a forest fire so she would know by now of his messy personal life: the bastard children, the marriage that never was. Then there was the complication of Emily, his supposed true love, so maybe Grace had decided that, with all the damage he'd wreaked, he wasn't worth wasting time on.

All Adam saw, however, was a disagreeable girl wanting in tact. Unlike Judith, a true friend in every sense of the word. 'What about France? Is it as beautiful as England?' he asked, turning to her for support.

'Well it's not called La Belle France for nothing. But come and see for yourself, I've invited you over often enough.'

Suspecting a feminine conspiracy a sullen look settled on Adam's face. 'Personally, I don't think there's anywhere on earth more lovely than this wood in springtime. It will never go for timber. And now it's coming on to rain.' He held out his hands and they heard the first pat, pat of rain on leaves. 'We'd better be getting back.' Feeling unappreciated after putting himself out on behalf of Miss Graceless, Adam was now anxious to be rid of her.

Unfortunately it wasn't in Grace's nature to be aware of other people's feelings. 'What's that horrible sickly smell?' she complained, as they tramped back through the damp undergrowth.

'Wild garlic, it's quite common in woods,' Adam answered tightly, for by now, every comment the girl made about his woods was a personal affront.

The trees had protected them against the worst of the rain but once they were clear of the woods, they discovered it was coming down in buckets and they were soon soaked through. 'Don't worry about coming with us, we'll find our own way home,' said Grace, as they ran towards the horses.

But Adam was torn between a wish to be rid of the girl and his duty as a gentleman to escort her back to Chenies Manor. 'Well ... I don't know...' he wavered. But before he could finish his sentence, Grace and her servant had mounted their horses and galloped off into the driving rain. Soon, all that could be heard was Grace's laughter, and as it resonated across the empty, water-lashed landscape, it seemed to Judith that locked within that laugh was a sound that mocked the world.

'So, what did you think of last night? Was it a success?' asked Matilda, coming into the office later that morning. But Adam wasn't listening. After returning from their ride, he and Judith had changed into dry clothes, breakfasted, then she and Harry had returned to Fern Hill. It was a short while after their departure that one of the tenant farmers had brought him some disturbing news.

'Adam, did you hear me?'

'Sorry, Mother, I'm a bit distracted. Amos Greasley came with some bad news, and I'm deciding how to deal with it.'

'Oh dear, what's that?' Matilda sat down. Although to all intents and purposes she had retired, she had run the estate for too long to be able to cut herself off from it entirely.

'You know that there's been this trouble recently with ducks and fowls being stolen from farms?'

'Yes.'

'Well, according to Amos, last night a lamb was slaughtered in one of the fields and everything taken except skin and entrails.'

'Good heavens. I trust you are not going to let the matter rest? It's a serious offence and it must be reported to the police.'

Adam stood up. 'That's what I intend to do, but I must go and investigate first. A watch will have to be organised, too, it's the only way we'll put a stop to it. I've also decided to send most of the lambs to the Leicester May Fair next Friday. That way they can't be stolen.'

'Before you go, tell me how you thought the dinner went?'

'Socially it was a great success, Mother.

But did you actually make anything out of it for the village school?'

'As a matter of fact I did. Several people dipped their hands in their pockets and Mr Bellamy wrote out a cheque for two hundred pounds, which I consider generous, particularly since he's a newcomer.'

'Pity he's got such a ghastly daughter, then,' Adam replied sourly.

'So you don't find her attractive?'

'Mother, really!' Although he knew it would be unwise to say so to his mother, in his opinion, Hattie was ten times prettier. In fact, he found that her invitation to visit the boys was frequently on his mind these days. And why shouldn't he get to know his children better? Where was the harm in it?

Matilda gave a small shrug. 'I just hoped...'

'I've told you, stop hoping. There isn't a chance in hell and please, can we drop the subject? Tell me, as the main benefactor, when do you plan to start laying the foundations for the school?'

'Soon, if the money keeps coming in, on that piece of land next to the church. But I don't intend to stint. I want a building that will still be there in a hundred years, and a good architect to design it. A Mr Claud Fry has been recommended, and since I hope you'll involve yourself in the project, I want you to go in to Leicester and talk to him first

– get an impression of him.'

'Mother, if we're going to have a spate of sheep rustling, I've got to concentrate on that. But I'll be going into Leicester on Friday for the May Fair; I'll look in then if I have time.'

'I know you'll do the best you can.'

'The people who you should be talking to are Clare and Christopher.'

'I'd hardly be so crass as to leave them out, particularly since they run the school,' Matilda retorted.

'Good, I don't want to be seen stepping on their feet.' Adam moved to the door. 'And now I must go and study those entrails and see what ghastly tale they tell me.'

Seven

It was the first day of the May Fair and carriers' carts, beasts, horses, sheep, street vendors and pedlars were squeezed into the main thoroughfares of Leicester, along with a goodly proportion of the population of the county. The greasy smell of cooking, bluebottles buzzing over bloody butchers' stalls, and the noise and stench of hundreds of penned animals made Adam feel hot and uncomfortable and he longed to undo his waistcoat and loosen his neckcloth. But such behaviour wasn't becoming in a gentleman, so he made do with removing his hat and wiping his forehead. In that unguarded moment a drunk fell against him. It was the oldest trick in the book and Adam pushed the man away. 'Don't you dare,' he threatened and quickly felt in his jacket pocket. Reassured that neither his watch nor purse had been lifted, he turned off into a side street and made his way towards the Town Hall.

When he reached it, Adam crossed the courtyard and pushed open a door. What he saw hardly represented law and order at its most efficient. As far as he could make out, there was only one policeman on duty and he was asleep in a chair. Adam lowered himself to the level of the man's ear. 'Can I have some assistance, please?' When there was no response, he gave him a slight shove, whereupon the peeler tilted slowly sideways on to the floor, where he remained, snoring loudly. Suspecting the man was drunk, Adam thumped hard on the desk. 'Where is everybody?' he bellowed in his most authoritative tone.

'Arright, arright, I'm coomin,' a voice announced and another upholder of the Queen's peace lumbered out of the gloom, jacketless and wiping his mouth with a handkerchief.

'Is that man on duty?' Adam pointed to the comatose figure.

'In a manner of speaking, sir, yes,' his colleague answered in between chewing and swallowing.

'He's drunk.'

'Beggin' your pardon, sir, a little fatigued, perhaps, for we work long hours, but not drunk,' he corrected.

'How is the crime rate ever going to be reduced in the county when we can't rely on our police force?' Adam demanded.

'It's bin difficult for us lately, you see, sir, with these bloomin' Chartists. There wa' another meeting last week at the Amphitheatre with that Irish troublemaker,

O'Connor. The Lion of Freedom they calls 'im, huh,' he snorted contemptuously. 'He comes with his bands, flags and mottoes, gets the poor folk of the town all worked up wi' promises 'e can't keep, then disappears back down to the smoke. Of course, there's no holding them afterwards. And who takes the brunt of it, I ask you?' He stabbed his chest with his forefinger. 'Why, us poor devils, of course. It gets so bad sometimes we need to drown our sorrows. So I hope, sir,' he wheedled, 'you'll see our point of view and let it go no further.'

'What is your name?'

'Police Constable Pegg, sir.'

'Well, it depends, Constable Pegg, on how you deal with a serious offence I have come to report. One of my tenant farmers had a sheep stolen the other night, and there has been a whole wave of poultry thefts in Halby.'

'It'd be them paupers from the Bastille. They've got work to go to in the stoneyards, but they're idle devils and would rather thieve. I ask you, what is the world coming to? They cause us no end of trouble wi' their beggin' around the streets and threatening people who don't pay up. And I can't tell you the number of houses that have bin broken into these past weeks.'

'Since you appear to know who the villains are, why haven't you apprehended them?'

Police Constable Pegg shook his head sagely. 'But it's proving it.'

'Well, you might be interested to know that Police Superintendent Sibson is a personal friend of mine.'

The constable paled. This could be the end of his career and there flashed before him the grim stoneyards. Quickly he found a pen and paper. 'Now, if you give me your name and address, sir, I will come over personally tomorrow and do a thorough investigation.'

The constable wrote down Adam's particulars then, obsequious and smiling he showed him out, reiterating that he would be in Halby at the crack of dawn and promising that he'd have the crime solved by the evening. Immediately Adam left, his mood changed. Striding over to the still snoring figure, he kicked him viciously in the ribs. 'Come on, Giggs, wake up. You've got me into a right load of bloody trouble and you'll be lucky if I don't report you to old Sibson.'

Walking back down Town Hall Lane, Adam's mood shifted from irritation to one of slight shame. He'd used his slight acquaintance with the superintendent to intimidate Pegg, which was hardly the action of a gentleman. By and large the police were pretty incompetent and the chance of one, not very bright, peeler solving the crime was about nil. The main thing was that, as a responsible landowner, he'd discharged his duty and Amos and the villagers would feel reassured. His next task now was to pay a call on the architect, Mr Claud Fry, on behalf of his mother. When he reached this gentleman's office in Rutland Street, however, Adam was informed by an aged clerk that the architect was out of town. He suggested that Adam should make an appointment for the following Monday afternoon, when Mr Fry would be available.

His business finished for the day, Adam was on his way back to the Bell to collect his gig, when he noticed the Pleasure Fair a bit further along in Humberstone Gate. When was the last time he'd visited it? Probably when he was about twelve, with his grandmother and Clare. Suddenly it came flooding back to him, that feeling of anticipation as he lay in bed the night before. He could recall each detail of the day, and the glimpse into a magic world. The excitement of actually being there, of watching with wide-eyed fascination fire-eaters and sword-swallowers, of screaming with laughter at the antics of the clowns, then the delicious terror of standing in front of a caged lion. To hear its roar, to stare into its great gaping jaw and see those enormous teeth its keeper assured them could tear a man apart, had made his spine tingle with fear. One of the booths had advertised a two-headed woman, and Adam remembered how he and Clare, little savages that they were, had tried to pull their grandmother towards it. He could still hear her voice, unusually firm, declaring she would not allow her grandchildren to see such a freak of nature. Instead, she hauled them off to the marionette booth, which she considered far more suitable entertainment for young minds. Those were such secure, uncomplicated times, Adam thought, and experienced a tug of regret for lost childhood days. And although his adult eyes saw through the sparkle and enchantment to its tawdriness, the fair still had a magnetic pull and he found himself moving towards it. He had reached the entrance and was about to pay the gatekeeper, when he saw a girl who was Emily's double walking towards him. Adam blinked. It *was* Emily and the shock was so intense, it took him a moment to notice that she was with Lily and her two children. The girl was having a real paddy, stamping her feet, screaming that she wanted another go on the roundabout, and declaring she hated everyone, in particular her mother.

People were staring and Adam thought, poor Lily. She'd obviously given up trying to pacify the child and, her face tight with anger, was dragging her unceremoniously towards the gate. Emily was a step behind, holding the boy's hand. As they reached the gate, the girl aimed a kick at her mother's shin, broke free and ran back into the crowd. 'Helen, come back here, this minute!' Lily ordered and went limping after her.

Engrossed in the drama, Adam hadn't moved and as Emily went to step through the gate, she saw him. They stared at each other wordlessly, then she pulled the boy back and said, 'Shall we go and see if we can find your mother, Peter?' But by now, Lily, her bonnet slightly askew, had reappeared with her snivelling daughter. Her reaction, when she saw Adam, was the exact opposite to Emily's. She smiled, straightened her hat and was about to speak, when Emily nudged her in the ribs. 'Come on, let's go,' she ordered and hustled Lily and the children past him.

But the boy was curious and he stared back at Adam. 'Who was that, Auntie?' he enquired, and in a clear voice, so that Adam would be sure to hear, Emily replied,

'No one of any consequence, Peter.'

That hurt, but what could he expect? Adam asked himself. She was hardly likely to say; 'The man I adore and should have married'. The encounter had made him lose all interest in the fair so he collected his gig and set the mare in the direction of Halby.

He then left it to her homing instinct to get them there, while his thoughts drifted back to the early days when Emily *had* adored him, in all her sweet trusting innocence. Enough to risk all and run away with him. But everything passes, everything changes, even his nagging unhappiness, he assumed, would fade in time. But did she love her husband with that same intensity, Adam wondered, as the horse trotted along Main Street. Because if she did, what was she doing in Leicester without him?

Monday was the day of the great Cheese Fair. The animals had gone, the streets had been thoroughly cleansed and the air had a fresh lactic smell. It was not permitted to bring cheeses into the market until two a.m. so farmers would have been rattling in on their wagons from the earliest hours to get the choicest pitch. Now, along the length of Granby Street and up into the market, great cartwheels of Stilton and Leicester, protected by beds of straw, were piled one on top of the other. Adam was constantly accosted and urged to taste and buy, but he'd decided it would be more sensible to wait until after his meeting with the architect before making such a purchase.

When he reached the Market Place, however, moved by an inner compulsion, his found his feet turning in the direction of

High Cross Street. A glimpse of Emily, that was all he wanted he told himself, it could do no harm. Then he remembered Clare's words to him, brutal but honest.

Police Constable Pegg had come out to Halby on the Saturday, as promised, had taken statements and gone away again after enjoying the hospitality of several villagers at the Weavers' Arms. But Adam's thoughts were more occupied with Emily that day than one stolen sheep, and since Clare was the only person he could confide in, and he knew Christopher was with his mother discussing the plans for the school, he walked up to Thatcher's Mount to see her.

She was in the garden planning the summer flower-beds with the gardener, but she stopped when she saw her cousin. 'Hello,' she smiled.

'Clare, can we talk please, in private?'

'Of course. Let's go inside.'

Adam didn't beat about the bush. 'I saw Emily, yesterday. In Leicester,' he said before he was even seated.

'Did you? I bumped into her recently, too. We had quite a long talk. She looks well, don't you think? And she's enjoying her new life in London, by all accounts.'

'You never told me,' Adam accused.

'Why should I have? Emily is a married woman. You no longer have any claim on her.'

129

'Was she with her husband when you saw her?'

'No, she was only here on a brief visit to see her father, who's not enjoying the best of health at the moment. That's probably the reason she's in Leicester again. And I beg of you, Adam, leave her alone. You've caused that girl enough heartache. Think of her for once instead of yourself.'

They were harsh words to hear, but honest, Adam had to admit. He had caused Emily grief, not once but many times over. And he was fooling himself when he said he only wanted a glimpse of her. What he really wanted to do was grab her, smother her with kisses and never ever let her go.

Emily had probably gone back to London by now, back to her husband and her exciting life in London, Adam told himself and retraced his steps. But he couldn't resist doing a quick circuit of the market, in case he bumped into her. He would even have been happy to see Lily, always a firm ally, but although his one circuit became two then three, he didn't see one familiar face.

Finally accepting that he was wasting time, Adam set off in the direction of Mr Fry's office. With his own preoccupations, he'd been unaware of a certain restlessness in the air. He was regularly accosted by paupers and, as a salve to his conscience, he always dropped a few coppers into their grubby paws. But now he noticed large groups of them, swaggering around the town and intimidating people with their foul language. The tension rose when one of them attempted to snatch a cheese, was caught and set upon by several stallholders and given a good beating. The public, sensing that trouble was brewing, began to drift away, farmers loaded their wagons and the market was soon empty of everything except small bundles of straw being tossed about by the wind.

And as usual, thought Adam, not one policeman to be seen. Deciding it would be wise to follow the example of everyone else and get his meeting over with as soon as possible so that he could start for home, Adam accelerated his pace. He was shown into the architect's office by the elderly clerk. 'Mr Bennett to see you, Mr Fry,' he said and an extremely tall gentleman in early middle age, unwound himself from a chair and held out his hand. Adam shook it and was about to sit down, when there was the sound of raised voices and feet thudding past the window.

The two men looked at each other. 'There's a very tense atmosphere in the town, Mr Fry, can you think of any reason why this might be? Is a politician expected? O'Connor, for instance.'

'Not as far as I know. But trouble has been

brewing for a while with the paupers at the workhouse.'

'So I heard.'

'It came to a head this morning at the stoneyards. It seems the Board of Guardians has changed the paupers' hours of work. They now have to start at six and finish at seven for ten pence a day. When they turned up at the old time of eight o'clock they found the gates closed against them, so they seized a truckload of bread. We just have to pray it doesn't get out of hand, that's all. Now, how can I be of help, Mr Bennett?'

Adam explained about the school, the size of the plot on which they hoped to build it, how they were looking for a suitable architect and how his mother had been given his name. 'We want at least three classrooms and we're hoping that eventually we'll be able to persuade parents to allow their children to stay on at school until they are at least twelve years of age.'

'That is an honourable aim, Mr Bennett. If only it could be achieved for every child in the country, we might not have this continual unrest. As it is, most people live in the darkest ignorance, spend all their wages in public houses and are unable to achieve their potential. I'm a member of the Temperance Society and although we regularly get people to sign the pledge, I'm afraid they often lapse. Hume is one of my successes. He once had a liking for rum, but he's been with me ten years and not a drop of alcohol has passed his lips in all that time.'

As Mr Fry finished, the subject of his conversation shuffled in. 'I think we ought to close the shutters on this floor, sir. There's going to be trouble before the day's out, I can feel it in me bones.'

'Well, your bones have never let you down yet, Hume, so you may close the shutters. It seems a little early to light lamps, so if you don't object, Mr Bennett, we'll continue our discussion in my living quarters and perhaps when you have a moment, Hume, you could bring us a tray of tea?'

Adam began to warm to the courtly man, and as he followed him up the stairs and into his sitting-room, he took an interested look around. There were no toys or pieces of sewing lying about the room, or any other evidence of a wife and children, and it was immaculately tidy. It was obvious that Mr Fry was a reading man, though, for a book-case ran from floor to ceiling and a copy of Charles Dickens' *Oliver Twist* lay open on the table. The room overlooked the street and a co-ordinated chanting drew Adam to the window. Almost at once he stepped back in alarm. 'Your clerk's hunch appears to be right. You were wise to put the shutters up. There's a great pack standing outside a

house a few doors down, baying for someone's blood.'

'Oh dear.' Mr Fry wrung his hands in
some agitation. 'That's the home of Mr
Wilks, the Chairman of the Board of
Guardians. I do hope he'll come to no
harm.'

Keeping up his commentary, Adam went
on, 'From what I can make out they're
demanding their wages. And good Lord,
this is serious ... some of the women are
collecting stones in their aprons and...'
Adam moved closer to the window,
'...others are pulling up garden palings.'

'Please come away, Mr Bennett, if they
throw a brick this way, you'll be injured.'

But although the noise and violence made
his heart thump, Adam couldn't drag
himself from the window, even when the
street began to ring with the sound of
shattering glass. 'Where are the police? Why
aren't they here doing their duty and
arresting the ringleaders?' Adam exclaimed
as he watched the mob take control; women
distributing stones as if they were sweetmeats, and men setting about, with vicious
intent, to smash everything in sight with the
palings.

Mr Fry's tall frame quivered like a leaf. 'If
they break into Mr Wilks's house, they are
quite like to murder the poor man. He must
be terrified.'

'They're here, at last.' Adam gave a gasp of relief as suddenly, if somewhat belatedly, what looked like the entire police force appeared at the end of the street. They advanced shoulder to shoulder, wielding their truncheons indiscriminately and felling people like trees. The whack of staves against bone, the groans of the injured and the terrified shrieks of women, so sickened Adam he had to move away. Amidst all the mayhem, Hume appeared with a tray of tea. The spoons tinkled slightly against the cups but otherwise the clerk gave no sign of fear.

'Your tea, gentlemen,' he announced, then went to the window, drew the heavy curtains and lit the lamps. 'You won't want to be listening to that din, it will put you off your tea,' he asserted, before disappearing again.

'He's a cool customer,' Adam commented, as Mr Fry poured the tea.

'Yes, he went to sea as a boy. I imagine that must have toughened him up. A riot is nothing compared with a full scale sea-battle.'

Adam was surprised how dry the inside of his mouth was and how much the tea refreshed him, and as he held out his cup for a refill, said, 'With a virtual battle going on outside, I can hardly see us concentrating on business tonight, do you, Mr Fry? So perhaps it would be better if I returned another day when we're less likely to be distracted.'

'I agree, it's hard to think clearly when the town has descended into a state of anarchy.'

Adam finished his tea and stood up. 'I'd better be getting home.'

'Mr Bennett, listen to it out there, they're baying for blood. I wouldn't dream of allowing you to leave this house. If you put a foot outside the front door the mob will tear you apart. I have a spare room and I shall be happy to put you up for the night.'

'That's most generous of you, Mr Fry,' Adam answered, for he, too had been wondering if he would make it back in one piece to Halby.

'I'll just go and tell Hume, then.' The architect disappeared briefly and when he returned, it was with some news. 'Hume tells me that the magistrate has just been to read the Riot Act. Let's hope they see sense and disperse, or it will be the military next,' he predicted and took up one of the lamps. 'I don't know about you, but I always retire early, so if you'll follow me, I will show you to your room.'

Mr Fry led the way up a further flight of stairs into a bedroom which was again at the front of the house, but well out of reach of any missiles. 'If the violence subsides you might get a little sleep, Mr Bennett, but in the circumstances, I won't wish you sweet

136

dreams,' the architect said a trifle wryly, and closed the door.

Adam saw that a night-shirt was laid out for him, long and lean like Mr Fry, and that hot water, soap and a towel had also been provided. He undressed, washed, and lay down on the bed. Although he was tired, Adam was resigned to a sleepless night, so he propped a pillow behind his head and picked up one of Mr Fry's books. But before he'd reached the end of the first paragraph, the print began to blur and the book fell on to his chest. He was on the edge of sleep, when a blast of bugles, then the insistent beating of drums, made him shoot up in bed. 'God almighty, what's that?' The mahogany chest of drawers, the large press, was not furniture Adam recognised and for a moment he was confused. He stared down at the overlong sleeves of his host's night-shirt, then it clicked in his brain where he was and he leapt out of bed. He pushed up the window and a chilling sight met his eyes. With bayonets fixed, about fifty Pensioners (army reservists) were marching in a straight line down Rutland Street. Christ! He'd wanted the riot controlled but not this, it would be outright slaughter.

Imagining the bloodshed, and knowing he couldn't stand by and allow it to happen, Adam grabbed his clothes, without stopping to consider what he could do as a solitary, unarmed man. He was stuffing the bulky nightshirt into his trousers, when outside an authoritative voice ordered, 'Stand fast, everyone.'

Adam went and leaned out of the window again. Hell bent on martyrdom, the rioters were moving with arms linked towards the advancing army. 'Don't be such damn fools! Run for it!' Adam yelled. No one took any heed of his warning but as the deadly bayonets advanced, their steps did falter.

Tension silenced the crowd and the order to, 'Stand fast,' was repeated. By now only a few feet separated rioter and Pensioner and the ugly blades were pointed straight at their stomachs. No, they couldn't! It was unthinkable in this day and age. Adam held his breath. Then wisely, self-preservation took over and one of the rioters broke rank and fled. In panic-stricken disarray the rest followed with the Pensioners in hot pursuit, until they disappeared into the network of alleys and backstreets, where no policeman or soldier who valued his life would ever dare to set foot.

Adam exhaled with relief. A tragedy had been averted. He undressed again, climbed back into bed, blew out the lamp and at last, slept.

Adam refused breakfast the following morning, thanked Mr Fry profusely for his hospitality, said he would be in touch again soon, opened the door and stepped out into a battleground. It was a grisly, depressing sight. A pall of smoke hung over the area and there was a stomach-churning smell of vomit and urine. Blood was smeared across walls, cobbles that had been dug up for ammunition were strewn across the street, gas-lamps had been smashed, gardens trampled underfoot, windows shattered. Policemen stood guard outside the most badly damaged houses and as Adam picked his way between shattered glass and broken window frames, one of them addressed him by name. 'Good-morning, Mr Bennett.'

Adam paused. It was Constable Pegg dressed in his uniform of blue tailcoat and top hat. 'Good-morning, Pegg,' he replied.

'I don't see us solving your crime for the minute, sir, not with this carry-on,' the policeman apologised.

'Yes, you've certainly got your hands full. It was a nasty business. Do you think it's the last we've seen of the rioters, or are you expecting more trouble?'

'Definitely more trouble. We've got a few of the blighters locked up in the cells at the Town Hall, so they won't be able to do any more mischief, but it's the ringleaders we want and they're still free. Oh yes,' he prophesied gloomily, 'they'll be out again tonight, maybe even during the day. Me, I'd have every rioter hung, drawn and quartered as an example. That would stop their nonsense.'

'No doubt it would, but a little extreme, perhaps.'

'You don't know these people, it's all they understand.'

'Yes ... well, I'd better be on my way, then. I don't want to be caught up in it again.'

'I should do just that, sir. Home's the safest place. Wish I wa' there,' Police Constable Pegg added plaintively.

Sensing a little encouragement would be in order, Adam said, 'Never mind, you're upholding law and order and doing a splendid job, constable.'

'Kind of you to say so, sir, 'cos to tell the truth, we in't appreciated.'

'Oh, you are.' With this final assurance Adam wished him good-day and walked on, noticing there was none of the usual bustle of commerce, and windows remained shuttered in a nervous expectancy of worse to come. He'd imagined some shops would be closed but the town looked as if had been hit by the plague. Struck by a sense of desolation at human folly, Adam was about to find comfort in a jug of ale at the Stag & Pheasant when the silence was broken by the ring of metal on cobblestones. Trotting towards him was a solitary hackney carriage, on its way, he assumed, to the station with a passenger. Glad of some human contact, as the cab passed, Adam gave the occupant a quick glance and found he was staring at Emily. She gazed back at him without a flicker of recognition, but undeterred Adam shouted, 'Emily,' and went chasing up Granby Street after the vehicle. He didn't catch up with the cab until it stopped outside the station and by then he was too out of breath to speak. While he drew air into his lungs, Emily paid her fare, picked up her bag and walked with rigid indifference towards the ticket office.

'Emily, speak to me please,' Adam called, when he'd regained his breath. She turned slowly, gave him a scornful look and disappeared inside the station. Deciding that, since she obviously loathed him, he had nothing to lose, Adam continued in pursuit of her. She was buying a ticket and her bag was at her feet. Seizing the opportunity, Adam bent and picked it up. 'Let me carry this for you,' he offered.

'No.' Emily tried to wrench the bag from his hand and there followed a slightly undignified tussle, until a porter, who'd obviously been watching them, came over and demanded, 'Is this gentleman pestering you, madam?'

Emily looked uncertain and Adam stiffened with embarrassment. Was she about to wreak revenge? 'Oh ... er ... no,' she faltered and unwillingly surrendered the bag to Adam. Satisfied all was well the porter moved away, but as soon as he was out of earshot, Emily hissed, 'Now, give me back my bag.'

Adam handed it to her. 'Can't you at least be civil to me, Emily?' he pleaded.

'Give me one reason why I should.'

'Because I love you.'

Emily stared at him coldly. 'In case it's slipped your memory, may I remind you that you are talking to a married woman.'

Adam moved closer and gazed into her eyes. 'Love's not something you can rip out and throw away.'

'Such beguiling words, but meaningless.'

'Why do you say such harsh things to me?'

Emily's eyes hardened. 'I thought you had more intelligence than to ask such an obvious question. But since, like most men, you have a selective memory when it comes to betrayal, I'll refresh yours. How is your wife? – Bad choice that, Adam – and the serving maid, and your bastard children?' Emily paused and waited.

'They were all mistakes,' Adam mumbled.

'Oh dear. You'll be telling me next you were an innocent dupe of scheming women.'

'In the case of Isabelle, yes. She lied to me from the first moment I set eyes on her.'

'You'll have to forgive me, but I've

developed a healthy scepticism of late.'

'I trust not towards your husband?'

Emily bridled. 'There are always exceptions. I couldn't have a more loving husband than Rory. Now, if you'll excuse me, I do have a train to catch and he'll be waiting for me at the other end.'

Eight

Whatever possessed me? Emily asked herself as she jumped into the carriage and threw herself down on the nearest seat. Where did I dredge up all that bitterness from? And the lies? Her heart and the wheels of the train beat in furious rhythm but she felt curiously elated. Adam knew exactly where he stood with her now and that was nowhere. She had at last buried the past and she would not waste another second regretting it. Besides, Adam diverted her from her main concern, which was her father. She hated acknowledging it but every time she saw him he looked more frail and she was beginning to seriously consider whether she ought to give up her job in London and return home. Neither parent had suggested it, but then neither of them knew that their son-in-law had taken himself off to America. Rory and her father were old political allies and every time she explained away his absence, her excuses sounded so hollow, she wondered why her mother didn't see right through them. And she would have at one time, because she had a sixth sense about matters of the heart, particularly her daughter's. Now, though, only one thing concerned her; and that was her beloved husband and his failing health.

Although she'd vowed to sell her wedding ring, she still wore it. *And if only Rory would write,* Emily fretted, *then I wouldn't feel like a deserted wife.* But was it more than mere coincidence that had caused her to lose two men to America? Perhaps there was some colossal fault in her character that drove them away. Emily tried to do an honest appraisal of herself and thought of her worst faults: bossy at times, yes, and stubborn, and her father had taught her to speak up for herself, answer back, and that was a trait considered unfeminine in a woman. Yes, she would admit to all those failings, but on the other hand she'd never attempted to commit murder, neither had she stolen so much as a groat, and she was a faithful wife. So where had she gone wrong? Emily puzzled about this for the next hour, but as she lifted down her bag to change at Rugby, she was no nearer to having an answer.

The letter had been slipped under the door. Emily snatched it up, saw that it was Rory's handwriting, and as she tore it open, her self-respect was restored. She wasn't the abandoned wife she'd feared she was, after all.

'My dearest, darling precious wife,' she read, 'I can't tell you how glad I am to be on terra firma. I'll spare you the details but travelling steerage is no joke, particularly when your travelling companions vomit every time the ship pitches. I miss you so desperately, Emily, and I can't wait for you to join me, although I promise that you will travel (third class) in a proper cabin. However, there is a problem about money at the moment. Quinn is paying me less than he promised, New York is expensive and most of my wages go on food and accommodation. As soon as I can I will send you a money order, which I want you to save to put towards your ticket. I can't wait for us to be together again, so that I can hold you in my arms all night long. There are so many opportunities out here (there is talk of large deposits of gold being found in California and people are moving west in the hope of becoming rich), so we have a chance to make a good life for ourselves, and with the family I know you want, Emily. I've never met so many Irish people before outside Ireland, many of whom came to escape the famine, so there's plenty of jaw, jaw about the auld country, but no drinking I promise, and it keeps me from feeling too homesick.

Don't lose faith in me, Emily. You're my last thought before I fall asleep and the first when I wake. I'll love you forever, and all I want is for us to be together again as man and wife...'

It was those final words, Rory's reaffirmation of his love for her, that did it and the tears came spilling out. They ran down her cheeks and dripped on to the letter, turning the loving phrases in to spidery smudges. Aching with loneliness Emily lay down on the bed and pressed the letter to her lips. 'Oh, Rory, I do miss you so much,' she whispered, then lay sobbing with quiet hopelessness into her pillow. The faults that had begun to irritate her, his unreliability, his restlessness, his drinking were forgotten in her aching need to feel his naked body pressed against hers.

Thoughts carnal were nudging their way into her brain, when there was a tap on the door and Prudence called, 'I heard you were back. Can I come in?' Without waiting for an answer, Prudence's fuzzy nob appeared, followed by the rest of her. Standing over Emily, she exclaimed, 'Oh dear, there ain't anyfink wrong is there?'

Emily sat up, adjusted her hair, blew her nose and didn't reply. Prudence was one of life's losers, but that wasn't how she wanted to be viewed and she had no intention of swapping confidences with Prudence, or allowing an intimacy to develop, in case it was catching.

'It's the letter, ain't it, it's upset you?'

Emily nodded.

'It was me who put it under the door. I

saw the American stamp so guessed it was from Rory. He's all right, ain't 'e?'

'He says he is. It's just me. I miss him,' Emily confessed, in spite of herself.

'Well that's natural enough.'

'But he's promised to send me the money for my fare soon,' Emily went on, brightening a little.

'Ain't you the lucky one?' Prudence gazed at Emily with open envy. 'But then there are some women who've got everythin': brains, looks, a decent bloke who looks after them and don't go sniffing around other petticoats.'

In comparison with Prudence she certainly was, Emily decided, imagining the horror of being saddled with the dire Edmund.

The warmer the weather got, the stuffier her room became and Emily was faced with two alternatives. She could keep the window shut and roast, or open it and be almost overwhelmed by the putrid, disease-carrying smells that wafted up from the drains in the yard below. Not unnaturally she had grown to loathe the room and tonight in particular, Emily knew she'd die if she stayed confined within its four walls. Before she left home her mother had pressed five shillings into her hand, and she knew it ought to go towards something sensible, like her rent. But she didn't feel like being sensible tonight. Instead she wanted to do something outrageously extravagant. But not on her own. She turned to Prudence. 'How do you fancy going out for a bite to eat?'

Prudence's face lit up. She wasn't a fool and she knew Emily despised her for staying with a man who treated her so badly. But it was easy to look down your nose when you had the support of a husband and family, and she felt like telling Emily so sometimes. She did have class, though, and if they could be friends, some of it might rub off on her, then she could find herself a nicer chap and tell Edmund to go to the devil. 'Ooh yeah. We could treat ourselves to an eel pie, it's one of me favourites. Get yer titfer on.' Prudence linked arms with Emily, then to prove she wasn't a completely downtrodden drudge, added with a conspiratorial giggle, 'Edmund's upstairs waiting for his dinner, but bugger him ses I, let's go and paint the town red.'

Hattie came across the journal that she'd kept during her time as Isabelle's personal maid, while she was searching through a drawer for some buttons. She'd almost forgotten about it, but immediately as she sat down and began flicking through the pages, she was engrossed. There was a lot of stuff about Isabelle and her carry-on with

Sir Austin but what gripped Hattie, and made her warm and excited, were the pages explicitly detailing what she and Adam had got up to in the hayloft. Did we really do all those things? Hattie giggled, but the moistness between her legs told her that she couldn't go on living a nun's life much longer. Sex was good, it was natural, she was young and she had two babies to show for her passion and naughtiness, but no man. She'd been waiting for Adam to weaken but he made sure he stayed well clear of temptation. She knew he was having to fight it, though, because if ever he came within a hundred yards of her he turned his horse around and galloped off as if she were a witch with magic powers to entrap him.

So Hattie had taken to keeping watch at her window and if ever she caught sight of Adam on the spare piece of land where the school was to be built, she would immediately dump the babies in the wagon and take a walk round the Green. As she passed she would wave and say loudly, 'Look boys, there's your papa,' then watch with pleasure as he blushed bright red to his ears.

Immediately he would turn his back on her and enter into an earnest discussion with a stork-like man who had what looked like plans of the new school spread out in front of him. But Adam had no wife now, and eventually old Hornington would start getting frisky. He'd have to have a woman then or burst, Hattie decided. And then he would come tapping on her door like a woodpecker and she would take him in, undress him and they'd make wonderful love all night long and maybe another baby. Hattie closed her eyes and sighed.

But if, by chance, he didn't come by, who else was there? Well certainly any married man in the village, if she had a mind, which she didn't. After Adam, whose linen was always spotless and whose skin was anointed daily with soaps that smelt of carnations and cologne, it would be hard to stomach an unwashed farm labourer with bad teeth who was likely to belch and fart through a quick poke. No, she'd acquired a taste for gentlemen, so from now on she'd stick to them, Hattie decided, and remembered young Gabriel Smith who'd caught her eye last time he was home from Rugby School. Half gypsy, he scowled a lot and he was younger than her, but he was already well built and she bet his man's thing was fairly bursting out of his trousers. But perhaps she needed to wait a year or two. He wouldn't have much idea about anything and she'd be happy to advance his education, but she didn't want to be accused of cradle-snatching and gain an even worse reputation in the village than she had now.

So who did that leave? Hattie searched

around in her mind. No one except Freddie, whom Clare had brought up. Well he'd done all right for himself. She remembered him from school, gangly and a bit of a swot and now he was away at university, lucky devil. She'd been pretty good at school herself, but of course, being a girl, education had finished early for her.

Hattie went to sling the notebook back in the drawer, then changed her mind. No, that was a sign of defeat. The book was asking to be written in again so why not keep a record of the boys' development? How much they weighed, and important landmarks such as their first teeth and first words. But it also needed information that made the pages sizzle, real gossip and immediately thought of Mrs Dowse and the hints she'd dropped regarding Adam's parentage. How awful if his pa had only been a common village lad and not the Squire, after all her bragging. What she needed to do was have a chat with Mrs Dowse, find out the true facts, or she'd never hold her head up again in Halby.

You could set your clock by Mrs Dowse. Punctually at twelve each day she came out of her house with a jug in her hand and made her way down to the Weavers' Arms. Hattie prepared herself by baking a seed cake, then she pushed the boys into the small front garden, sat down on the bench with her sewing box and a shady hat and waited for the gossipmonger to come by.

'My, they grow bigger by the day,' a voice said eventually.

Hattie looked up from sewing lace on to a baby's cap with a show of surprise. 'Oh hello, Mrs Dowse. Yes, they do, don't they?' She folded away her sewing and stood up. 'They're right guzzlers, too, so they'll be wanting their feed soon, but I was thinking of making myself a cup of tea first. Would you like one?' Hattie invited.

'That's very kind of you, me dook,' answered Mrs Dowse, and pushed open the gate. Following Hattie inside, her sharp, inquisitive eyes surveyed the room and Hattie knew she was recording every detail, down to the pattern on the plates. It would be relayed back to the neighbours, of course, but that was exactly what Hattie wanted. She'd taken the rough end of the stick from many of the villagers when she was in the family way and it gave her immense satisfaction to think of them looking at their own meagre possessions and turning green with envy. In their sanctimonious eyes, it was wrong that a bad lot like her should be profiting from her sins.

'My, you've got this nice.' Mrs Dowse swung around, peering up at the ceiling, then into the darkest corners to check there were no cobwebs or mice droppings.

'Do you think so?' Hattie answered modestly.

'And that dresser's got a lovely shine on it.'

'Yeah, I polish it every week with beeswax and turpentine,' Hattie informed her as she took down cups and saucers, put the kettle on the fire and sliced the cake. 'Most of the furniture came from the big house,' she bragged, hoping this would get back to the neighbours.

'I can remember Trent Hall when it were nearly falling down. The Squire couldn't afford a new roof until he married Matilda. Old man Pedley, her pa, had to pay a high price to get her off his hands.'

All ears, Hattie handed her guest a cup of tea and a slice of cake. Mrs Dowse paused to take a bite then went on, 'To look at her now with her la-de-da ways you wouldn't guess what Miss Matilda got up to when she were young. I was only a girl at the time, meself but I remember seeing her coming out of church one day, and I'll tell you this, by the state of her, she hadn't been in there praying.'

Hattie was goggle-eyed. 'Are you saying...?'

Mrs Dowse shook her head in sorrow at such sinfulness. 'I am.'

'In God's house?' Even by Hattie's standards that was impressive.

'Disgusting in't it? But that's gentry for

you. Although, of course, Matilda was only a hosier's daughter, and that brother of hers were even worse. He tried to take advantage of me once. I tell you, no girl in the village was safe, and poor soft Polly went to an early grave 'cos of him. He was hounded from the village, in the end, and serve him right, too, an–'

'Who was Matilda with in the church that day?' Hattie interrupted before Mrs Dowse strayed completely from the point.

'I couldn't say definite. But Captain Bennett were around a lot at the time. The Squire were his uncle, ye see. Oh, you have should seen him. He was the handsomest man I ever saw in my life in his soldier's uniform. And those eyes! Blue as the heavens, they were.' Mrs Dowse let out a long sigh of regret. 'There wasn't a girl in the village who wouldn't have lifted up their skirts for him. We were all in love with him.'

'Are you saying Mr Bennett is Adam's pa?'

'That's a question only his mam can truthfully answer.'

'But it's a pretty good guess that he is?'

'Don't ask me to make things up, Hattie Bonner,' Mrs Dowse chided sanctimoniously. 'Anyway I must go. The old man goes on something dreadful if his dinner in't on the table in time and I in't been for his ale yet.' She gave her bosoms a hitch and stood up.

Hattie showed her out then hurried back to feed the twins. It had been a fruitful half hour, and as she put her babies to her breast, she whispered to them, 'You've got a grandpapa you can feel proud of boys. He's a man of substance, a Member of Parliament and he was a soldier, too. Fought in wars, won medals, and if you do half as well, I'll be well-pleased with you.' She kissed them, laid them in their cradle for a nap, opened her notebook at a fresh page, ran her finger down the spine, dipped her pen in the ink and started to write at great speed, anxious to get the facts down while they were still fresh in her mind. When she'd finished, Hattie re-read the piece, thinking with a complacent smile, I bet I now know more about Mr Adam Bennett than he does himself, and it will certainly come in useful if I feel like stirring up a bit of trouble in the future.

Nine

What with all the worries and stresses of the new school, constant meetings with the architect and builders, Clare hadn't paid any attention to the changes in her body and it wasn't until she was violently sick one morning that she realised it was two months since she had her last menses. Hardly daring to hope, she felt her breasts. Yes, they were tender. She stared in the looking-glass at her wan features. It wasn't a silly fantasy, the hours on her knees in prayer hadn't been wasted, and what she'd so longed for had finally happened. She was with child. A whole woman and not the barren husk she'd come to view herself as. 'Thank you, thank you, God,' she whispered, then calling, 'Christopher! Christopher!' she flew down the stairs, paused when remembered the precious gift she carried, and descended in a manner more in keeping with her interesting condition.

Christopher, who was reading in the drawing-room, heard his wife call and rushed out into the hall. 'Whatever is it darling?' He asked in alarm as she ran into his arms.

'I'm ... I'm...'

'Ill?' he finished for her.

'No, no!'

'You're getting yourself into a state. Come and sit down and tell me calmly,' Christopher suggested and led her to a chair.

Clare's face glowed. 'Oh Christopher, it's happened at last, I'm going to have a baby.' She watched a flicker of doubt cross his face, then he knelt down beside her and grasped her hand.

'Are you sure?' he asked earnestly.

'As sure as any woman can be.'

'Oh my sweetest, cleverest girl.' Overcome with emotion he buried his head in her lap.

Clare stroked his hair and said dreamily, 'Yes, we're going to be parents. Have a child of our own at last.'

'Of course, you'll have to give up teaching,' said Christopher, becoming practical again. 'And there's to be no more running around worrying about the new school, either.'

'Yes, Christopher,' Clare answered obediently.

'And I want to arrange for you to see a doctor in Leicester. Your aunt will know a good man, and we'll drive in and see him as soon as we can make an appointment.'

Clare stood up. 'Let's go and see Aunt Tilda now.'

'Will you be able to manage the walk, my darling?'

Clare laughed. 'Christopher, I'm going to have a baby, something millions of women do. It doesn't mean I've lost the use of my legs.'

'All right. I'll go and fetch your cloak and we'll stroll down to the Dower House at a very gentle pace.'

Since the architect, Sir Charles Barry's decision to rebuild the Houses of Parliament in the Gothic style, it had become all the rage in house building. However Matilda considered it over-ornate and had refused to consider it when she was having the plans for her own house drawn up. Instead, she'd decided that the Dower House would be built in a design similar to Trent Hall, using the same Charnwood granite, but on a smaller scale. Neither was the heavy furniture that was so much in vogue, to her taste and she'd stuck to a simpler style that harked back to an earlier age. However, she had made some concessions to modern living, and the kitchens and her bathroom with its water closet were the most up to date, most envied and most copied in the county.

Matilda was awaiting the arrival of Mr Fry with the final plans for the school, but he was late and she was standing by the window wondering what could have delayed him, when she saw Christopher and Clare coming up the drive. Oh dear, she thought, I do hope they haven't come with yet more suggestions for the school. Since they would be running it once it was built, Matilda had considered it only fair that they should be fully involved in the project. However, she quickly discovered the truth of the saying that too many cooks spoil the broth. Conflicting opinions could cause serious delays. In the end she'd had to be ruthless and take control. One of her cleverer ideas was to decide to have the name of every benefactor carved on a frieze around the outside of the school and, at the promise of this bit of immortality, people had come running with their moneybags. And now she was growing impatient. She wanted to see the foundations laid, and at least the shell of the building completed before winter set in.

But as Clare and Christopher were shown in it was apparent from their smiles that it was not the new school they had come to talk about. Matilda often felt a jolt of remembrance and guilt when she looked at her niece, and as Clare hurried towards her, her brown eyes glowing with happiness, Matilda was reminded painfully of Polly and the wrong that George had done to her.

'Oh Aunt Tilda we have the most joyful news,' Clare burst out. 'I am *enceinte*.'

Dear Lord, no, thought Matilda. This was something she'd hoped might never happen but she managed to arrange her face in a smile and kiss her niece with deep affection. 'I am so happy for you both, you've waited such a long time,' she congratulated them, deciding she must look on the bright side. After all, everyone had expected the worst when Clare was born, hadn't even thought she would live. But she'd survived to become a fine young woman and so could this baby.

'This is the first of many,' Christopher predicted, standing tall as a grenadier. 'Just you watch, that new school will soon be so full of young Harcourts, you'll have to build another one.'

'I do hope not, this one is causing me enough of a headache,' Matilda laughed.

'Perhaps we'll stop at six then. But what we've come for is to ask you for the name of a doctor in Leicester, one you could recommend. We would like to have the pregnancy confirmed as soon as possible.'

'Well there is a Doctor Welland, who looked after Hattie. He's reliable, with modern ideas. I'll give you his address.' Matilda went to her writing desk, found the doctor's card and handed it to Christopher.

'Thank you. I'll write immediately and arrange an appointment for Clare. There is also another problem. Obviously Clare can't continue teaching. It would be improper. But I'm going to find it difficult to manage on my own. Would you be agreeable to advertising for another teacher?'

Since Clare came free and a new teacher would require a salary, Matilda had to think about this. 'I am being stretched financially at the moment, Christopher. Couldn't one of the older girls monitor the little ones?'

'Probably. But when the school is finished we'll need another teacher anyway, it just means bringing it forward a few months. I'm hoping Freddie might consider taking up teaching, but he's still at university so that's some way off.'

'I feel a bit awful letting you down like this, Aunt Tilda, and if it would help, I could carry on for another month. No one knows but us that I'm with child, so I won't offend anyone,' said Clare.

'If Christopher doesn't mind, that would be a great help, dear, and you're quite right, we'll have to appoint someone else eventually.'

'And no doubt the Good Lord will provide,' said Clare, sounding uncannily like her late grandmother.

'In the meantime I'd better put an advertisement in the Leicester *Chronicle* for a qualified teacher,' said Matilda, thinking wryly that it was more likely to be one of her better pieces of jewellery financing the new teacher rather than the Good Lord.

A week later, Clare and Christopher drove into Leicester for their appointment with Dr Welland. Clare had heard of women, desperate for children, having phantom pregnancies, so at the back of her mind there had lurked a fear that her symptoms might be little more than wishful thinking. Therefore, when, after a thorough medical investigation, the doctor confirmed her pregnancy and also told her she was in excellent health and would have a fine baby, Clare wanted to embrace him. She restrained herself, but walked out of the doctor's consulting rooms clutching Christopher's hand tightly and feeling somehow unique. She was also bursting to tell the world of their great achievement. 'There's no reason why we should keep it a secret any longer, is there, Christopher?' she asked.

Christopher, conscious of his new responsibilities, gave this question some thought. 'None at all, my dear,' he said at last.

'So can we go and see Jed and Rachel?'

'Of course, my dearest.' Christopher had heard that when a woman was in a certain condition it was the husband's duty to indulge her every whim, so he was happy to assist Clare into the trap and turn the horse in the direction of Jed's shop.

But not, apparently, without a stop en route, because when they reached Cheapside, Clare touched his arm. 'Stop here, outside Sharpe's,' she commanded. 'I've told Hattie she can make me a couple of dresses, so I need to purchase some material.' Clare disappeared into the shop and when she re-emerged half an hour later, she was accompanied by an assistant carrying several very large packages.

'I bought a few things for the baby as well,' Clare explained, as a place was found in the trap for the parcels.

Christopher laughed indulgently. 'So I see.'

'The prettiest little garments, I'll show them to you when we get home.' Clare's face already had a dreamy, maternal quality and Christopher wanted to kiss and hug her there in the street for what she'd given him; after a lonely, miserable childhood a loving and happy marriage, and now a child. But out of a sense of propriety he restrained himself, squeezed her hand instead and ordered the horse to walk on, and a short time later they came to a halt under a swinging sign that read, Jedediah Fairfax, Bookseller.

'That's strange, the closed sign is up, and the blinds are down. It's not the dinner hour, is it?' Clare asked.

Christopher consulted his pocket watch. 'No, it's only eleven-thirty.'

Clare got down from the trap and went to

the window and tried to peer in. 'I can't see a thing. I'll try the side door.' She went and pulled the bell, then stood, expecting to hear footsteps descend the stairs. However there was only silence.

'They must have gone out,' said Christopher.

'I doubt it, they have a business to run.' Clare put her ear to the door and gave the bell another tug. She was about to give up, when she heard a shuffle then the bolts being shot back. The door opened a fraction and Emily's ravaged face appeared. 'Oh ... oh Clare,' she faltered, and burst into tears.

With instinctive compassion, Clare reached out a hand to her friend. 'Emily, my dear, what is wrong?'

'Papa ... he is dead.'

'Oh no!' Clare took a shocked step backwards and tears filled her eyes. Not Jed, he'd always seemed somehow invincible, a man who could cheat death. And she hadn't even said goodbye to him. 'I knew he was poorly ... but I never guessed...' she stumbled.

'It was his heart...' The words finished in a sob and Clare opened her arms, Emily fell into them and they clung to each other sobbing quietly.

Christopher was saddened to hear of Jed's death because he had been a good man but selfishly, his main concern was for his wife and their unborn child. He had a terror of something going wrong and Clare needed calm, not an emotional upset on this scale. Although Christopher didn't want to appear cold-hearted he knew he had to get her away. 'We are so sorry, Emily, but we don't want to intrude on your grief...' he tried, lost his nerve and tailed away.

Guessing the general drift of her husband's thoughts, Clare disentangled herself from Emily, wiped her eyes and blew her nose. 'Jed was kin and I must offer my condolences to Rachel,' she insisted.

'Yes, of course,' Christopher answered and had no option but to follow the two women up the stairs.

Here it was a twilight world. The blinds were down and Rachel sat in a chair dressed in deepest widows' weeds, looking small and insubstantial. Natalie sat bolt upright in the chair opposite, bright hair glowing like a candle in the gloom, and on her young face a look of bewildered misery.

Clare quickly crossed the room, crouched down and took Rachel's small work-scarred hand. 'I am so sorry, Rachel.'

'He shouldn't have gone and left me, not just yet.' Rachel twisted a small black bordered handkerchief compulsively.

'I know. But the dear Lord called him,' Clare answered softly, for like her grandmother, she had a simple, but sustained faith in God.

'My Jed was a good, honest man, he did all he could to improve the lot of his fellow men, and it wore his heart out in the end. But he didn't believe in God and I could never get him to church, even in the last month. So do you think he'll go to heaven?' Rachel looked at Clare half fearfully. 'I couldn't bear it if I thought he wasn't.'

'He'll go to heaven, I'm sure of it. The good we do here on earth doesn't go unnoticed.'

Natalie suddenly shot out of her chair. 'Stop talking like this. Papa's not dead, I tell you! He's not dead!' she screamed and ran from the room.

'Sorry, that was a bit rude, but she's young and she's taking it very hard, like we all are. Papa was our rock and I don't know how we'll go on without him,' Emily apologised.

Clare, who was beginning to feel she was intruding in this house of grieving women, asked, 'What about Ben and Simon? When will they be here?' She was going to add, 'And Rory?' but decided against it.

'This afternoon.'

'We'll go, then.' Clare bent and kissed Rachel, then Christopher moved over and rather stiffly offered his condolences to Rachel.

Emily saw them off the premises and as they embraced, Clare asked carefully, 'When is the funeral, Emily?'

'The day after tomorrow at eleven o'clock.'

'We'll be there,' Clare promised, but she was silent on the journey back to Halby, her thoughts focused on Rachel and the tragedy of her loss. She and Jed had had such a solid marriage, and now she was doomed to go through the rest of her life on her own, like a rudderless ship. Clare glanced at her husband. How would I be able to endure it, she wondered with a shiver, if Christopher were taken from me? But she must stop dwelling on such gloomy matters, it wasn't good for her, or the baby, and anyway, Clare told herself, she and Christopher were still young, blessed with good health and they had years ahead of them. A marriage that didn't look in such good shape was Emily and Rory's. Rory's continued absence was mystifying and when Emily was in most need of his support, why wasn't he at her side? Surely he would be at the funeral to pay his last respects to his father-in-law, a man he considered a friend as well as a political ally.

As was to be expected of someone of Jed's standing, the church was full. Fellow Chartists, friends, (but not Rory as far as Clare could make out) foes and adversaries alike had turned up to pay their last respects to a man who had been both admired and vilified in the town. Family and close friends followed the coffin to its last resting place and as the priest intoned: 'Man that is born of a woman hath but a short time to live...' Clare could hear the quiet sobbing of Rachel and her two daughters. Earth was scattered on to the coffin, the priest recited the final prayer and it was over; a man's life, his achievements laid in a box in the ground.

The final 'Amen,' was just too much for Clare and she put her hand to her mouth and turned away.

'Let's go home,' said Christopher quietly, and he guided her down the path between the lichen-covered gravestones. They had about reached the street when Emily caught up with them. Her eyes were puffy, but she was fighting to keep control of her emotions, and it was obvious it was going to be her task to get the family through the rest of the day.

'Thank you both for coming. My mother is almost in a state of collapse and Simon and Ben are looking after her at the moment, but I want to ask you a great favour. I shall have to return to London in a few days, Natalie is too young to cope, and I'm rather concerned about leaving Mama, so if ever you're in Leicester, could you look in and see how she is, Clare?'

'You know we'll do anything to help,'

Clare answered immediately. 'We'll come in at least once a week, won't we, Christopher?'

'We certainly will.'

'Oh, thank you, that's a great weight off my mind. Here, this is my address.' Emily handed Clare a scrap of paper. 'If you have the slightest doubts about Mama's health, write to me immediately and I'll come home.'

'Don't worry, we'll keep a close eye on her, and Natalie.'

'I didn't see Rory. Wasn't he able to make it to the funeral?' Christopher rather daringly asked.

'No. It was a great pity, but his editor has sent him to Ireland,' Emily lied.

'I imagine he must have been upset, not being able to pay his last respects to an old friend.'

'He's deeply distressed. I must go.' To avoid further awkward questions, Emily kissed them both and walked quickly away, fighting her way against the tide of mourners leaving the churchyard.

'Well, what do you make of that?' Clare asked, as she tucked her arm through her husband's. 'Strange, was it not?'

'Most curious,' Christopher answered. 'In fact, Rory appears to have vanished off the face of the earth.'

The following day the boys left; Simon to return to his regiment, Ben to London and his wife. Natalie rarely moved from her bedroom, wouldn't eat and refused to go to school. Emily let her be. Her younger sister was bewildered and hurt; it was the first major tragedy in her life and she needed to mourn in her own way. The loss of a few day's lessons was neither here nor there, and she had enough flesh on her not to die of starvation. Anyway, Emily's main concern was her mother. Rachel had always been a little vain about her looks, but she'd lost all interest in her appearance and didn't even bother to dress her hair in the morning; instead, leaving it hanging down her back in a long plait.

At first Emily avoided mentioning her father, fearing it would drive her mother into an even deeper depression. But then she discovered Jed was the one person Rachel did want to talk about, and in particular, their life together.

'Do you know the first time I set eyes on your father?' she asked a day or so after the funeral.

'No, tell me.'

'When he was setting fire to one of Joseph Pedley's corn ricks. I was a servant in the house at the time.'

'Papa? An arsonist? I can't believe it.'

Rachel almost smiled. 'My Jed was quite a

hothead in his youth. For a long time I was so convinced he was a Luddite and would get caught and hanged, I tried to stop myself falling in love with him. Those were very uncertain times.'

'Did he ever tell you why he did it?'

'It was retribution. Joseph Pedley ruined Jed's father and he died in the debtors' prison a broken man. That was the start of all the enmity between the two families and it just got worse. The Pedleys committed many more wrongs against us, but I'm not going to drag it all up again. There's been enough bitterness, and the feud prevented you and Adam from marrying, which wasn't right. It was no fault of yours and it all happened before either of you were born.'

'That's certainly water under the bridge, and I'm probably not cut out to be a land-owner's wife. Can you see me fitting into that sort of society; me, with my outspoken opinions?'

'It would do them good to hear a few home truths. They're all too complacent.'

'Well I'm glad to be who I am. We're humble stock, sturdy but humble.'

'Well, Adam hasn't got a great deal to boast about. His great grandfather was a drunken turnkey at the prison.'

'Was he now? Well that puts that mother of his in her place.'

Rachel thought of the many other disclosures she could make about Matilda: the question of Adam's parentage, for instance, but it all seemed pointless now and she wasn't a vengeful type. She'd said nothing so far, but it was Emily's marriage that most concerned her. Rory's non-appearance at the funeral couldn't be overlooked, and Emily's excuses lacked conviction. Although Rory wasn't the man her daughter truly loved, with their shared political interests, she had hoped they could make a go of it, but now she was genuinely worried. An unhappy marriage must be the equivalent to hell on earth. But whatever the problem, Emily obviously didn't want to share it or she wouldn't be making up all these feeble excuses And there probably wasn't a marriage that didn't go through a bad patch, so maybe, in time, the problems would sort themselves out. Of course, a baby might help.

'Have you decided yet when you are going back to London?' Rachel asked.

'Rory will be returning from Ireland on Saturday, *and* with all his dirty washing, no doubt, so I'd better say Friday,' Emily answered, thinking to herself with something like shame, what an adept liar I'm becoming.

Matilda had several replies to her advertisement for a schoolteacher, but after sifting through them she found only one promising candidate, a young man by the name of John Brown, who hailed from Nottingham. His ambition, right from when he was a small boy, was to be a teacher, he informed her in his letter. He then went on to describe how he had started on this road, beginning at thirteen as a pupil-teacher. When his five-year apprenticeship was completed he sat for the Queen's Scholarship and was fortunate enough to be offered a place at a training college. Here he was proud to gain his 'parchment', which finally qualified him to teach. He finished his letter by saying he was available to be interviewed at any time.

His credentials were so impressive, Matilda wrote back by return post, inviting him to an interview on the following Tuesday at two in the afternoon, informing him Jenkins would fetch him from Loughborough in the gig.

Matilda had arranged to conduct the interview at Trent Hall, so that if Mr Brown proved satisfactory, she could take him down to the school to meet Christopher. It was only fair, she felt, that he should have the final say since he would be working with him.

When he was shown into the office, Matilda saw a young man of about twenty-four, built like an oak tree and with light

174

brown hair. He was also impeccably turned out, wore his hair quite long and was sporting side-whiskers, a fashion that hadn't yet reached Halby. Thinking to herself that he was going to be wasted in such a small village, Matilda invited him to sit down, picked up his letter of application and quickly re-read it.

'I must say, I'm impressed with your qualifications, Mr Brown.'

'Thank you, Mrs Bennett.'

'You don't think you would find Halby a backwater?'

'No, the country life will suit me well, Mrs Bennett, I like to observe nature and I paint in my spare time.'

'Oh, good. The children have never really done art, so perhaps that could go on the curriculum. The reason I advertised for a teacher is that my niece who assists her husband, Mr Harcourt, is, for personal reasons, giving up teaching, and I am also having a new school built. The village has a small one already, in two converted cottages, but we're outgrowing it. I'm determined to have the best equipment we can afford and good teachers who will inspire the children.'

'I hope I will be able to do that, Mrs Bennett.'

'The foundations are about to be laid, but until the school is finished, you would have to teach in rather cramped conditions and I don't know how that would appeal to you.'

'I find the idea of a new school very exciting, so I think I could put up with less than ideal conditions for a while, Mrs Bennett,' the young man smiled.

'Accommodation is also provided. There's a cottage next door which is quite comfortably furnished,' Matilda added as a lure, although she had the impression that Mr Brown was as keen to take up the position as she was to employ him. The only stumbling block was Christopher. If he didn't take to him it would be back to square one. Matilda sighed inwardly. Had she over-reached herself with this new school? she wondered. Bitten off more than she could chew. It sometimes felt like it. She stood up.

'Shall we take a walk down to the school, where I will introduce you to Mr Harcourt and then he can explain how the school is run.'

When they arrived the children were chanting their tables, but they leapt to their feet when the visitors entered.

'Good-afternoon, children.'

'Good-afternoon, ma'am,' their young voices piped. When she saw them like this, bright as buttons, Matilda's doubts receded, and she knew that what she was doing for the village was right. She was helping to dispel ignorance. What could be more important than that? Of course, not everyone in the community shared her ideals. For them, education was a very bad idea. It made the lower orders dissatisfied with their lot, and where would they hire their farm labourers and servants from, they grumbled, if they all went trotting off to the towns with big ideas and the silly notion that they could make their fortunes?

'You may go now,' said Christopher to the children. 'But quietly and in an orderly manner, please. There's no need for a stampede.'

Matilda noticed that there was a tolerant smile on Mr Brown's face as they filed out. Well, at least he appears to like children, which wasn't always true of teachers, she mused, remembering the many vicious raps inflicted on her knuckles by one particularly diabolical teacher. When the last child had departed, and she'd checked that there were no sharp little ears pressed to the door, she said to Christopher, 'This is Mr Brown and I'm going to leave the two of you to talk on your own for a while. It is important that you see eye to eye over your teaching and disciplinary methods.'

'Yes, it might strike you as strange, but we don't go in for caning here, Mr Brown,' said Christopher.

'That suits me very well. I have never

condoned the idea of teaching by fear,' answered John Brown.

Matilda left them talking about various methods of education and although she didn't want to be over-optimistic, she took this as a good sign. To kill time she decided to take a walk around the Green. She set off, saw Hattie collecting water from the village pump, and quickly turned back. She loved Adam dearly, but Hattie was an embarrassment to her and a constant reminder that she had a son whose choice of women, in one way or another, had been a total disaster. Who also, out of sheer cussedness seemed determined not to provide a legitimate heir. Hattie existed, indeed had given her two grandchildren she doted on, but for her own comfort, she preferred not to acknowledge this link. Seeing Hattie struggling down the road with a heavy pail of water, Matilda turned her back on the girl and began tapping her foot impatiently. How much longer was Christopher going to take to come to a decision, for heaven's sake? To her, Mr Brown seemed like the ideal candidate, but if Christopher didn't share her view, she'd have go through all the inconvenience and worry of re-advertising the position then interviewing more candidates. And Clare certainly couldn't continue teaching for much longer; it would be highly improper and people would begin to talk.

Growing tired of being kept waiting, Matilda, was about to barge in and interrupt the two men when the school door opened. They paused on the step chatting amicably and when Matilda hurried over to them, Christopher said, 'I was just pointing out to Mr Brown, where the new school will be.'

'Yes, I hope that by this time next year it will be finished and we'll have moved in, but of course we are at the mercy of builders and the weather,' Matilda replied.

Christopher turned to lock the school door, then put the key in his pocket. 'I'd better get home to Clare, it's the maid's afternoon off and I don't like her being on her own at this time.' He held out his hand to Mr Brown. 'I hope we will meet again very shortly,' he said cordially, and hurried off home to his wife.

'How did it go?' Matilda enquired.

'Well, Mr Harcourt and I appear to have very similar ideas on education.'

'Oh, that's good.'

'He also said that if I decided to take the position, he would like me to start work next week and my answer to him was that if you offered me the job, Mrs Bennett, I would be very happy to accept it.'

Ten

Once the weather looked set to remain fine, Adam ordered the haymaking to begin. After this it became a fight against time, and every villager who could walk was expected to turn out to give a hand. Working from dawn to dusk and pausing only to whet their scythes, the mowing team made their way up the meadow in rhythmic unison, sometimes cursing, sometimes singing, while the rich grass fell in swathes before them. The womenfolk, their faces protected by huge sun bonnets, followed close behind, turning it with their hay-rakes to ensure that it dried well and retained its sweetness and colour. After this it was carted away and built into haystacks, which children considered it was their moral right to slide down. Although it was arduous work, it was a matter of pride with the mowing team that they didn't stop until a field was completed. And fortunately the weather remained kind, with unbroken sunshine. Children, now riding astride the hay wain like mahouts, would look back through the mists of nostalgia and remember unending sun-drenched days. The smell of newly mown hay would forever induce in them a poignant sadness for the lost joys of youth. So would the sound of skylarks with their sweet and piercing song, and they'd remember with particular clarity walking tiredly home in the twilight and watching a sliver of moon appear in the darkening sky, hanging there as if suspended on invisible wires. Shaking their adult heads sadly they would recall these magical times and declare, 'We don't have summers like that any more.'

Needless to say, Halby was like a deserted village and the eerie silence soon got on Hattie's nerves. She was gregarious by nature and she felt out of it; denied the comradeship, the broad humour and the banter that always went on between men and women whenever they got together. She tried to find comfort by reminding herself that she was now a cut above a common field labourer, but it didn't help. Hattie stuck it for a day then she dumped the twins in the stick wagon, but by the time she'd dragged them over several bumpy fields, they were howling with rage.

'Hush,' Hattie urged as she spread a blanket out under a tree and laid them on it. Deciding there was no chance of them catching a chill in this heat, she removed most of their clothes and freed from the restricting garments, their mood improved instantly. Tears turned to beatific smiles.

The world around them was beginning to mean something now and if a small bird, butterfly or falling leaf caught their eye, they would reach out to try and grab it.

Adam was a good provider and Hattie noticed some kegs of beer in the shade of a tree waiting to be drunk by the workforce. As soon as the church clock chimed one o'clock they wiped their faces with their red handkerchiefs and sat down with weary groans. Hunks of bread and cheese and raw onion were unwrapped and the kegs of beer handed round. Hattie, who had a bit of a thirst herself, edged her way over to a group sitting under a hedge. 'Would you like to try some fruit loaf?' she offered, because she'd had the sense not to come empty-handed.

'Well, thank you very much, Hattie,' one of the men answered, and reached out a work-calloused hand to take a slice. He then un-stopped the keg, carefully wiped it with his forearm and offered it to her. 'Here, have a sup, m'dook.'

'Thanks.' Hattie took the small barrel, threw back her head and drank deeply before handing it on. Hattie was encouraged to moisten her throat on its several circuits round the group and when she returned to her maternal duties, she was surprised how uneven the ground under her feet was. Her bonnet slightly askew, she eased herself down, leaned back against the tree and stared at her babies and wondered how she suddenly came to have triplets. Oh Lord, now there were four! Was she tipsy? Well maybe a little, she decided, giggled and gave a wide yawn. The haymakers had started back to work and were at the far end of the field, which dipped down to a small stream, and their voices had receded and the afternoon had taken on a somnolent air.

Hattie dozed, for how long she wasn't sure, but she was awoken by voices, then two riders passed close by. When she saw who they were, Hattie was immediately awake and sober. Mmm, Miss Grace Bellamy and her Indian servant again. Now where are they off to? she wondered. And those parents of hers were certainly daft, letting them go off on their own. She supposed it was unimaginable to them that their well-bred daughter could be attracted to a servant, least of all a dark-skinned one. Well they were wrong, because she'd caught them kissing in the woods one day. So passionately they didn't notice her, and she'd had time to creep away. She'd been a bit shocked at first, but live and let live was Hattie's motto, and she soon got over it, particularly when it dawned on her that she could score Miss Bellamy off her list of possible rivals for Adam's affections. As an outsider herself, Hattie's sympathies were with the young couple, so she'd kept her knowledge to herself, fearful of what would happen if word got out. Mr Bellamy, with his red face, looked like the sort of bully who would have the boy flogged, and heaven knows what he would do to the girl, shut her up for life, most probably.

Hattie adjusted her back more comfortably against the tree, pushed a pillow behind her head and was about to close her eyes again when from somewhere above her an unfamiliar voice said, 'Good-afternoon.' She looked up, shading her eyes. A solidly built young man was holding a sheet of paper towards her. 'For you,' the stranger said.

Puzzled, Hattie took the paper, and saw that it was a very skilful pencil sketch of her and the twins, the boys kicking their feet in the air, she asleep against the tree. 'Did you do this?' she asked, a little put out that he'd done a likeness of her without her knowledge or permission. If someone was going to sketch her, she would have at least liked to have been sober.

'I did.'

'You had no right, you know.'

'Sorry, but it was such a lovely scene I couldn't resist it. Here, if you don't like it, I'll tear it up.' He held out his hand for the drawing.

But Hattie thrust it behind her back. It was rather flattering, she supposed, that a

184

stranger had found her interesting enough to sketch. 'Maybe I'll keep it, it's good of the boys, and it will remind me of what they were like at this age.'

'I'll sign it for you then, in case I ever get to be famous,' said the stranger and, without waiting to be asked, he squatted down beside Hattie and inscribed his name with a great flourish.

Hattie peered at it. 'What does it say?'

'Can't you read?'

Hattie was deeply offended. 'Of course I can. I was a good scholar. It's your handwriting, it's nothing more than a scribble,' she retaliated.

'I'm sorry, I should have known that in a village like Halby most of its inhabitants would have had some schooling. Anyway, the name is John Brown, plain John Brown.' He held out his hand and as Hattie took it, he added 'And I'm the new schoolmaster.'

Hattie's attitude towards the young man changed immediately. This put a very different complexion on things and Hattie regarded him with new respect. 'Oh, I expected you to be a lot older.'

John Brown laughed. 'Why did you think that?'

'Well, Mr Harcourt is quite old.'

'He's probably in his middle thirties, which hardly makes him Methuselah,' John Brown protested, then gave Hattie's smooth young face his full attention. 'Still, at your age I suppose anyone over twenty-five is ancient, Miss...?'

'...Hattie Bonner,' she supplied.

'And are you the children's nurse, Miss Bonner?'

Hattie looked him directly in the eye. 'No, I'm their mother.'

Rather thrown by her confession, and clearly embarrassed, the young teacher cleared his throat. 'I'm ... I'm sorry, I didn't mean to pry.'

'The village biddies would have told you soon enough, so I'll spare them that pleasure and tell you also that Adam Bennett is their father.' While he digested this further startling revelation, Hattie stood up, folded the blanket away and deposited the twins in the wagon. Deciding he would no longer wish to engage in conversation with a fallen woman, she adjusted her bonnet, brushed strands of hay from her dress and wished him good-day. But Hattie was darned if she was going to scuttle away in shame, and she set off down the field with her head held proud and high.

John Brown watched her for a moment admiring her courage and honesty. It was obvious that Adam Bennett, using his position in the village, had taken advantage of an innocent working girl, and left her to pay the price. What an utter cad, he thought contemptuously and went hurrying after her.

'Here, let me do that,' he said, when he caught up with Hattie and rather master-fully wrested the handle from her.

'Why, thank you.' Hattie smiled at him in gratitude for having the courage to be seen with her and Adam, passing them on his way to the top meadow to check on the progress of the haymaking, was rather put out by how uncommonly domesticated Hattie, *his* sons and the new schoolmaster looked together.

As promised, Clare tried to visit Rachel at least once a week, and although the shadow of loss lay heavily on her, Clare knew she was struggling to get a grip on herself. 'Without Jed, I'll never be more than half a person,' she confessed to Clare on her first visit, 'but I'm the sole breadwinner so I have to keep the shop running. Customers are fickle and if I'm closed for too long they'll go down to the booksellers in the Market Place and not come back.'

By Clare's second visit, Natalie had become Rachel's main concern. 'I don't know what to do about her. She hardly eats, refuses to go to school and won't move from her room. Frankly, I'm at my wit's end.'

'Perhaps a change of scene would help Natalie,' Clare suggested. 'I'm not working now, so I've a fair amount of time on my hands and she'd be welcome to come and stay with us in Halby. We have plenty of room.'

Rachel looked doubtful. 'It's kind of you to invite her, but I doubt whether she'd come.'

'Ask her, you might get a surprise. Some good country air would help to get her back on her feet again.'

'And revive her appetite,' Rachel added. 'She also needs to talk to somebody outside the family about her grief. She just freezes if I even touch on the subject. It would also do us both good to have a break from each other.'

'Perhaps she realises that, too. So speak to her,' Clare urged, 'there's nothing to lose.'

'What about her schooling, though? She's lost a lot of time recently, and I do want her to keep up her education.'

'That would be easy to sort out. Christopher will set her lessons each day, and I'll supervise them. Don't worry, there won't be any malingering. I'm used to dealing with children.'

'It seems strange to think she might soon be staying as a guest in the house where I was a maid. You'll be able to show her the attic room where I slept. Cold as charity up there it was.'

'Maybe you could take a trip out and see

it for yourself?' Clare suggested.

'Well, perhaps.' Rachel wouldn't be so rude as to turn down Clare's invitation outright, but Thatcher's Mount was the last place on earth she wanted to revisit. It held too many dark memories of George and his attempted rape and even from the grave, he could still make the hairs rise on the back of her neck. But she mustn't forget that Clare was still his daughter. Such a lovely girl, too, and not a nasty bone in her body. But what about this baby that she was having? Supposing the bad blood skipped a generation? When Clare had told her that she was with child, she'd been delighted and said so, at the same time expressing regret that Emily appeared to have no plans to make her a grandmother.

'But Emily's only been married a year, Christopher and I have been waiting for this baby for over ten years,' Clare had pointed out.

'I know, dear, I'm sorry, it was a tactless remark, but I am concerned about Emily's marriage and I sense all is not well.'

Although Clare shared Rachel's doubts she saw no point in adding to her anxieties by saying so. She was also of the opinion that a baby was hardly likely smooth out any difficulties in the marriage, rather the opposite, in fact. 'Don't worry, they'll sort themselves out. The first year of marriage is always difficult, as you probably remember yourself. It means adjustment for both and the smallest row can be blown out of all proportion. You end up convincing yourself that you hate him and the marriage is a terrible mistake.'

'Yes, you're right I suppose,' Rachel answered, although she was certain she and Jed had never once thought that way about each other. 'Perhaps Rory will come with her next time she visits us and prove me wrong. But I still think it's a terrible tragedy that she and Adam never married.'

'I always imagined you were against it.'

'Jed and your aunt yes, because of their family feud, but not me. Mind you, Emily was saying a while back that she didn't think she would have fitted comfortably into country life.'

'She would in time and Adam still loves her, I know that. If he hadn't been so stupid with Hattie, they might have had a second chance.'

'That's men for you, weak where the flesh is concerned.' Adam was certainly a chip off the old block, thought Rachel, remembering Harry's persistent wooing of her.

'And Adam's got two children to prove it,' Clare retorted.

Rachel gave a resigned shrug. 'Well that's water under the bridge. Mistakes were made, wrong turnings taken. It would be wonderful, wouldn't it, if we could turn back the clock? Unfortunately we can't and good or bad, all of us have to get on with the life that we've made for ourselves.'

Remembering how restricting and narrow she had found Halby herself when she was young, Clare suspected that when the suggestion was put to her, Natalie, who was quite a young madam in her way, would toss her copper locks in disgust at the very notion of burying herself in the countryside for two whole weeks. Even when Natalie wrote a few days later, thanking Clare for the invitation and saying she would really love to come and stay at Thatcher's Mount, she suspected the enthusiasm was a little forced and that Rachel had been standing over her when she penned the letter.

However, plans were finalised and on the Saturday morning Christopher drove into Leicester to collect her, leaving Clare wondering why she had ever issued the invitation in the first place and with a nagging worry that she was going to have a bored, sulky girl on her hands for two weeks.

Well, it was too late now, she decided, and went to have a final look at the bedroom she'd had made ready for Natalie. It had been her bedroom when she was single and before that Aunt Tilda's, and her grandmother's touch was still very evident. The pretty little writing desk, for instance. How many billet-doux had been written on it, or hidden away in its secret drawers? she wondered. And how fortunate inanimate objects could never offer up their secrets.

Deciding her thoughts were getting a bit fanciful, Clare wandered back downstairs and called into the kitchen to check that there was no last minute panic with Mrs Bunyon, who came up from the village to cook. She knew at a rough guess how long it would take Christopher to ride into Leicester and back again, so when it was near the time, she called Jelly and went down to the gate to wait for them. When she saw the trap coming up the hill, she waved and unlatched the gate to allow Christopher to drive straight through.

'Here we are,' he said, 'one young lady.'

'Hello, Auntie Clare,' Natalie called, then without waiting to be helped, she jumped down from the trap and gazed about her, her young face alight with curiosity. So this was where Mama had been at the beck and call of the spoilt Miss Matilda. Right from when she was a small girl, her mother's many stories of Thatcher's Mount had fed her imagination. She knew the exact position of her poky room under the eaves and she had built up such a vivid picture of the house she was sure she would recognise every brick, every door, every lintel. But what her imagination hadn't allowed for was the size of it. 'What a large house!' she exclaimed. 'Did Mama have to clean this all on her own?'

Clare laughed. 'I don't think so. There were others to help.'

Christopher, who had taken Natalie's bags from the trap, was now walking towards the house. 'Come on Clare, let's have some of that lemonade you promised. I've been thinking about it all the way home and I'm absolutely parched after the journey.'

'It's so warm, I thought we'd have it in the garden. There are homemade biscuits, too,' Clare added, for she'd decided that one of her missions this holiday would be to get Natalie eating again. And she *was* thin, she decided, eyeing her up and down; like a beanpole in fact.

Jelly, who considered it was about time he was shown a bit of attention, gave a peremptory bark. 'What a dear little dog,' Natalie cooed, bent to stroke him and Jelly, who adored flattery, gave his heart to her.

'Yes, he's Freddie's really, but he's up at Oxford.'

'Oh yes.' Natalie vaguely recalled a shy, gangly young man coming into the shop once with Clare - looking for books on dull subjects such as Latin, she seemed to remember.

'Still, we'll soon be seeing Freddie again,

won't we?' said Clare addressing the small dog.

At the mention of his master's name, Jelly grew so excited, he started to spin around like a top, trying to catch his own tail.

'Oh dear, I shouldn't have mentioned his name.'

'He does seem to love Freddie.'

'Yes, but then that boy has the kindest heart in the world, especially where animals are concerned. He's coming home next week for the summer vacation so you'll have someone nearer your own age to talk to.'

Freddie sounded like a bit of a swot to Natalie so she doubted if she'd have much in common with him, although of course, she wouldn't be so rude as to say so to Clare.

'Now come on, let me show you your room; it used to be mine before I married,' Clare called over her shoulder, as she lead Natalie into the house and up the stairs. Her rather shabby bags were standing in the middle of the bedroom and Natalie gazed around her with an unforced delight.

'Oh, this is lovely,' she exclaimed, and found herself rather shamefully making a comparison with her own very modest bedroom at home. Every item had obviously been chosen with care and to please the feminine eye; the half tester bed spread with a white lace counterpane, the paper hangings patterned with pink roses and the muslin curtains tied back with matching pink ribbon. Already Natalie could feel the dark cloud of sadness, which had seemed to flatten the life out of her ever since her father had so suddenly left them, begin to lift. Not that she'd wanted to come, and when her mother first mentioned the invitation, she'd flounced about a bit declaring she would die of boredom and nothing on earth would induce her to go to Halby. But her mother had been unusually insistent, had actually stood over her while she wrote the letter, explaining how it would do her good to get away. 'Do you want rid of me then?' she'd snapped. Rachel had thought about this. 'Not exactly, but we should have a break from each other and you need to get out of yourself and meet new people.'

Her mother's comments had hurt Natalie at the time, but from this distance she could see her point of view, because in a way, they fed on each other's misery. Her mother would now have time on her own to reflect, and she would get a fresh perspective on life. As they said goodbye this morning her mother had kissed her then said quickly before both of them got tearful, 'Now enjoy yourself and don't forget to write.' And she might even do that, she thought, enjoy herself, even if she was stuck out in the wilds of the country.

'You'll want to freshen up, but leave your unpacking, Phoebe will see to it,' Natalie heard Clare say. 'Come down into the garden when you're ready.'

When Clare had gone, Natalie thought, fancy! A maid! Wait until she wrote and told Mama. And two of their rooms at home would fit easily into this bedroom, although perhaps it would be better not to mention that, she decided. She skipped over to the open window and leaned out. The view was perfect. A short distance away there was a small wood and she could hear rooks cawing in the high swaying branches, while further on a lone horseman cantered across green undulating fields. Wondering idly who it was and whether they would ever meet, Natalie was about to withdraw her head, when she saw a girl in a maid's uniform, Phoebe she assumed, carrying a tray loaded with glasses and a jug out into the garden. That'll be the lemonade, Natalie decided and, reminded of how thirsty she was she withdrew her head, poured water into the wash-basin, quickly splashed the dust of the journey off her face, then pulled a brush through her hair, which she still wore down. When she was finished she rummaged around in her bag, found a wide-brimmed straw hat and tied it securely under her chin. With her pale skin there was a risk of freckles, horrible disfiguring things.

Natalie found Christopher and Clare already in the garden, sitting in the shade of a tree.

'Lemonade, dear?' Clare enquired, as she sat down.

'Ooh yes, please, I'm dying of thirst.'

'Try one of these biscuits, as well. Cook has just made them and they're delicious.' Natalie leaned across to take one, and as she bit into it, she noticed a rather handsome gentleman, strolling towards them.

'Hello, Adam,' Christopher called. 'Would you care for a glass of lemonade.'

'I've been sent by my mother for some accounts you apparently have for her. But a drink strikes me as a much more sensible idea in this heat.' The gentleman, removed his hat, wiped his brow, while gazing with open curiosity at Natalie.

'Adam, this is Miss Natalie Fairfax,' said Clare to put him out of his misery.

'How do you do, Miss Fairfax,' Adam inclined his head slightly then shot a questioning glance in his cousin's direction.

'Natalie is Emily's sister,' Clare explained. 'She's come to stay with us for a while.'

Of course, the red-headed baby girl who'd been found with her dying mother in the snow. He recalled, too, several occasions in Lily's garden when Emily and he had played at being her parents, although they'd been hardly more than children themselves. Why was it everything seemed right about those times, everything wrong with the present? Adam asked himself, staring morosely into his glass. He knew Jed Fairfax had died, and he wasn't going to pretend to be upset or offer words of commiseration to the girl; that would be hypocritical. The man had never done him any favours in life. Quite the opposite, actually. In fact, he'd rather mucked it up.

Her own recent sorrows had made Natalie more sensitive to other people's moods and watching Adam over the rim of her glass, she thought, poor man, he does look dreadfully unhappy, I wonder why. Has he lost a dear one, like me? Or has his heart been broken? And how did he come to know her sister? Then in a flash of total recall, she was back in the church at Emily and Rory's wedding. It was *him*, the man who had shouted out in front of the whole congregation that he loved Emily and tried to stop the marriage going ahead. What a fuss it had caused, although she'd thought it very romantic. Papa, though, had threatened death by strangulation if he ever set eyes on him again. Because grown-ups thought children should be kept in the dark about such matters, all her questions were brushed aside. Maybe if she kept her eyes and ears open during this holiday, though, she'd find a few being answered. What was really puzzling, however, was that if Emily was sweet on Adam and he on her, why did she marry Rory?

'Natalie.'

'Eh... Yes?'

'Penny for them,' Clare laughed, 'You were miles away.'

'Sorry, was I?'

'I was just saying to Christopher and Mr Bennett that I've got to find out what your interests are so that we can entertain you while you're here,' Clare said.

Remembering the horseman, Natalie said instantly, 'I'd love to learn to ride.'

'Well, that can be easily arranged. We have an excellent stables in the village, run by Mrs Jane Smith and her son Gabriel. They'll teach you in no time. We'll take a walk down there later and have a word with them. You can borrow one of my riding habits, I won't be using it for a while, although it will probably need some adjustments, but Hattie would see to that.'

'Who's Hattie?' asked Natalie with youthful curiosity and noticed that this seemingly innocuous question produced an awkward silence.

'Oh, Hattie Bonner is a girl from the village,' Clare replied casually, 'she's rather handy with the needle.'

Adam hurriedly gulped down his drink and stood up. 'Thank you for the refreshment but if you don't mind, Christopher, I'll collect those accounts from you and be on my way.'

Christopher stood up as well. 'They're in my study. I'll get them for you.'

Adam bid Clare and Natalie good-day, followed Christopher into the house and while he stood waiting for him in the hall, mulled over the recent conversation. That sister of Emily's certainly asked some awkward questions, he decided and wandered over to watch the two women from the window. They were chatting away, but what about? Him? Well he'd given them plenty of material. *Stop it*, he rebuked himself, you'll go mad if you keep imagining everyone is whispering about you behind your back.

Adam moved away from the window and began striding restlessly up and down the hall. There was a letter lying on a small table and out of idle curiosity he glanced at it. The name Mrs R. Aherne, didn't register for a second, then his heart gave a thump. Of course! Emily's married name. He picked it up, quickly memorised the street name, then flung it down when Christopher's door opened and he emerged from his study with the accounts. As Adam moved forward to take them from him, he was already planning his visit to London. It would be a business trip, naturally. An urgent one which would require him there as soon as possible. And if by chance he happened to take a stroll past Emily's place of residence and bumped into her, wouldn't it be the most natural thing in the world to stop and talk?

Eleven

As soon as she thought she had the emotional strength, Emily sat down and wrote to Rory, telling him of her father's death. She explained how he'd gone, extinguished like a light while sitting in his chair. But it was pure agony putting it down on paper, reliving her loss and she had to dash away the tears that welled up in her eyes. She signed the letter, *'with love'*, but as she sealed it she thought resentfully, why aren't you here, Rory, by my side, then I wouldn't have to keep lying to my mother? And where's the money you promised for my fare? Not that it mattered so much now that she had made up her mind that she wasn't joining him in the New World, a point she'd failed to mention in her letter. But he knew she'd never been that enthusiastic about leaving England for an uncertain future in a strange country. Rory wasn't so heartless either that he'd expect her to leave her mother so soon after her father's death, and he'd probably read between the lines anyway, Emily reasoned. Where this left their marriage, she didn't know, but it was a problem she tried not to dwell on too much.

Her life now had its own rhythm, and after the initial loneliness, Emily had discovered the pleasures of a solitary life. As soon as a room at the front of the house became vacant she persuaded the landlord to let her have it. It cost more but it was worth every penny because it was away from the stinking back yard, where a wind in the wrong direction blew smells and bluebottles across from the pigsties and stables. She'd set to immediately with a pail of whitewash, bought some cheap rugs in the market to cover the floorboards and nailed a few pictures over the cracks in the wall. When it was finished, Emily looked about her and adopting the cockney jargon said with something like pride, 'Well it ain't much but it's 'ome.'

Like her father, Rory had been virulently anti-church, but after his departure Emily found the bells calling her back on a Sunday morning and she was once more a regular churchgoer. Her employer, Mrs Haig, was also a member of the congregation. She had introduced Emily to several other ladies and gradually she found herself being pulled in to help with various good works.

The Reverend Basil North's latest crusade, was the 'Fallen Sisterhood'. Distressed by the sight of them in the streets all around him and concerned about their spiritual welfare, he had arranged a tea for them in a hall adjoining the church later that day. The function had been well advertised so he was expecting a good attendance and although Emily was doubtful that he would succeed in making many conversions, she had agreed go along and give a hand. But Saturday morning was put aside for the weekly ritual cleaning, when she and Prudence went down to the wash-house to launder their clothes and afterwards step next door to enjoy a wallow in the baths.

While she waited for Prudence's knock, Emily bundled her dirty linen into a pillow-case, remembering to add a lump of soap before she tied it up. She was ready to go now, but where was Prudence? Emily looked at the clock on the mantelpiece and tut-tutted. 'Late again,' she sighed. Prudence's timekeeping irritated her, for she wouldn't get herself out of bed even though she knew that if they didn't get there early, all the wash places would be gone. Well, I'm not hanging around any longer, Emily decided, picked up her bundle and was going out through the front door, when behind her Prudence called,

'Em, 'ang on. Why were you goin' without me?' she huffed, when she caught up with Emily.

'You know why. If we don't get there in

good time, the tubs will be taken, which means a long wait.'

'Don't tell me off, Em, I've got a bit of an 'angover,' Prudence whined.

'And I have a busy day ahead of me at the church. Loaves of bread to slice and butter, teas and coffee to make. Why don't you come and give a hand?'

'With this head? No thanks. Anyway, Edmund ain't got time for bible-thumping vicars and he would laugh 'is bleedin' head off at the idea of me trying to convert some whores to Christianity.'

'Who cares what he thinks?'

'I've got to live with him, you ain't.'

And I thank God for it, Emily said to herself. Her attitude towards Prudence swung between irritation and concern and she was constantly urging her to leave her lover. 'I've told you before, you do have a choice.'

'Leave it off, Emily, I don't need preachin' to,' said Prudence truculently.

'Oh, all right,' Emily snapped, walked on ahead and joined the end of a long line of women, all weighed like beasts of burden with their family's washing. 'It's looks as if we'll be lucky if we get in.' There was a reprimand in Emily's voice.

'Nah, look we're nearly there,' Prudence chirped, and sure enough, a moment later they had paid their pennies and were inside the hot, steamy atmosphere of the wash-house. It was a high glass-roofed building with huge deep tubs running down its entire length. Condensation dripped down the walls, and it always took Emily's nostrils several minutes to get used to the powerful combination of gas, soap and wet washing. But that was outweighed by the convenience, the unlimited supply of hot water and the wringers that removed excess water, so that the washing was almost dry when you took it home.

The wash-house was also a real Tower of Babel, and the high roof echoed with the sound of women's tongues wagging nineteen to the dozen. For wasn't there a week's gossip to catch up on? Useless husbands to complain about and remedies to exchange to deal with certain unspecified women's matters. Given the choice, Prudence always preferred a bit of tittle-tattle to hard graft, so she tipped her dirty washing into the tub, said to Emily, 'I think I'll leave it to have a bit of a soak,' and wandered off. But as far as Emily was concerned, much as she disliked it, it was a job to be done and, bent over the tub, she soaped and scrubbed and rinsed. Because of the heat, she always left off her corset, but it didn't stop the sweat trickling down her face and she could almost hear the curl falling out of her hair. What kept her going was the thought of going next door and luxuriating in a hot bath.

With a sigh of relief, Emily gave her sheets and clothes a final rinse and eased her aching back. She smiled at the women at the next tub. 'Nearly finished now,' she said and began feeding each garment through the wringer while she turned the handle at the same time. When she had a pile of clean smelling, almost dry laundry, she stood back and regarded it with satisfaction.

'Have you finished already?' Prudence, who had just sauntered back, stared in disbelief.

'Nearly.' Emily was now folding the washing into the pillowcase, ready to take home and iron. 'That's it for another week,' she said at last and picked up her bundle. 'I'm going next door now for a bath.'

'Bleeding 'ell, Emily, you can't go wiv out me,' Prudence wailed.

'You shouldn't spend all your morning gossiping, then,' Emily shot back. 'So you'd better be quick if you want me to wait.'

Prudence sloshed her washing around in a half-hearted fashion, peered at the murky water, said, 'It must be clean, it's bin soaking long enough,' then without bothering to give it a rinse, she said, 'Here, give us an 'and, Em, and turn the 'andle,' and began shoving the washing through the wringer. 'There you are, done in no time.' Looking pleased with herself, Prudence tied the washing up any-old-how in a sheet, slung it over her shoulder, grinned and said, 'Right, ready when you are.'

The baths adjoined the wash-house and cost tuppence, with a scratchy towel and minute piece of soap included in the price. Emily eased her aching back down into the hot water and gave a sigh of pleasure. If ever she became rich, she decided, she would bath every day. She soaked until her skin turned lobster pink, then on an impulse, decided to wash her hair. She hadn't thought about the size of the towel, however, and she soon found out it wasn't up to the task of drying it. Emily then also remembered that she had to be at the church hall at two o'clock. Hastily she piled her soaking locks under her bonnet and when she emerged from her cubicle with it dripping uncomfortably down her back, it didn't help when Prudence exclaimed, 'What have you done? You look like a drowned rat.'

Emily picked up her laundry. 'Thanks for the compliment, now can we hurry? I haven't much time to spare and I want to get home and dry it.'

'It seems a pity that you're gonna to be stuck buttering bread for them old bags on a nice day like this. We could have gone to St James's Park and listened to the band. Maybe found ourselves a couple of blokes,'

Prudence said as they made their way back to their lodgings

'Prudence, I'm married,' Emily admonished.

'You don't know what Rory's up to, do you? After all, he's a long way from home,' she said slyly.

'I can assure you, I trust my husband implicitly.'

'Well, perhaps he's different from the rest.'

'You are so cynical.'

'You would be, too, if you lived with Edmund.'

'Well, I don't and neither would you if you had any sense.'

'No, and that reminds me.' As Emily pushed open the door of the lodging house, Prudence shot past her up the stairs. 'I'd better go an' see about his dinner before 'e starts mouthing me off.'

Emily had paused to remove her bonnet and tease out her damp hair with her fingers, when above her a door opened and she heard Edmund in his normal abusive tone, bellow, 'Where the devil have you been, woman?'

'To the wash-house, Edmund, to do your laundry.' Prudence's voice was small, apologetic, all the spirit knocked out of her.

'You should have been back hours ago. Do you want me to die of hunger, or something?'

'Yes, please,' Emily murmured fervently, continuing on her way up the stairs, and wondering how long it would be before Edmund's verbal attacks on Prudence became physical.

'I'll need some money, Edmund.'

'Here, take this!' he snarled and as Emily dumped down her washing to open the door, there was a sudden rattle of coins then a sixpence and several pennies rolled down between the banisters and landed at her feet. She was about to bend and pick up the money, when she heard him add, 'Get me a meat pie, and look quick about it.'

'Ye–yes Edmund.'

When Emily heard the wobble in Prudence's voice, she wanted to shout up the stairs, 'Where's your cockney gab? Tell him to get lost, can't you? Or sod off, like you'd normally do,' but she knew she would probably make it worse for her friend. Emily heard Prudence scrambling around picking up the coins like some beggar in the street, and gave a resigned sigh. What was she to do, when it was obvious that one of the main pleasures of Edmund's life was publicly humiliating his mistress, and when she almost conspired in his nasty little game. He showed her neither love nor affection and for him, Prudence was just a dog for him to kick.

Not wanting to add to Prudence's mortification, Emily left the coins where they were, picked up her laundry and went into her room, pushing the door shut with her foot. 'Why in the name of heaven doesn't she leave him?' she said out loud as she spread her washing out to dry along the fire guard.

She gave this some thought, then answered her own question. 'Because she's indolent by nature and it's probably easier to stay with Mr Obnoxious than to go searching for work.'

Since she started living alone, Emily had been given to talking to herself, and the great advantage of this was that she always got very satisfactory answers to her questions, plus there was never any disagreement. She gave her hair a good rub with a dry towel, separated it into strands and while she twisted it round heated tongs, she thought a bit more about Prudence and her problems. There was a father somewhere, although from what she could gather, he was a drunk who'd beaten Prudence so badly when she was a child, she'd run away from home at the earliest opportunity. Living with Obnoxious was probably cushy in comparison, so perhaps she shouldn't be so quick to criticise. How sheltered her own life seemed in comparison, although she hadn't cared at all to hear Prudence questioning Rory's faithfulness. Once put into your head, ideas like that took hold and festered away under the surface like a carbuncle.

Her hair was now dry and sprung back in glossy ringlets, so with time passing, she quickly ironed her undergarments, spread them across the guard to air, then had a think about which dress she would wear. The day had grown warmer and Emily enjoyed the freedom of walking around naked except for a wrap and the idea of having to trap her flesh again in a stiff-boned, restricting corset suddenly struck her as abhorrent. But who says I have to truss myself up like a fowl ready for the oven? she asked herself and decided to leave it off. She sorted through her small store of dresses and pulled out the pale green one she'd worn the day she'd gone with Rory to watch the aeronaut make his magical ascent in his balloon. That had been such a happy day. Emily gave a wistful sigh and as she stepped into her clean drawers and petticoats, she wondered if she would ever again enjoy such days.

The one looking-glass in the room was small and mottled with age but after Emily had dropped the dress over her head, she gave her hair a final brush then went to take a look at herself and tie on the leghorn bonnet that went with the dress. Her image was blurred but she supposed she looked all right and after all, the vicar's fallen women were hardly likely to criticise.

Emily paused on her way out, but all was quiet from upstairs. Probably made it up and gone to bed, she decided and set off to do her good deed for the day with an easier mind.

As she stepped out on to the cobbles, the hot soupy air engulfed her and Emily wondered what she was doing sacrificing her Saturday afternoon to fallen women when she could be in St James's Park with Prudence. It was, she decided, way beyond the bounds of Christian duty. She disliked the church hall too, with its fusty smell of piety and for a moment she was tempted to turn back. But it went against her nature to let people down and her promise to the vicar and Mrs Haig kept her going.

By the time she reached the hall, most of the helpers were already there and Emily stood at the entrance watching them for a moment, struck by the uncommon sight of well-bred ladies, who would have their own servants at home, laying out cups and saucers and plates onto large trestle tables for women of the night. Well, we're all sisters under the skin, Emily decided, and marched on in to do her bit.

'Over here, Emily,' Mrs Haig boomed from the other side of the hall. Her employer was busy slicing bread, and when Emily reached her and enquired what she should do, Mrs Haig pushed two large piles of bread in her direction. 'You could start buttering these,' adding after a glance at Emily, 'you do look charming, my dear, in that dress, but you don't want to spoil it, so why don't you put on one of those?'

She pointed to a pile of white aprons and after removing her hat, Emily slipped one on over her head and started buttering.

The Reverend Basil North was a diminutive gentleman with an egg-shaped, perspiring bald pate, which he wiped so frequently with a handkerchief it had begun to shine like the melting butter on the slices of bread. He was rushing from table to table making encouraging remarks to his band of helpers, but doing little constructive otherwise. 'It was very good of you to come and help us out, Mrs Aherne,' he beamed, when he finally reached the table where Emily and Mrs Haig were working.

'Well I hope it all gets eaten, Vicar,' Emily answered bluntly, eyeing the mounds of bread she'd laboured over.

'Oh it will, it will, Mrs Aherne, you must have faith. I'm expecting a large crowd. But one must be prepared to fail, for it is the good that one tries to do in life that matters.' He smiled beatifically before moving on to offer spiritual comfort to the ladies slicing cake and filling enormous teapots with boiling water. Emily thought of her good friend William Jackson, toiling away in the intense heat of India because of his beliefs. She hadn't heard from him for a long time and she wondered how many conversions to Christianity he'd made, and whether his faith had ever wavered.

The various tasks now completed, the vicar clapped his hands for silence, took out his pocket watch, waited a moment, then with something of a flourish, went and flung open the doors. If he was expecting a swarm of converts he was mistaken, for his only customer to saunter in was a small street urchin.

'Coo blimey!' the boy exclaimed and gazed around him as if he'd entered Aladdin's cave.

'Well ... er ... yes.' The vicar put his hand to his mouth and coughed delicately. 'Today is for ladies only, I'm afraid, young man.'

'You mean old bags, don't ye?'

'A boy of your age should not be using such vulgar language,' the vicar admonished. 'In my eyes, they are ladies. Now, will you please go.' It would have been unchristian to send the boy away empty-handed, so the vicar pushed some cake into his hand, then guided him firmly out through the door.

'Can I come back later, rev? When them ladies 'ave gorn.' The boy bargained.

The vicar's band of helpers were now

struggling not to collapse into a state of unseemly mirth and, sensing he was losing control, he snapped, 'Yes, I suppose so!' gave his pate an agitated polish, went and sat down, and took up his bible for spiritual refreshment.

It went quiet again, the rays of the sun filtered in through the dusty windows, but absolutely nothing else happened. Emily gave Mrs Haig a glance. 'It looks as if that young scallywag will be able to bring all his friends with him at this rate.' She kept her voice low so as not to upset the vicar.

'It just needs one to walk through the door, then the others will follow,' Mrs Haig answered. And indeed, as she spoke, a young woman moved uncertainly into the hall. Blinded by the sudden change of light, she blinked and before she had a change of mind, the vicar descended upon her. 'My good lady, come in, come in,' he urged and drew her towards his helpers, who were all gazing at the young sinner with intense interest. 'Have some bread and butter, and ... and some cake,' he urged and proceeded to pile her plate high with food. Two more women now appeared, giggling and pushing each other in a slightly embarrassed way, and Emily wondered if they had been waiting outside. The vicar, who could barely contain himself, deserted the first prostitute to dash over and greet them.

Suddenly women were pouring into the hall. 'There, what did I tell you?' said Mrs Haig, smiling round at the packed hall. 'Faith can move mountains, although it's probably food they are looking for, so let's get these plates of bread and butter handed round,' she said in her practical way.

The women were milling around chatting amiably to each other and sipping tea - it all seemed as sedate as a vicarage tea party. Emily watched them in bemused silence, hardly able to credit that these were the same women who fought and cursed under her window at night, who were despised by society and regarded as lower than the beasts in the field. But here they were, decked out in their best clothes and weighed down with large amounts of gaudy jewellery. Some of the prostitutes were young, and the expression on their crudely painted faces was one of confidence, and Emily guessed that just as soon as they had enough money put by, they planned to give up the business. As a dire warning there were their older sisters, sad, raddled creatures; them in ten year's time, if they didn't get out of the game.

'Poor things,' Emily heard her employer say.

'My thoughts exactly, Mrs Haig.'

'But the vicar is a good man, if he can bring just a few to God, he will make sure they go to a place of refuge where they will be looked after.'

The Reverend Basil North was nothing if not patient, so he waited until the last slice of bread and cake had been consumed and the teapots were empty before attempting to convert these Mary Magdalenes.

'Oh dear, some are leaving already.' Mrs Haig gave a disappointed sigh as she watched the vicar climb on to a chair and clap his hands. 'We will now say the Lord's Prayer,' he said and as he bowed his head, Emily noticed a few more slip out. But enough stayed and after prayers he spoke feelingly of those women who had strayed from the path of virtue. 'Jesus understands, and He is your friend and saviour. If you repent your sins you will find salvation, happiness and spiritual fulfilment with Him,' he adjured and from the audience Emily heard several quiet sobs.

'I do believe we have some converts,' Mrs Haig squeezed Emily's hand excitedly, and as the meeting broke up and they began to clear away, Emily could see the vicar deep in conversation with two young women.

'Two seems a pretty small number,' said, Emily, who'd imagined conversions in the biblical sense. Baptisms and everything.

'If we just save two souls from that terrible existence, then this afternoon hasn't been wasted,' explained Mrs Haig as she wiped

218

down the tables. Emily thought of hers and William's efforts to rescue their own Mary and wished the Reverend Basil North better success. That had been quite a cruel lesson for her, but it had taught her that, no matter how dreadful people's lives might be, there was a security in them that they often feared losing. Well-intentioned people with their good deeds often left nothing but damage in their wake.

When the tidying up was done, Emily went to the door with the few scraps of food that were left. The little street urchin must have been hanging around all afternoon, for he shot out of a doorway, grabbed the food and was gone, without as much as a thank you.

Emily gave a shrug. 'Oh well, never expect gratitude,' she sighed and went and found her bonnet. The vicar had disappeared with his rescued women, the verger had taken down the trestle tables and was now waiting to lock up.

'Goodbye, Mrs Haig.' Emily had vaguely hoped that her employer might invite her round for supper, but she was busy talking to a close friend and she just turned and waved.

'Goodbye dear, and thank you. I'll see you in church tomorrow, I trust?'

'You will,' Emily assured her then, although she had all the time in the world, she set off as if she were on her way to an important destination. She found Saturday evenings extremely difficult to cope with, for everywhere she looked she saw couples on their way out for a night of fun, their pockets jingling with the week's wages. It emphasised her own loneliness and it was a sad reminder of the grand times she and Rory had shared. Whatever his faults, he had always known how to give her a good time and he always had some plan up his sleeve. A theatre and a meal afterwards in a small Soho restaurant if they were flush, or if money was tight they would invite friends round to their rooms; someone would be sent out for a few jugs of ale and they'd feast on jellied eels, bread and butter and conversation. Suddenly Emily felt a deep itching need for her husband and a restlessness she couldn't contain. It was late afternoon and although the shadows had lengthened the heat was still intense. The gutters stank with rotting vegetables and horse dung, she had spent the best part of the day either bent over a wash tub or in a church hall and she was suddenly gripped with a longing for the sweet air and rolling landscape of Leicestershire. The nearest large open space was St James's Park, but the only time she'd tried walking there on her own, she'd been accosted by some weird looking men who'd assumed her body was for sale. But Prudence would go with her, Emily decided and set off for her lodgings at a fair pace, to catch her before she went out.

When Emily had first arrived in London, Rory had warned her that there were places in London where sensible people should never venture. 'Evil characters lurk there,' he explained, 'who'd think nothing of cutting your finger off for your wedding ring, so never leave the main thoroughfares.' Today, because she was in a hurry and it was daylight and there were people about, Emily rashly ignored his advice and turned into a narrow alleyway of lock-up shops, with washing strung out across the upper storeys. Almost immediately she regretted her decision for she sensed she was being followed. She gave a nervous glance over her shoulder and sure enough there was a man several yards behind her. She tried to increase her speed but her terror had almost immobilised her. Emily's brain began to work feverishly. There was only him and her. Was he a cut-purse or a murderer? Would she be a corpse in a minute? Should she fling down what little money she had with her and try and persuade her legs to make a run for it?

'Emily,' the man called.

She froze momentarily, thought, good God, he even knows my name, and then took to her heels. Grateful to reach the main thoroughfare unharmed, she leaned against a wall, panting noisily. By a stroke of good fortune a peeler was approaching and as he reached she gulped, 'There ... there's a ... a man...' Emily pointed to the alleyway.

'Calm down and get your breath back, madam,' the peeler suggested. Emily inhaled deeply, filling her lungs and was about to continue when, to her astonishment, Adam turned the corner and stopped in front of her.

The peeler eyed him suspiciously. 'Is this the man who was pestering you?'

'Ah ... um ... er,' Emily stuttered, completely flummoxed, and rubbed her eyes. Was it Adam or had the heat and her ordeal brought on a brainstorm?

'It's all right, Constable, this lady and I are acquainted.'

'Is that correct, madam?'

Emily nodded, recognising Adam's voice.

'Well, that's all right, then.' He gave Adam a funny look and, swinging his truncheon, walked on.

'Why did you run off like that, Emily?' Adam asked.

Emily straightened, annoyed at his question. 'What is a woman supposed to do when she's convinced she's being pursued by a murderous villain?' she snapped. 'Do you make a habit of going around terrorising women?'

'I didn't realise, it was foolish of me. I apologise profusely.'

'Anyway, what are you doing in Soho?'

'Looking for a restaurant. One I was recommended.'

Emily gave him a withering look. 'You came all the way from Leicester to try out a restaurant?'

'No, I'm in town on business but I still need to eat. I was told to try The Capri.'

'And you just happened to bump into me?'

'Don't be hard on me, Emily.'

'Why ever not?'

'Because it's not like you. And whenever we meet we go over the same old ground. I'm quite aware of the damage I've done, but what I want to do now is make recompense. I have no other motive, I swear. We shouldn't continue like enemies.'

Emily started to walk on and Adam kept pace with her. 'Words, Adam, words. But if you do want to be open with me you can start by being honest. How did you find out where I was?'

'I found a letter Clare had written to you and I memorised the address,' he admitted. 'Now, you answer my question, Emily. Are you and your husband still together?'

'Why do you ask that?' she bridled.

'Clare let slip that she never saw him around.'

She stopped and gave him a fierce look. 'Oh did she? Well you needn't think my marriage is on the rocks, because it's not. Circumstances have separated us. Rory's work as a journalist has sent him to America, but I shall be joining him shortly. I haven't mentioned it to my mother yet because I don't want her upset, so I'd be obliged if you kept the information to yourself.'

'I give you my word. Actually, I've toyed with the idea of going back there. Often there seems to be little in England for me.'

'Except two sons.' Emily shot back, for she had decided she wasn't going to spare Adam. 'But that's men for you, they find it easy to walk away from their responsibilities, don't they?'

'Actually, I am aware of mine. The twins are well provided for and so is Hattie.'

'Why don't you marry her?'

'Please, Emily, stop punishing me. But if you would like to know, I have made the decision never to marry again.' By now they had reached Golden Square and with its flowers and trees and grass it was like coming upon an oasis in a desert. Even the heat seemed less oppressive and there was a suggestion of a breeze.

'If you really can't bear my company, Emily, I'll go. Otherwise, I suggest we sit down,' Adam said, then, without giving her a chance to decide, he took her arm and guided her to a seat under the shade of a tree.

Immediately Emily felt the anger flowing out of her.

'Can hostilities cease for a while?' Adam suggested tentatively.

'I suppose so.' Emily removed her bonnet and began fanning herself with it.

'I remember that dress and that hat.'

'Do you?' Emily turned to him in surprise.

'At the cricket ground. You were with Rory and looked so pretty I was eaten up with jealousy.'

'And you were with your wife.'

'She was never my wife. You must know she married me bigamously.

'I had heard.'

'Everything about Isabelle was a lie. She even tried to poison me when she found another man she considered a better prospect.'

Emily began to feel a sort of pity for Adam creeping in, but she stamped on it firmly. 'Why isn't she in prison, then?'

'She got away. And no doubt she's gulling some old codger even as we speak. But I hate even mentioning her name. Tell me instead when you plan to leave for America.'

Emily plucked a date out of the air. 'The ship sails on the first day of September.'

'Can we make our peace with each other

before you go, then?' Adam pleaded. 'Over supper at The Capri.'

He was watching her intently but Emily wavered, knowing that if she wasn't careful, she could be pulled into Adam's orbit again. But it was rather a grand restaurant, not one she would normally be taken to, and being wined and dined beat spending a solitary evening in her room. She'd never make the mistake of falling for Adam's charms again, and if she ever found herself weakening, all she had to do was recite to herself the many ways in which he failed her and that would pull her up short. 'All right, I'll come, but I'd like to go home and freshen up first.'

Adam's expression relaxed and he smiled at her. 'Good girl.'

'Wait here. I'll be back in about half an hour.' Emily stood up and Adam followed suit.

'This isn't a plot is it, Emily? You're not planning to give me the slip?' He was anxious again.

'You should know me better than that,' she answered severely. 'I have failings, Adam, but dishonesty isn't one of them.'

'Sorry,' he said contritely and sat down again. 'I'll wait here patiently for you.'

It only took Emily a few minutes to reach her lodgings and as she let herself into the dark, dusty hall, there was a Saturday evening silence to the house. No squabbling couples, no crying babies, no smell of cooking. At the top of the stairs, she stopped and listened. It was the same with Prudence and Edmund, not a murmur. They must have gone out, Emily decided, as she unlocked her door. But supposing she bumped into them this evening? How would she explain Adam away? Say he was her brother maybe, Simon, whom they'd never met. But it was ridiculous to panic, hell would freeze over before Edmund took Prudence to The Capri. It would be a waste of good money as far as he was concerned.

Emily rinsed her face, washed her hands, tidied her hair, dabbed her wrists with eau-de-Cologne and was on her way out, when she noticed the corner of an envelope sticking out from under the rug. 'Now, how long has that been there?' she asked herself, picked it up, recognised Rory's handwriting and felt a jolt of guilt. He probably imagined her sitting alone doing womanly things like sewing or reading and here she was, off out to spend the evening with another man, one she'd once loved and eloped with. Already Emily felt like an adulteress.

She tore open the letter and saw from the date at the top of the page, that their letters must have crossed. Which meant that the sad news that her father had passed away still hadn't reached Rory. However, as she read on down the page, it became clear that it was unlikely he would ever return to England. Stunned, she re-read the letter to help it sink in.

'There's no point in you coming out here at the moment, Emily. My job has folded – a long story, that – and I'm off to the Californian goldfields. The gold is there for the taking and people are pouring out West. All you need is muscle and a pick and a shovel. Well, I'm not short of muscle and I can buy the tools. We'll be rich soon, I promise you, Emily. I'll come back to England and build you a splendid home in Stoneygate, with servants to cater for your every whim and a fine carriage to ride out in, which will make you the envy of all the Leicester matrons...'

He signed off with his deepest and undying love, and Emily gave a disparaging, 'Huh.' What did you do with a man like Rory? It was promises, promises and meaningless sentiments, all mashed up together in a hotch-potch of typical Irish blarney, which he probably believed himself. In the meantime, another job had gone. Enraged Emily screwed the letter up and hurled it at the fire. But it had gone out, so she searched around for a lucifer, struck it, held it to the letter and as she watched it blacken and curl, she sloughed off any remaining guilt. When it was ash, she picked up a light shawl, locked her door and walked towards Golden Square with a sense of anticipation and a light heart. She was going to enjoy herself this evening, she decided; the good food, which she had precious little of these days, and Adam's company.

It was obvious he'd been watching for her, for he jumped to his feet and came towards her. 'I've been on tenterhooks, wondering if you'd changed your mind.'

'Have I ever done anything to make you doubt me?'

Adam's answer was heartfelt. 'No, never.'

Emily swallowed the urge to snap back, 'Unlike you,' because, on her way to meet Adam, she had made a pact with herself. She'd had her say today, and she did not want to spoil the mood of the evening with further recriminations. Neither would she mention Rory's letter and his latest hair-brained scheme. If Adam started spooning out sympathy, there was no telling where it might lead. The thing to do was keep the tone of the evening light and steer the conversation away from anything personal. That way they could go their separate ways afterwards with no harm done.

'Shall we be on our way then?' she heard Adam say. 'Although it might be a good idea if you act as guide. I tend to get lost in this maze of streets.'

The Capri attracted very wealthy customers. They would sometimes draw up in their carriages when Emily was on her way home from work, give indolent instructions to their driver to be there waiting for them at such and such a time, then sweep in through the doors. If she was lucky, before the door swung closed, Emily would get a glimpse of the interior, all mirrors and red plush, and she'd pause to savour the delicious mouth-watering smells that wafted across her nostrils. In all this time Emily had never dreamed she would become part of this exclusive clientele; that she too would pass through its doors and that a waiter, as if he had anticipated their arrival, would leap to attention and relieve her of her rather modest shawl.

'Good-evening, madam, sir. A table for two?' he enquired, and already Emily felt like a trespasser and she wondered if the waiter had her down as wife or mistress.

'Yes please, but one at the side, not in the middle.' Adam gave his instructions in the manner of one used to being obeyed. It wasn't so much arrogance, as an assumption that people would always jump to his bidding. Which, of course, they did and it came from being born to wealth.

The waiter led them to a table, Adam held her chair while she sat down then, as he took his own seat, he said, 'Bring a bottle of your best champagne.'

The waiter hurried away and came back with a green bottle buried in a bucket of ice. He eased the cork with a pop, poured wine into both their glasses and little bubbles floated to the surface. Adam waited until the man withdrew, then lifted his glass. 'What shall we toast to?'

Ignoring his question, Emily, who was anything but at ease with herself, looked around the restaurant. The women were elegant, dressed in haute couture which immediately made her feel small and poor and shabby. Leaning across the table she whispered rather miserably, 'I don't feel suitably dressed.'

'Nonsense, you look absolutely lovely.' Adam's glance swept round the room. 'I bet there isn't a women in this restaurant who wouldn't swap their diamonds for your youth and beauty. In fact I'll drink a toast to that. To Emily's youth and beauty.' He saluted her with his glass then emptied it in one go. Immediately the waiter was at his side re-filling it.

'Come on drink up. With a few glasses of bubbly inside you, you won't give a tinker's cuss about anything.'

Emily took a tentative sip. It was cold and the bubbles broke under her nose and made her sneeze.

Adam laughed. 'Bless you.'

Emily took several more sips, decided she

rather liked champagne and quaffed it down. Suddenly her insecurities, like the bubbles, drifted away and she no longer felt like a disadvantaged waif amongst all the opulence. But then another waiter presented them with two large menus and when she opened hers, Emily was dismayed to see that it was in French. 'I can't understand a word of this.' She spoke in an undertone, terrified the waiter would hear.

'Never mind, I'll tell you what there is.' Adam studied the menu for a moment, then asked, 'How does melon with lamb cutlets to follow, take your fancy?'

'It sounds fine.' The waiter came back to take their order and Adam called for another bottle of champagne.

'We should do this more often,' Adam said, when the melon had arrived, a half each, scooped out into little rounds, and nestling in a bowl of chipped ice.

'I expect you're out wining and dining all the time.' A melon ball found its way to Emily's mouth as she spoke and it was sweet and juicy with a faint taste on the tongue of something alcoholic. How she wished she lived in that sphere of society where food like this was commonplace, instead of having to exist on a monotonous diet of herrings and bacon, with lots of bread to fill up the empty corners.

'No, I'm not. Who would I go with?'

'I'm sure your mother would find you someone.'

'She attempts a bit of matchmaking from time to time and she recently tried to palm me off with a rather obnoxious creature who's recently returned from India. A frightful girl.'

Emily laughed and took another sip of champagne, hardly noticing that a hovering waiter was constantly re-filling her glass. 'I hear you've met my sister, Natalie. It was nice of Clare to invite her to stay with them.'

'Yes, and the visit has been extended. Riding lessons appear to have something to do with it. She's a lively girl, isn't she? And that hair, it's so vibrant; I think she'll soon be making an impression on young men.'

Emily looked alarmed. 'Oh, we don't want that complication yet.'

'It will be impossible to avoid. Nature tends to step in. You weren't much older the first time I met you.'

'I bet I didn't make much of an impression.'

'Perhaps not. But you certainly did the second time. I fell hook, line and sinker.' Adam leaned across and took her hand, but Emily quickly withdrew it.

'Adam, I'm married,' she warned. 'Don't spoil the evening by making me regret coming out with you.'

'Sorry.'

This was just the situation Emily wanted to avoid, so she was glad of the diversion of the waiter bringing the cutlets to the table. Each slender bone was decorated with a frilled choirboy ruff, and there were peas and tiny new potatoes. For pudding Adam chose chocolate mousse, the like of which Emily had never tasted before, and to finish the meal there was coffee in small cups, and when Adam pressed a liqueur upon her, Emily only made a feeble protest.

The bill came, Adam counted out a great wad of notes and tipped the waiters lavishly. Her shawl was draped over her shoulders for her as if it were the finest fur cape; Adam's hat was brushed before it was handed to him and they were seen off the premises with much bowing and scraping.

Out in the street, Adam immediately hailed a cab, for which Emily was glad as there was a curious sensation in her legs which made it difficult for her to walk in a straight line. She expected Adam to give the driver her address, but instead as he helped her in, she heard him say, 'Westminster Bridge, please.'

Emily sank back in the seat. 'Everythin's goin' round and round,' she slurred, hic-cuped twice, then gave an embarrassed giggle.

Adam smiled. 'I think you're the teeniest bit tipsy.'

'Am I? Well, it's rather nice.'

Adam realised he'd pressed her to drink far more than she was used to. It had been to relax her though and not out of any ulterior motive, he told himself, although in the dim intimacy of the cab he could barely keep his hands off her.

Emily's eyes were closed now. 'Are you tired?'

'Mmm.'

'Here, lean on me.' Adam moved a little closer and in a stealthy movement, slid his arm around her waist. Through the thin material of her dress he could feel her soft flesh and was aware of an absence of whalebone, a discovery which had an startling effect on his manhood. Embarrassed, he withdrew his arm, picked up his hat from the seat and quickly covered his shame with it.

The cab slowed down and the driver called from his seat, 'Which side of Westminster Bridge do you want, sir?'

Adam peered out of the window, saw the new, almost completed, Houses of Parliament looming out of the twilight and answered, 'We'll get out here.' He paid off the driver, helped Emily down and asked, 'Can you walk?'

Emily tested her feet against the hard ground. 'I think so, but I'd better hold on to you, just in case,' she said and linked her arm through Adam's. Walking with her towards the bridge, Adam felt like a god astride the world, and it didn't even matter that she let go of him as soon as she could support herself against the parapet.

'Ooh, it's lovely and cool here,' said Emily, throwing back her head. 'And my head's clearing a bit.'

'Have you enjoyed yourself?'

'The food was good.'

'What about the company?'

'Passable.'

'Ouch!'

'You shouldn't go hunting for compliments,' Emily laughed. 'Of course I enjoyed your company.'

'Thank you,' he answered gravely.

They stood side by side in silence for several minutes, gazing at the huge gothic edifice of the new Parliament rising in front of them, then Emily asked, 'Do you think it will ever be finished?'

'Eventually, although I hate to think what it's costing. It's so ornate that I'm not even sure I like it.'

'Oh I do. I love all those turrets, and the intricate carvings, it reminds me of a fairy-tale castle.'

'Let's not discuss architecture. Tell me what you will be doing tomorrow instead.'

'Let me see now. I'll go to church in the morning, and if the girl upstairs I'm friendly with is around, we'll take a stroll in the park in the afternoon.'

'We could take a steamer to Greenwich instead, if you like?'

'I thought I heard you say that you were returning to Halby tomorrow?'

'Well, there's no one waiting for me, so another day away will hardly make much difference.'

Emily turned to him with a doubtful expression. 'Adam, this evening has been really special and I don't want to spoil it, but nothing can come of it.'

'I know that, Emily. But why can't we just enjoy each other's company in this lovely weather? We've neither of us any ties, so what harm can it do?' Adam moved a fraction closer to her. 'Imagine sitting on the steamer with a cool breeze on your face,' he said persuasively.

'It would be nice,' Emily mused.

'So you'll come?'

Emily pretended to dither. Although the idea of a day on the river really appealed to her, she enjoyed keeping Adam guessing for a minute or two.

'Please say yes.'

'All right, then, yes.'

'Oh, you are an angel.' Adam grabbed her hand and kissed it.

'Wait for me in Golden Square.'

'What time?'

'I'll be there at half-past nine.'

'Do you know something, Emily? You've just made a marvellous evening perfect.'

Twelve

Deciding it would be something of a misfortune to bump into Prudence and Edmund, as they approached the end of Franklin street, Emily called to the driver, 'Can you stop here, please?'

'You'll let me see you to your door,' said Adam as the cab came to a halt and she reached for the handle.

'I daren't risk it. The people upstairs are friends of Rory. There's no love lost between Edmund and me and he'd like nothing better than to have the chance to spread gossip.'

'But we've done nothing wrong.' *Unfortunately*, Adam thought to himself.

'That won't bother Edmund. He'll make something up.'

'All right, if you insist, but I don't like the idea of you walking about these streets on your own.'

'I'll be fine, it's only about a hundred yards to my lodgings.'

'And now I've got long hours to wait until I see you again,' Adam sighed.

'You'll be sleeping most of them,' Emily answered practically, for Adam's voice had taken on a sentimental tone and she knew where that could lead.

'And we'll have a wonderful day together, tomorrow, I promise. I'll bring food, and when we get to Greenwich we'll have a picnic and afterwards walk up to the Royal Observatory, where there are some wonderful views.'

'It will be nice to get out of London,' Emily agreed. 'I miss Leicestershire in this weather – it must have been eighty in the shade today and the odours are getting pretty ripe in Soho. There are pigsties in the house behind us.'

'Heatwaves often bring epidemics. You ought to get out of it, go home.'

'I don't want to. I've got a job, and most of the time I like it here. I shall be leaving for America, soon, anyway,' she remembered to add.

'Oh yes, America.'

Outside the cab driver coughed impatiently. 'I think that's a hint to us that he wants to go.' Emily went to open the door but her hand was grabbed by Adam. Hello, what's this? she thought, as he pulled her towards him.

'Aren't I to get a kiss?'

'Adam, you promised...'

'Just on the cheek,' he pursued.

Emily gave a sigh of resignation. 'Oh, all right.'

Leaning across, he gently brushed his lips across her skin and unwelcome darts of desire shot through her. 'You taste of honey,' Adam murmured.

Emily quickly pulled away before her body lost control. 'I must go,' she said, leapt rather ungracefully from the cab and hurried up the street, noticing, even in her flustered state that several of the women who had attended the tea-party were back on their usual spot.

'Night, duckie,' one of them called.

'Night,' Emily answered and thought, so much for the Reverend North's conversions. They must know they'll end up diseased sooner or later, so why do they stay, how can they endure it? But she asked herself this question every time she walked past them and the simple answer was, while men were willing to pay for sex, there would always be women to provide it.

Had Adam ever had sex with a prostitute? Emily wondered as she reached her front door. She was about to let herself in, when the subject of her thoughts called from the cab as it rolled past, 'I'll see you tomorrow.'

Irritated by his lack of discretion, Emily ignored him, climbed the dark stairs, reached out to put her key in the lock, stumbled on something solid and nearly went flying. 'What on earth...?' Fearfully, she reached out to touch the object. Her immediate assumption, that it was an injured animal that had crawled in to find sanctuary, was quickly put in doubt by the very human noise of someone crying. Emily bent closer. 'Prudence? Is it you?'

Prudence mumbled something indistinguishable and Emily thought with disgust, she's blind drunk. 'Come on, stand up,' she ordered, holding the door open with her foot, while at the same time, trying to drag Prudence to her feet. She was a dead weight, but Emily struggled with her into her room and dumped her down on the bed. A street light shone through the window and she was about to give Prudence a lecture on the evils of drink, when she noticed her battered face and gave a gasp of shock.

'What's happened? Have you fallen? Been in an accident?' Emily asked in alarm, for Prudence's lip was split and bleeding and one eye was so swollen it was closed. Quickly, she lit the lamp, drew the curtains and went and sat down by her friend.

Prudence's shoulders sagged and she began to sob. 'It ... it was Edmund, 'e beat me up.'

'Beat you up?' Emily repeated. 'Why? When?'

Prudence wiped her cheeks with the back of her hand. 'After you'd gone out. Just 'cos I brought back a meat pie instead of an eel pie. I swear it's what 'e asked for.'

'He did that to your face because of a blinking pie? The vile bloody brute!' Emily rarely swore but she was beside herself with rage.

'Oh Em, I thought 'e was gonna murder me. It was worse even than when me pa used to hammer me.'

'Has he hit you before?'

'A coupla times. But not bad, just some bruises on me arms.'

'Wait here. I'm going to deal with him.' She went to make for the door but Prudence grabbed her arm.

'No don't, please. You'll only make it worse for me.'

There was such a look of abject terror on her poor, bruised face, Emily moved away from the door, but reluctantly, for she was in a fighting mood, and nothing would have given her greater pleasure than to tell Edmund to his face that he was a bullying thug. 'All right, if you'd rather I didn't say anything, I won't. But let me bathe that eye and lip.'

Emily went to the washstand, poured water into a bowl and tore a clean piece of linen in half. As she applied the cold compress to Prudence's misused face, the girl said frightfully, 'Can I stop 'ere tonight, Em? I won't be a nuisance, I promise, and I'll sleep on the floor.'

'You'll do nothing of the sort. The bed's narrow, so it'll be a bit of "When mother turns, we all turn", but we'll manage.'

Prudence couldn't quite manage a smile. 'I wish I 'ad a mum. I wouldn't be in this bleedin' mess, then.'

'What happened to her?'

'She died when I was six of the smallpox. I can tell you've got a nice mum though cos you've bin bought up decent and you speak nice. That's how I'd like to be, a lady.'

'My mother's lovely, the best in the world. But her life didn't start off well. It was worse than yours. She was born in the poorhouse, never knew either of her parents and was put out to work as a little skivvy when she was five. But she got over these setbacks and so can you, Prudence, but as I keep telling you, you've got to break away from that rotter upstairs.'

'But I wouldn't know where to go, what to do.'

'You must get a job.'

'Yes, but what?'

'You could be a housemaid, and you'd get a nice uniform.'

'It ain't somethin' I really care for, cleaning.'

That was apparent from the state of their rooms, thought Emily. 'A factory, then?' she suggested.

Prudence shook her head.

She tried again. 'What about dress-making?'

'I've never been good with the needle. It's no good, I can't do nothing.'

Emily heard the defeated tone and decided to let the matter rest. This was no time to push Prudence, and if she continued she would only make her feel even more inadequate.

'I expect you're tired.'

'Yeah, I am a bit done in.'

Emily went to her drawer, pulled out a clean cotton nightdress and handed it to Prudence. 'You can wear this,' she said then for modesty's sake blew out the lamp.

The pair of them rustled around in the dark getting undressed, Emily checked that the door was locked, dragged up the window to let in some air, then they climbed into the narrow bed and lay together like spoons. 'Ain't this cosy?' Prudence giggled, almost forgetting her misery in the novelty of it all. 'G'night, Em, and thanks, I feel really safe here,' she murmured and a moment later she was asleep.

Emily lay there hardly daring to move in case she woke Prudence. But it was hot with two bodies in a narrow bed and she began to sweat and her limbs grew stiff. To block out the discomfort she went back over her evening with Adam. She'd loved the pampering, the good food, Adam's company, but when she'd been caught in his web before, she'd always been the loser. So was she playing a dangerous game in agreeing to go on this boat trip with him tomorrow? Well, if she was going to be honest with herself, of course she was. Adam wanted her, he'd deliberately pursued her, and he was a man used to getting his own way with women. Her intense, girlish love for Adam hadn't survived the many blows he'd delivered to her self-esteem, and he was no longer her white knight, but a man with his share of human failings. But what was to stop her having a more basic relationship with him, one that satisfied her own sexual needs? There had been several things wrong with her marriage but sex had never been one of them and she missed it, so why should she have to endure years of enforced celibacy, just because her husband had chosen to remove himself to the other end of the earth? Emily asked herself.

She wouldn't be going to Adam as an inexperienced girl, but as a woman who knew how to give pleasure to a man, and it would be a mutually fulfilling relationship between two adults, where the word love would never be mentioned. That way, she could not be made a fool of again. And this time she'd see to it that she played piper and he danced to her tune. But where would they conduct this illicit affair? Certainly not here. Lying in the dark, Emily let her fantasies take flight. Adam would rent an apartment in a discreetly anonymous building in one of the best parts of town, and their bed would be a huge four-poster and they'd have satin sheets and they'd make love in it all day, only getting up for champagne and oysters. Emily smiled. By this time tomorrow she could have committed adultery and yet she didn't feel a whiff of guilt. But then, Rory was hardly an ideal husband and she had more than a passing suspicion that he was trying to shake off his responsibilities and disappear from her life, for without an address how would she ever trace him? Papa had warned her that he was a rolling stone, but she'd made the mistake of thinking that marriage and responsibilities would tame him, so in a sense she was to blame.

Emily yawned, and was trying to stretch her cramped leg, when Prudence suddenly shot up, yelled, 'You bugger! You bugger!' then fell back on the pillow and began to snore loudly.

'Must you frighten the life out of me, Prudence?' Emily grumbled to the sleeping girl then, deciding she'd had enough, she got out of bed, dragged off a blanket, wound it round herself and lay down on the floor near the window. Although there was a faint breeze, the floorboards dug into her shoulderblades. 'God, this is even more uncomfortable,' she moaned and, knowing she'd never get a wink of sleep, prayed for morning to come. And there's still to-morrow night, she was thinking when she became aware of a far off sound of banging. Emily sat up and blinked. She would swear she hadn't closed her eyes all night, and yet there was sunlight streaming through a gap in the curtains. How strange, she thought, and there it was again: a great thunderous noise that vibrated in her head.

'Prudence, I know you're in there. You've ruined all my canvasses and I'm warning you, you'll pay for it, and I don't care if I swing for it.'

'Oh God, it's 'im!' Prudence was sitting up in bed, holding the blankets in front of her as if for protection. Her frizzy hair was all over the place, and although her black eye and swollen mouth hardly added to her beauty, it did make her look heartbreakingly vulnerable.

Emily struggled out of her cocoon and went and put a comforting arm around her. 'It's all right. He can't get in. The door is locked.'

'He'll break it down. I know,' Prudence whimpered as they watched the door bulge under the violence of the attack. 'And he will kill me, like 'e said.'

'No, he won't, I'll protect you,' Emily

promised, although she had no idea what with. The frying pan perhaps? But Prudence, who had an excessive faith in her abilities, was calmed by her assurances and by now anyway, other inhabitants of the house, fed up with having their Sunday morning lie-in disturbed, had come out on to the landing.

'Shut yer din, mate, or it'll be you who gets yer head knocked off, not yer old woman,' a male voice threatened and being a cowardly creature, Edmund must have taken this warning seriously and slouched off upstairs, because it all went quiet again.

'See, he's gone.'

'Yeah but for 'ow long?' Prudence answered gloomily.

'Hey, did you really ruin his paintings?' asked Emily.

'Yeah. After 'e beat me up I waited until 'e'd gone out then slashed every single one of them wiv a knife.'

Emily was deeply impressed. She would never have credited Prudence with that much initiative and she began to grow in stature in her eyes.

'He can't paint for toffee nuts, anyway,' Prudence sneered.

Emily laughed at such honest criticism.

'Do you know, I can paint better than 'im.'

'Really?'

'Yeah, ten times better. I always bin a good

drawer. I'll show you one day.' Prudence slid out of bed. 'Have you got a piss-pot I can use, Em?'

'No, sorry.'

Prudence gripped herself between her legs and danced up and down. 'Ooh, ooh, I'm dying for a pee. Do you think I dare risk goin' down to the jakes?'

Emily's reply was blunt. 'Well, I don't want you doing it on my floor, so you'll have to.' She held her ear to the door. 'Quiet as the grave out there, so if you're quick and don't make a noise, you should be safe.' She unlocked the door, opened it a fraction, peered out, then beckoned to Prudence. 'It's all clear.' She pushed her out into the hall, turned the key as a precaution, but stood ready to let her back in immediately she heard her footsteps outside.

But Prudence took such a time, Emily grew impatient and decided to have a quick wash. She emptied last night's dirty water into a slop pail and was about to pour fresh water into the basin, when shouts and screams made her jump with guilt. *Oh God, Edmund.* If he killed Prudence, it would be her fault for abandoning her post. Emily ran to the door and wrenched it open, forgetting in her haste, that in her nightwear, she was hardly properly dressed for combat. In the half-light of the landing she quickly took in the situation. Edmund had Prudence pushed up against a wall and was laying into her with his fists and snarling at her, 'You whore! You cow!' while Prudence sobbed,

'Stop it, Edmund for Christ's sake, you'll kill me,' and tried to protect her face with her arms.

Without stopping to think, Emily flung herself upon Edmund and began hammering her fists upon his back. 'Lay off her, you bastard!' she screamed, then when he took no notice, she stood back and gave him a hard kick up his backside. It was thin and bony and it must have hurt, because he gave a yelp, let go of Prudence and turned his rage on Emily. She backed away, looking for somewhere to run, but he'd got her cornered. This is it, he's going to beat me black and blue, she was thinking, when the man whom Edmund had had the dispute with earlier, appeared at his door. He was wearing a shirt and socks, otherwise there wasn't much to distinguish him from a gorilla. He glared darkly at Edmund then strode across the hall.

'I thought I told you, I don't like noise,' he bellowed, grabbed Edmund by the scruff of the neck, turned him round and socked him hard on the jaw. Emily couldn't resist it, she gave a loud cheer as Edmund staggered back, lost his balance and fell to his knees. 'That's it, mate, pray, although I don't think 'im up there will be much help,' his opponent advised.

Edmund gingerly felt his jaw, scrambled to his feet then turned to Prudence. 'You'd better not ever come back if you want to live.' His eyes stared out with hatred from under his pink, crusty lids.

Prudence wiped her hand across her nose. 'You needn't worry, you've seen the last of me. I'm not gonna be your skivvy any more. You can do yer own dirty work or find another mug. And d'you know somethin' else?' She leaned forward to make her point, 'Yer painting's crap. That's why you don't sell none.'

'Why, you...' To have his genius questioned was the last straw and Edmund made a lunge at Prudence. But Emily, anticipating this, grabbed Prudence by the arm and pulled her into the room. She secured the door then leaned against it panting heavily.

'You shouldn't needle him, he's dangerous,' Emily warned as she fixed the back of a chair under the door handle as an extra precaution.

Prudence adjusted her nightdress. 'I've put up wiv 'im for long enough, I'm getting me own back.'

'Did he hurt you?' Emily studied her face.

'I reckon there'll be a few more bruises before the day is out,' Prudence answered philosophically.

'The pig!'

'Yeah, now that you mention it, he has got a bit of a piggy face.'

'Could you manage a bit of breakfast with that cut lip?' Emily asked, knowing that beneath the cockney bravado there was a very frightened girl.

'I'll have a try, I'm famished.'

'Right, since that's all I've got, we'll have tea and toast.'

'And I'd better get me things on. Do you know Em, yer a real duck, helping me like this,' Prudence said with great sincerity as her head came through the neck of her dress.

Emily turned from lighting the fire. 'If I was in a fix, you'd do the same for me, wouldn't you?'

'Course I would. You're me best mate, ain't you?'

'That's nice to know. You need people you can rely on. Now, come and hold this while I get dressed.' She handed Prudence the toasting fork. 'And don't burn it,' she warned. 'It's the last of the bread.'

Only the corner of one piece of toast was slightly charred, which by Prudence's culinary standards was pretty good. There was a scraping of jam but no milk for tea, and in spite of her injuries, Prudence consumed everything in sight, including a crust Emily left at the side of her plate.

It wasn't until they'd finished their meagre

meal that Emily remembered she should be somewhere and glanced at the clock. *Oh heavens, Adam,* she thought with a jolt of guilt, and jumped to her feet.

'Where you going? Yer not leaving me are you, Em?' Prudence stared at her protector with a frightened expression.

'No, no.' Amidst all the drama and hullabaloo it had completely slipped Emily's mind that she'd arranged to meet Adam in Golden Square. And that was over two hours ago. But nobody would be expected to hang around that long, she reasoned, so even if she went this minute, he'd have been long gone. Remembering how close she'd come to breaking her marriage vows, Emily broke out in a cold sweat. She'd really had a close shave. Fortunately, fate had intervened, not in the most pleasant way, but at least she'd been spared the indignity of making a fool of herself again with Adam.

Adam arrived early at Golden Square to allow himself the exquisite pleasure of savouring that first glimpse of Emily as she turned the corner; to delight in the lightness of her step, to watch the way the skirt of her dress swayed slightly but oh so erotically as she walked. And when she reached him she would smile and he would have an un-controllable urge to gather her up in his arms, kiss her and swear his undying love, except that he knew that it would be very unwise. For he mustn't forget for one second that she was a true and loving wife.

It was quiet in the square and Adam leaned back on the seat and stretched his legs in front of him. For the first time in a long while, the nagging unhappiness that was his constant companion had lifted, probably because he had a whole day to look forward to with Emily. And there could be others, as long as he didn't overstep the mark and frighten her away, a point he must constantly remind himself of.

He sat there for a half an hour waiting and then the bells of a nearby church started to peal. Adam shifted uneasily. Emily was never late. Worshippers were now arriving for the morning service and Adam skimmed the various family groups, hoping she might be amongst them. There was a sudden surge of latecomers, who managed to slip in just before the verger closed the church door, then the street was empty and the service began, prayers were recited, familiar hymns were sung. Adam waited for another half hour then stood up. Something must have delayed her, he decided, and began to walk towards her lodgings. Aware that, for her sake, he shouldn't make his presence too obvious, he walked past on the other side of the street, trying to keep his manner as casual as possible. What struck him about her lodging house, was the absence of any sign of life and curtains were still drawn across most of the windows. Perhaps Emily had overslept. Or maybe he'd missed her and she was now waiting for him. Adam turned and galloped back to Golden Square, but except for some pigeons it was empty. He dashed back and forth again and this time when he returned the service had finished, people were filing out of church and standing talking in groups before going off to their homes.

By insisting on kissing her had he overstepped the mark and put her off the idea of spending the day with him? If so, what exactly am I achieving, running around like a headless chicken? Adam asked himself. Just accept it, she's not coming. He let this disagreeable idea sink in for a few minutes, then it slowly began to occur to him that Emily was probably, at this minute, sitting at home having a good laugh at his expense.

'Damn and blast all women!' Adam cursed, in an explosion of fury, and as his voice echoed round the empty square, there was a soft flurry of wings as the pigeons flew out of harm's way. Adam strode back to the hotel stiff with resentment and thinking: that's the last time a woman makes a fool of me. He packed, caught the next train back to Leicester, but Emily's perfidy was still chafing at him when he reached Halby. As

Adam drove down Main Street, past the Green, he glanced in the direction of Hattie's cottage. Now there was a woman who would make him welcome, if her hints were anything to go by, and she'd always had some very pleasant ways of making him forget Emily for an hour or two. By now in no state to stop and consider whether his actions were wise, he turned the trap in the direction of her cottage. She was in because the lamp was lit and the curtains drawn. In a state of pleasurable anticipation, Adam knocked and waited. There was rather a long pause and a shuffling noise, but Hattie eventually came to the door and she looked rather taken aback to see him.

Adam lifted his hat and gave her his most charming smile. 'Good evening, Hattie.'

'Oh ... hello.'

Adam had expected a much warmer greeting than this but he ploughed on. 'Would it be convenient to come in and see my boys?' he asked.

Hattie looked acutely embarrassed. 'Well, no it wouldn't actually,' she said, with a glance over her shoulder.

It was now Adam's turn to feel uncomfortable, for it suddenly occurred to him that Hattie must have a gentleman caller. He had a strong suspicion who it was, too: the new schoolmaster. And being a man himself, he would understand exactly

Adam's real motive for calling, and he could hear in his own ears, how feeble his reason for being there must sound. Certain he could hear suppressed laughter in the background and deeply mortified, Adam hastily bid Hattie good-night and climbed into his trap. Before he moved off, he stared hard at the curtained window. What were they up to in there, Hattie and her amour? Well, from his own experience it didn't require much imagination to guess, Adam concluded, and drove home with a burgeoning resentment against the whole of the female sex.

Presided over by Clare, Natalie applied herself diligently to her schoolwork; composition, arithmetic plus some geography and history. This took up a good part of the morning, but once it was done, she had the rest of the day in which to do as she pleased.

Like she'd promised, Clare took her down to the stables and introduced her to Mrs Jane Smith and her son Gabriel soon after she arrived in Halby.

'Fairfax,' Mrs Smith ruminated, 'that name rings a bell.'

'Natalie is Rachel and Jed's daughter,' Clare explained. 'She's come to stay with us and while she's here she's keen to learn to ride.'

Mrs Smith's weathered-roughened face

broke into a smile. 'The best occupation for any gel, and my son's the one to teach you,' she boomed. 'He's a splendid horseman and my poor old bones aren't up to it now. I'll go and get him.' She limped across the stableyard and called, 'Gabriel, could you come here, please?' and a moment later a dark-haired youth of about Natalie's own age appeared and something about him told her he was the lone rider she'd seen from her window on the day she arrived. He was dressed like a field labourer in moleskin trousers and a dark blue open-necked shirt, and his brows were drawn together in a scowl.

'Yes, Mother.'

His mother, who in contrast to her son was relentlessly cheerful, smiled fondly at him. 'Dearest, this is Miss Natalie Fairfax and she wants to learn to ride.'

The young man turned and regarded Natalie with such a hostile expression, she thought she was about to get an outright refusal. Instead, in a cultured voice that was quite at odds with his manner and dress, he enquired, 'When would you like to start?'

Natalie turned to Clare. 'When would be a good time?'

'As soon as Hattie has finished altering that riding habit.'

'She told me I could collect it this evening.'

'Right, how about tomorrow then, Gabriel?'

'Yes, but could you be here early please, Miss Fairfax?'

Natalie glanced at Clare. 'I have school-work in the morning.'

'Schoolwork?' Gabriel sounded aston-ished that anyone should wish to indulge in such a pointless pastime.

'Yes, Natalie's mother was anxious that she should keep on with her studies while she's with us, so she has lessons with me every morning. The afternoon is hers, though.'

'I could come at two o'clock,' Natalie suggested.

Gabriel thought about this rather longer than necessary, in Natalie's opinion, then gave a nod, which she supposed meant, yes. 'May I go now, Mother?'

'Of course, dear.'

He had enough manners to wish them good-day but as he sloped off, Jane gave a slightly apologetic shrug, as if to say, what am I going to do with this son of mine?

Jane invited Natalie and Clare inside for some of her homemade elderberry wine as a sort of apology and later walking back up Blackthorn Lane, Natalie said in her blunt youthful way, 'Gabriel's not a very friendly person, is he?'

'No, a chip off the old block, really. His

father rarely opened his mouth, except to talk to his horses. Rugby School has banged some manners into Gabriel, otherwise he'd be completely wild.'

'Where is his father?'

'No one knows. He left one day, vanished into thin air. He's never been seen or heard of since.'

'Poor boy.'

'Well, he did inherit one talent from his father, superb horsemanship. He might not have much to say for himself, but you've got the best teacher in the county. Just don't expect much in the way of conversation. Freddie is due home the day after to-morrow. You'll like him, everyone does, and you'll find him great company. He's interested in everything, loves all wild things and he'll have you roaming all over the countryside, so I hope you've brought some stout shoes with you.'

They had reached the house now and Clare paused before opening the gate. 'I'm a little tired, so I'm going to have a rest. What time does Hattie want you down at her place?' she asked.

'Not until about eight. She wants to make sure the twins are asleep.'

'Right, I'll take you down but I need to go and have a word with my aunt, so I'll drop you and pick you up again later. Perhaps Hattie will find time to give me a second fitting, while I'm there. In the meantime, can you entertain yourself for an hour or two?'

'I'll sit in the garden and read. I've brought some books with me.'

'Good, I'll see you at about four o'clock for tea.'

Hattie had just finished putting the final dart in the jacket of the riding habit when Natalie arrived. She let her in then went and sat down again. 'Sorry, I'm a bit behind, I'm afraid, Miss Natalie. I don't know if they are sickening for anything but the boys have been fractious all day, and I didn't get much of an opportunity to do any sewing.' She rubbed her eyes tiredly. 'I must get on with Mrs Harcourt's dress as well.' Hattie nodded in the direction of a half finished dress. She was about to add, 'Or she'll have had her babby before I'm done,' when she remembered that such delicate matters weren't mentioned in front of young girls, although she'd discovered for herself early enough that they weren't found under gooseberry bushes. She sewed the last stitch, bit off a length of thread, stuck the needle in her dress and handed the jacket to Natalie. 'Now, go upstairs and try on the whole outfit then come down and show me what a fine lady you are.'

Natalie liked the idea of being thought a

lady and she'd already written excited letters to her mother and Emily, telling them of her plans to learn to ride. Wearing clothes of quality, made by a high class tailor in London was very much to her taste and when she'd changed, Natalie went over and studied herself in the looking glass. The habit was sage green, a perfect colour for her vivid hair and although her figure was still girlish and her breasts were almost non-existent, the clever darting in the jacket made her slender body look quite curvaceous. Natalie twirled an imaginary riding crop, tilted her head and tried a haughty stare. Was it her fancy or did she have the look of a young lady of the county? Furthermore, would she make any impression on Gabriel? Probably not. Natalie giggled. Not unless she learned to neigh, eat hay and paw the ground. She could toss her mane, though, as well as any horse.

She was on her way down to show herself off to Hattie, when she heard a conveyance of some kind draw up outside, then knocking on the door. Assuming it was Clare, she was about to continue on down when a voice, masculine and deep, made Natalie pause. Whoever it was, Hattie obviously had no intention of inviting him in and there followed a few intense minutes of conversation on the step. Although she strained hard, Natalie didn't catch one word except good-night. The door closed on the visitor and, deeply curious, Natalie hurried to the window, lifted the curtain a fraction and peeked out. It was Mr Bennett. Now, what's *he* doing here? she wondered as she watched him jump in his trap, stare hard at the cottage then flick the reins and drive off in a manner which suggested that Hattie had said something to upset him.

When Hattie didn't mention the visit, neither did Natalie. What callers she had were her own business and she wouldn't thank her for poking her nose into what didn't concern her, Natalie decided. To amuse her, though, she adopted an exaggerated pose and took a few steps around the small parlour. 'Well, how do I look?'

Hattie studied Natalie for a moment then made quite an acute observation. 'You'd better be careful, Miss Natalie, or you'll start getting a taste for this toff's life.'

'I'll never do that,' Natalie protested without conviction. 'I'm here for two weeks, but after that I know I shall be homesick for Mama and the bookshop.'

'Well, town life would always win hands down with me. And that's where I aim to be before long, in Leicester with my own dress shop. I don't want to rot here.'

'I shall buy all my dresses from you, I promise, Hattie. You're a wonderful seamstress. Look how beautifully you've altered this outfit.'

'I'm glad you're pleased. Now run and change, Mrs Harcourt will be here soon, and she'll be wanting a fitting.'

Later as they drove home, Natalie was on the point of mentioning Mr Bennett's visit to Clare, but then some instinct stopped her. She was still considered a child, so such things were never discussed in her hearing, but there were undercurrents here that she didn't quite understand. And where was Hattie's babies' father? People said nothing ever happened in the country, but that wasn't true in Halby. And tomorrow she would write to her sister and tell her all about it.

Thirteen

Being the sort of girl who despised wilting violets, to find herself squealing, 'I'm going to fall, get me down off this horse!' the moment she climbed on its back, was a humbling experience for Natalie.

'Muffin is a pony, not a horse,' Gabriel corrected her, 'and she's too sweet tempered to throw anyone, and I promise you won't fall. Take a few deep breaths, make sure you're sitting comfortably then we'll take a turn or two round the yard. And hold the reins like this,' he said, adjusting them in her hands, 'but not too tightly or you'll hurt Muffin's mouth.'

Gabriel spoke quietly to the mare, Natalie felt a jolt to her spine as Muffin moved off, then with Gabriel holding the leading rein, they began a steady amble round the yard. But Natalie felt awkward, ungraceful and not at all in control and the ground still seemed miles away. She also had to struggle to remember Gabriel's instructions, and she was certain he was laughing to himself and thinking, what a complete dunce. Slowly, though she began to move in rhythm with the pony, but just as she felt she was beginning to get the hang of it, Gabriel announced, 'That will be enough for today. But do you want to go on with this anyway? There's not much point if you don't enjoy it.'

'In other words, I'm no good so I'm wasting your time.' Natalie unhooked her leg from the pommel, slid to the ground and stood staring him straight in the eye.

'I didn't say that.'

'Not in so many words, no. Even you stop at that. But I do want the truth.'

'All right. You'd learn in time, but some people have a natural affinity with horses. You don't. Perhaps it because you're a town person.'

'At least townfolk have manners,' Natalie shot back, deciding it was time to bring this arrogant young man down a peg or two.

Gabriel scowled at her with such ferocity his black eyebrows met across the bridge of his nose. 'I'm not rude.'

'Well, you certainly don't put yourself out to be pleasant. You might have a few friends if you did.'

'The horses are my friends. I don't need anyone else.'

'Glad to hear it,' Natalie retaliated and strode out of the yard.

'You can come back tomorrow if you like,' Gabriel called after her.

The temptation was strong to ignore his invitation, but it was an olive branch of sorts, and she did want to be able to boast to her mother that she had learned to ride when she returned to Leicester. She stopped and turned. 'What time?'

'Two o'clock, the same as today, Miss Fairfax. There, was that polite enough for you?' he taunted.

'It will do,' Natalie answered, with a toss of her tawny mane, and decided that tomorrow she would bring carrots for Muffin, then at least she'd have one ally, even if it was of the equine variety.

When Natalie returned from her second riding lesson, she knew at once that Freddie was home. Although there was no sign of him, luggage and books were piled high in the hall and Jelly was running around in berserk circles. 'Come on Jelly, calm down.' She bent to pick up the small dog, but he wriggled from her arms and tore off up the stairs.

Laughing at his antics Natalie followed him, and halfway up Clare's head appeared over the banisters. 'As you've probably worked out by now, Freddie is home.'

A door opened as Natalie reached the landing, someone called, 'Come here, Jelly,' and the dog sped along the corridor in a state of frantic excitement.

Clare smiled. 'How's that for devotion?'

'He does seem to love Freddie,' Natalie agreed, but then, she thought, dogs are never critical of their owners.

'So how did the riding lesson go today? Was Gabriel any more forthcoming?'

'Not really. But I think I'm beginning to get the hang of it. And Muffin's such a lovely pony, I wasn't frightened.'

'When you meet Freddie you'll find he's the absolute opposite to Gabriel...' Clare didn't finish her sentence, instead she gave a little, 'Ouch,' and pressed her hand into her stomach.

Natalie leaned towards her with a worried expression. 'Aunt Clare, are you all right?' she asked, for she was biting hard into her lip.

Clare gave her stomach a rub and managed a smile. 'It's a bit of indigestion, don't worry, I'm prone to it.'

'Why don't you have a lie down?'

'And have Freddie think he's come home to an invalid? Certainly not. Now, off you go and change. I've told Freddie, tea is in a quarter of an hour.'

When Natalie entered the drawing-room a little later a young man, grown much taller than the one she remembered coming into the shop, rose to greet her.

'Natalie, this is Freddie.'

They shook hands, mumbled a rather self-conscious, 'How do you do,' and sat down some distance from each other.

'We won't wait for Christopher,' said Clare. 'The workmen have finally started on the school foundations, and he's so excited that his school is finally going to be built, he can't bear not to be there.' She laughed indulgently, went to pick up the teapot, exclaimed, 'Oh dear me,' and slumped back in her chair with her eyes closed.

Immediately Natalie and Freddie were at her side. 'Aunt Clare, what's the matter,' Natalie cried, in a frightened voice.

'She's fainted,' said Freddie tersely, undid the collar on Clare's dress and started fanning her with a small napkin.

'She wasn't well earlier. I told her to rest but she wouldn't because you were home.'

This remark sounded in Freddie's ears, something like an accusation. But he didn't respond because Clare's eyelids were moving, a sign that she was coming round. 'Quickly, go and open her bedroom door,' he ordered, then picking Clare up as if she were a doll, he carried her upstairs.

Feeling totally inadequate, Natalie turned down the counterpane, and as Freddie laid her down on the bed, Clare opened her eyes. Obviously confused, she blinked several times. 'What happened?' she asked.

'You fainted.'

'Did I? How silly of me, it must be the heat.'

Natalie hurried to the door. 'I'll tell Phoebe to run down to the village and fetch Uncle Christopher.'

Clare pulled herself up in bed. 'No. And please, both of you, don't mention anything about this to him.' Her voice was agitated.

Freddie looked doubtful. 'But Aunt Clare, you might need to see the apothecary.'

'Christopher has enough on his plate with the school, I don't want to give him more worries with my silly faintings.'

'If you insist,' said Freddie.

Clare lay back on the pillows. 'I do. I need to rest for an hour, then I'll be right as rain. Leave me now and go and finish your tea and I'll see you at dinner.'

Clare turned on her side, and by the time Natalie had pulled the counterpane over her legs, drawn the curtains and moved to the door, she could hear Clare's regular breathing. 'I think she's sleeping,' she whispered and they tiptoed from the room.

But the incident had left Natalie feeling upset and uncertain. It was so soon after her father's death that any sign of illness frightened her. Morbid thoughts started to press in and fearing that she might be pitched into that deep dark hole of melancholy again, she tried to occupy herself by pouring tea for them both. She tasted hers and made a face. 'Ugh, it's cold. Shall I ring for some more?'

'I don't really want any, thank you. I think I'll take Jelly for a walk instead.' Freddie stood up.

'Can I come, too?' Natalie couldn't face being left alone with her own thoughts.

'If you like. But it's over the fields and the ground is uneven.'

'I've got boots with me, I'll go and change into them,' said Natalie, who sensed Freddie was trying to put her off. Clare had kept emphasising how friendly he was and what a good companion he would be to her, but he didn't show much sign of wanting to get to know her. But then she supposed an undergraduate at Oxford, years older than she was, and used to the company of clever people, would probably find having a schoolgirl tagging along a bit of an embarrassment.

She half expected him to disappear over the horizon while she was changing her shoes, but he and Jelly were waiting for her at the gate and they set off immediately down Blackthorn Lane. Because Freddie was tall, his strides were long and Natalie was soon panting from trying to keep up with him.

'Can you slow down?' she pleaded.

'You townies are all the same,' Freddie mocked, 'no stamina.'

'And you country types give yourself superior airs,' she shot back. 'But don't worry, I won't trouble you with my company any longer.'

First Gabriel and now Freddie! In high dudgeon, Natalie went to turn back, but Freddie put out his hand to restrain her. 'Sorry, it was only said in jest.'

'Could you keep your jests to yourself, please? I get enough of that sort of talk from Gabriel Smith. I don't feel I should be pitied because I live in Leicester.'

'He's a strange lad, Gabriel. Definitely a one-off. Marvellous with horses, though.'

'So I'm always being told. But not much good with human beings.'

'Perhaps not, but I get on with him well enough. Now, shall we continue? There's a stile a bit further down and a path across the field that takes us to the river. If we're lucky we might see some kingfishers.'

A picture of total doggy happiness, Jelly bounced along in front of them like a furry ball, pausing and turning every now and then to reassure himself that his beloved Freddie was close behind.

When they reached the stile Freddie went first and held out his hand to help Natalie.

She ignored the proffered hand. 'I can manage on my own, thank you,' she said and with a gazelle-like leap, was over.

In the field, Jelly went sniffing around like a hound dog, then came running up with a stick clamped between his jaws. He laid it at his master's feet and Freddie picked it up and sent it spinning in the air. Jelly went tearing after it, retrieved the stick and came rushing back, waiting with furiously gyrating tail for a repeat performance.

'He does love you, doesn't he?' Natalie observed.

'Yes, and I love him,' Freddie answered unselfconsciously. The ritual continued until they reached the river, where Jelly abandoned the stick and hurled himself into the water. He swam around for a few minutes, until something else caught his attention, then he came running out and shook his long coat all over them.

'You are a holy terror,' Natalie laughed, glad that she'd had the forethought to change into one of her older dresses.

They followed the bank for a while, until they came to a natural seat formed by the trunk of a fallen tree. 'Let's sit down here,' Freddie suggested, 'It's a good place to see a kingfisher.'

Natalie picked some stones and aimed them at the water. 'Do you think Aunt Clare is all right on her own?' she asked, for she was beginning to worry that she should have stayed with her.

'She was sleeping, that's always a good sign. And I know she asked us not to, but I think I might tell Uncle Christopher about her fainting fit.'

'But that's breaking a promise.'

Freddie glanced at her. 'Natalie, do you know what is wrong with Aunt Clare?'

'Yes, indigestion.'

He smiled. 'You're a bit young so I don't know whether I should be telling you this.' He paused.

'Tell me what?'

'Clare is going to have a baby.'

Natalie mulled over this information. At school, a great deal of time was taken up in the playground, discussing where babies came from. The gooseberry bush was a favoured source, although she had always been more inclined to her mother's explanation that the stork brought them. Recently, however, she'd become more observant and she had begun to notice how women's stomachs became all swollen up, a baby would arrive and they'd shrink back again to a normal size. Natalie hadn't quite fathomed out the mechanics of this but she intended to quiz Emily about it next time she came home. She had no intention of displaying her ignorance to Freddie, however, so she threw another stone in the water and answered casually, 'Oh, is she? How do you know? Did Aunt Clare tell you?'

'No,' he admitted, 'but I know how animals give birth and I'm going to train to be a doctor at the Leicester Infirmary when I come down from Oxford, so I've made a study of such matters. She might need to see the apothecary and it would be terrible if anything went wrong.'

Went wrong. The words had a frightening ring to it. 'What shall we do?' Natalie asked.

'The more I think about it, the more I'm sure Uncle Christopher ought to be told.' Freddie stood up and called to Jelly, who'd been snuffling away in the undergrowth. 'Let's go down to the school, I expect he's still there.'

Deferring to Freddie's age and experience, Natalie followed him back across the field and down the lane. Even before they reached the village, they could hear the excited babble and when they reached the school plot, they found it swarming with people. The children were having the time of their lives, scrambling up piles of earth or tumbling into trenches, while their parents stood and watched fascinated as the navvies heaved great sods of earth out of the ground.

'This is a big event in their lives,' Freddie explained, 'There's been so much talk about the school – this is proof that they are actually going to get one.'

Scanning the crowds, Natalie asked, 'But can you see Uncle Christopher?'

'No, but Mr Bennett's over there. You wait here, I'll go and have a word, he probably knows where he is. Come here, Jelly.'

Freddie held out his arms, Jelly leapt into them and they pushed off through the crowd. Left alone, Natalie realised how much of a stranger she was here and she looked around for someone she might know even vaguely; Gabriel, for instance. But he would never involve himself in a gathering like this, she decided, not where there were *people*. But then in a breach in the crowd, she noticed Hattie and the twins. She's always friendly, I'll go and have a chat with her, Natalie decided and was about to make her way round to where Hattie was standing, when she noticed a smartly dressed young man walk up to her and raise his hat. Blast! He'd beaten her to it. They stood talking amiably, then he must have said something funny, for Hattie threw back her head and laughed, quite loudly, and a short distance away Natalie noticed Mr Bennett turn and stare at them with a disapproving frown. Now, why should he do that? Natalie mused. But Freddie was now speaking to Adam and she saw him direct him to a small group some distance away. Freddie hurried over to them, there was a further brief discussion then Christopher separated himself from the group and, looking extremely agitated, tore off up Blackthorn Lane.

Natalie wasn't sure whether to follow him or wait for Freddie, but people kept stopping him, obviously proud to be able to lay claim to a young man, schooled in Halby, but so clever he was at one of the great English universities; a pinnacle to which their own boys might aspire with the new school.

'Sorry, but I know a lot of people,' he apologised, when he finally reached her. 'I think we did the right thing, though. Uncle Christopher is really worried. You see, they've waited a long time for this baby,' he confided.

'Oh, What shall we do? Stay here or go back? I don't want to be in the way.'

'I think I should get back, Uncle Christopher might want me to ride over to fetch the apothecary.'

'I'll come with you. Staring at a hole in the ground soon loses its novelty, and there I might be able to help in some way,' Natalie answered, almost immediately regretting her decision. Because as they were passing the stables she saw Gabriel come out of the gate and walk down to the village.

'Hello, Gabriel,' Freddie called and he answered with a brief nod. 'Doesn't change, does, he?' Freddie observed with a tolerant smile.

There was a lot Natalie could find to criticise about Gabriel; in particular, his indifference to her chafed. She was popular with boys, had several admirers at school, and she was vain enough to want him to like her. Also, she didn't know why, but there was something about his scowling black eyes that caused a strange sensation in her stomach and drew her in a way that made her shiver with a mixture of agitation and excitement.

Hattie felt pleased with herself. John Brown was paying her attention and she could tell from the way Adam was glaring at them that he was furious. Jealous? It would be nice to think so. Of course, he'd jumped to the conclusion that she was entertaining another man when he'd knocked on her door that night, but let him think that if it got him more interested. Obviously, her mistake in the past had to been to make herself too readily available to Adam. If she could use John Brown as a bait, without letting it go too far, perhaps it would bring Adam to his senses and he would decide he couldn't live without her. She could see it vividly. In a rush of love, he'd fall on his knees and ask her to marry him, and after all, plenty of girls from lowly beginnings moved up in society. There'd be a grand wedding and her boys would no longer be tainted with the word 'bastard'.

'Would you care to take a turn round the Green, Miss Bonner?' the schoolmaster asked, breaking into her daydream.

'Why thank you, Mr Brown, I would like that,' Hattie answered and gave Adam a quick glance. Yes, he was glowering at them and that was promising.

'By the way,' the schoolmaster said, as he took the handle of the stick wagon from Hattie and started to pull it down Main Street, 'call me John, and if I may I will call you Hattie.'

'Well, John, do you know you've started the gossips' tongues wagging?'

'Why?'

'Because you're respectable and I'm not fit to be seen with.'

'I'll decide with whom I keep company, not these ignorant people. My mother, God rest her soul, had me out of wedlock and paid dearly for it. But she was determined that I would have the best and it's because of her that I'm now a teacher.'

While Hattie chewed on these few facts, they continued on round the Green and eventually came to a halt outside her cottage. John manoeuvred the wagon through the gate, closed it then leaning on it, said, 'I thought I might go up to the river on Sunday. There's a particularly picturesque stretch that I'd like to paint. Would you and the twins care to join me?'

'Oh yes,' Hattie answered eagerly, 'and I'll make a pork pie and bring it with me and some of the parsnip wine I've made.'

'Sounds like a real feast. I'll call for you after church.' He smiled, wished her good-evening then continued on to his own cottage, which was just a few doors down from hers.

Later, while she fed the babies before putting them down for the night, Hattie wondered what John Brown's game was. Did he reckon that because she was damaged goods, she would be easy to seduce? Well, he could think again. One thing was certain: in this relationship *she* was going to retain the upper hand.

Adam stood watching Hattie and John Brown suspiciously as they strolled off down Main Street, and he didn't take his eyes off them until Hattie went into her cottage and closed the door. The trouble was, she and that schoolmaster lived too close to each other and John Brown had been sniffing around Hattie since the day he arrived. Hattie's own overt overtures to him had been embarrassing until recently, but, his sexual desire had been fanned by the frustration of being turned away from her door and the thought that another man was after her. But if John Brown got there first, Hattie wouldn't want him any more, so what was he to do? Well, tomorrow she would be bringing the children up visit their grandmother, which left her with enough free time to spend it with him in the seclusion of the hayloft – if he could persuade her, of course.

While he planned his campaign of seduction, not far below the surface, Adam's conscience troubled him. He knew he was focusing on Hattie out of pure animal lust and because Emily remained unattainable. And there were numerous dangers in involving himself with a woman he'd already made pregnant. If it happened a second time, he'd be almost honour bound to marry her. Restless and uncertain, his head tussling with common sense and lust, but with lust winning, Adam strode home and ordered one of the stable lads to saddle Whitesocks. Whitesocks was a hunter and Adam, wanting to let off steam, gave the horse his head and they thundered across the fields, flying over fences and ditches with ease. Exhilarated, his head cleared of all the debris swilling around in it, Adam slowed to a canter and decided to go and see how the barley was ripening. He tied Whitesocks to a post, climbed over a gate and walked a little way along the edge of the field. The sight of a field of corn standing high and healthy always pleased his farmer's eye and a faint whisper as the wind moved over the ears of barley, calmed him. If it kept fine, in another month the barley would be ready to go to the Maltings, Adam decided.

He was about to turn back when he noticed a path had been carelessly trodden through it, obviously by human feet. He thought he could hear a noise, too, children, he didn't doubt. Well, when he got hold of them he would box the little devils' ears for their destructiveness, and, following the path, set off to find the miscreants and deal with them firmly. It wasn't children he found, however, but to his utter astonishment, two naked bodies: one a smooth brown, the other white, stretched out on the ground and coming noisily and frantically to climax. 'Good Lord in heaven!' Adam exclaimed, unaware that he had spoken out loud, and went to back away.

Grace pushed Anil off her, sat up and in her wilful way, gave Adam a bold stare. 'What can I do for you, Mr Bennett?' she enquired with an insouciance Adam had to admire. Her breasts were large and firm and he felt a splutter of desire, not for her, but any woman.

'Have you any notion of what you are up to?' he asked in a rather schoolmasterly tone.

'I know exactly what I am up to. I have just been most enjoyably engaged in sexual congress with my black servant. You yourself, I hear, have a penchant for servants. So uninhibited, don't you agree? Besides, white skinned men disgust me. Whereas Anil

283

here,' She ran her hands slowly down the boy's smooth flesh and he lowered his eyes in embarrassment. 'Isn't he beautiful?' she asked.

'Well, not quite my type,' Adam murmured, almost as embarrassed as the boy, who was now trying to get dressed.

'You're going to keep our little secret I trust, Mr Bennett?'

'Of course, of course. But the scandal if you were found out–'

'We're quite discreet.'

'Not discreet enough, or I wouldn't have found you. Putting in bluntly, if you go fornicating around the countryside, you'll be caught eventually. Then it will be all over the county. And what about your parents? Don't they suspect?'

'No, they're actually rather stupid. Anil and I grew up together and they see him as my protector.'

Glancing at the young Indian, Adam realised this was a tragic situation, particularly for the young man, and he suspected that however their relationship had started, Grace had initiated it. 'But there can be no future for you.'

'I know.' Uncharacteristically, Grace dropped her head and began to sob. Anil threw his arms protectively around her and glared at Adam.

'We love each other, Mr Bennett, and

nothing will part us,' he asserted.

Uncomfortable, uncertain how to deal with it, Adam retreated.

'You promise not to say anything,' Grace called after him.

'I promise,' Adam called back, but he rode home with a strong sense of foreboding. He wished he had someone like Judith to discuss this disturbing matter with, but since Paris was no longer in a state of revolution and the barricades had come down in the boulevards, she had decided it was safe enough to return and had left for France the previous week.

Fourteen

After a second uncomfortable night squeezed together in the bed, Prudence had gone back upstairs to Edmund. He'd come down on the Sunday evening and knocked on the door, but his tone was now conciliatory instead of threatening.

'Prudence,' he called in a wheedling voice, 'I'm really sorry for what I did and it won't happen again.'

Prudence, who'd commandeered Emily's chamois leather buffer and was polishing her rather grimy fingernails with it, paused. 'Oh, yeah?' she sneered. 'Tell me another.'

'I'm a reformed character. Truly.'

'Is that since yer fire went out?'

'No.'

'So it ain't gone out?'

'Yes, it has, actually.'

'I thought so. And you can't get it to light, 'cos yer bleedin' useless and you need a slave to fetch yer supper. Well, go and find another half-wit. I told you, I'm done wiv you,' answered Prudence, and made a rude sign with her fingers at him through the closed door.

Pleased at her defiant attitude, Emily

smiled her approval. She was learning to stand up to that blighter at last.

They didn't hear any more from him that night and Emily went off to work the next morning, leaving instructions that Prudence wasn't to open the door to anyone, least of all Edmund. However, when she returned the room was empty and she knew Prudence had gone back to him.

She came down a little later to explain her change of heart, but Emily was so irritated she could hardly bear to listen. 'Please don't start making excuses, Prudence, I don't want to hear them.'

'You've got to. You know I couldn't have stayed 'ere for long, you ain't got the room, and where else could I 'ave gone?' Prudence asked.

'I told you earlier, you need to find work. I can't understand why you don't.'

'Probably 'cos I'm a lazy cow.'

'You said it, not me.' Emily turned her back on Prudence. 'And next time he beats you up, don't come crying to me.'

'He's promised he'll never touch me again. But thank you for helping me out, Em, yer a good mate, but I ain't got much choice, really.' Prudence paused then went on, 'You're different from me, you see, Em. You're strong, and clever and you know what you want. Me,' Prudence gave a helpless shrug, 'all I've ever wanted is a quiet life with a nice bloke, but I can't ever see meself gettin' one. So, I've got to make the best of what I have, and that's 'im upstairs. And looking at it positively,' she grinned, 'at least you'll 'ave a decent night's sleep tonight.'

After this it was a bit cool between them for a few weeks, but then one day, Prudence came knocking at her door again. 'Here, take a gander at this.' She handed Emily a sketch of Edmund, which was a good likeness and skilfully done.

'What do you think of it?' Prudence asked.

'It's good.'

'I did it.'

'You?' Emily looked disbelieving.

'I told you I could draw, didn't I? And with you keepin' on at me to get a job, I decided I'd give it a go and see if I could make some money from it. And you know that café on the corner of Greek Street?'

'The Parthenon?'

'That's it. Well, I showed them this picture of Edmund and they want me to go in an' do drawings of any customer who wants it. They take fifteen per cent, whatever that is. But I get to keep the rest. It means I'm earning real money.' She looked jubilant. 'Aren't you pleased with me, Em?'

'I certainly am. When do you start?'

'Tonight. Only one thing worries me. Edmund. What's he gonna get up to when I'm out?' Prudence lowered her voice.

'Mind you, as soon as I've got a bit of tin put by I'm off.'

'Good for you. I'm glad you're seeing sense at last.'

'But first of all, I'm going to tog myself out in some new clothes. These I've got on are nothin' but rags bought off the market stall.'

Prudence's sketches did very well, and she soon had a cupboard full of new dresses and hats. She was more generous to Edmund than he had ever been to her and he went out dressed like a dandy these days. They also had frequent parties. Emily was invited but she always refused, for however much Prudence might have forgiven Edmund, she knew she never could or would. Emily also doubted that Prudence was saving much, for they were a profligate pair and a lot of spending went on. But as she told herself, what Prudence did with the money was her own affair and at least she had earned it.

Since Rory's letter telling her of his intention to go to California, Emily hadn't heard a word. However, the papers were full of stories about the gold rush, and how gold could be picked out of the rock with a knife and how sailors were deserting their ships, farmers their land for the promise of great wealth. So, perhaps Rory would strike it rich and come back and buy her a large house like he'd promised, Emily thought, although she decided not to set her heart on a house in Stoneygate just yet.

She did have a letter from Natalie, though, packed with news, but light on the comma and full stop.

'Although I'm not supposed to know Aunt Clare is going to have a baby,' she wrote, *'and that is something I want you to tell me about for it's no good asking Mama all she does is fob me off with stories about storks so you've got to promise you'll explain all about it next time you come home. Aunt Clare seems quite ill it started while I was staying at Thatcher's Mount and they had to get the doctor and he told her she had to stay in bed so that meant I had to come home and that was sad because I was having a lovely time. I thought before I went I'd be bored in the country but I wasn't at all and I was learning to ride and a boy called Gabriel was teaching me and Freddie who is a sort of son of Aunt Clare's and Uncle Christopher's but isn't, came home from Oxford for the holidays and I was just beginning to get to know him. I also met Mr Bennett, he's handsome isn't he? And Hattie and the twins who are fat and adorable...'*

The letter prattled on and Natalie finished by saying that Clare had invited her to come out for the day over the Christmas holidays, with Mama.

Emily folded the letter away thoughtfully. She wasn't sure how much Natalie knew about her and Adam, or Adam and Hattie for that matter. Children picked up titbits, though, and Natalie was curious about everything. She might even start questioning her on her own life soon, as well as where babies came from. The most troubling piece in the letter, however, was the news about Clare's health. What a tragedy if she lost the baby after waiting so long for it.

Deciding a letter would cheer her friend up, Emily sat down and wrote to Clare. She thanked her for having Natalie to stay, and said how much her sister had enjoyed herself. She even found herself promising to visit Clare on her next visit home, even though in the past she had always avoided going anywhere near Halby.

September came, then October and although the days grew shorter, autumn brought with it cooler days, some of the more offensive smells subsided, and London became a pleasant city to reside in. But November was escorted in with the dreaded pea-soupers. The thick and yellow fog hung around for days and seeped through the cracks in window-panes. It sank into her pores and no matter how hard Emily scrubbed, she never felt clean. There was a constant low moan of foghorns on the river, people kept their mouths covered, and when she went out, Emily often lost her bearings and wandered around quite lost, bumping into people, who emerged from the fog like wraiths and immediately disappeared again. The lungs of the old and frail gave out and burial grounds couldn't cope with the extra custom. And then Emily fell sick herself. It started with a runny nose but soon developed into such a hacking cough, Mrs Haig grew concerned.

'Have you any linctus, my dear, for that?' she enquired one day as Emily barked into her handkerchief.

Emily paused and drew breath, gasped out, 'No, but I'll buy some on the way home tonight,' then resumed her coughing. But the medicine did nothing to relieve the symptoms and the next morning when she put her feet out of bed and stood up, the room began to tip and she had to cling to the bedpost until it righted itself. Every bone in her body also ached, but she managed to dress and drag herself to work.

Mrs Haig took one look and her and ordered her straight home. 'You are ill, my dear. You must go to bed immediately, and don't come back to work until you are fully recovered,' she said firmly, pressed some money into her hand, called for a cab and helped her into it.

When she reached home, Emily crawled up the stairs, fell into bed and lay shivering and sweating by turn, too ill to light the fire or eat and wishing she were home being fussed over by her mother. Luckily, on the second day, Prudence poked her head round the door, saw her huddled under the blankets and hurried to her side.

'I heard that graveyard cough, so I thought I'd look in.' Prudence peered down at Emily. 'Gawd you look like death, Em,' she observed brutally.

Emily levered herself up in bed. 'Thanks,' she croaked, 'you've really made me feel better.'

'Is it yer bronchials?' Prudence asked.

Emily nodded and blew into some sheeting she'd torn up for handkerchiefs. 'And my head aches and my throat's raw,' she added and fell back on the pillow, exhausted from the effort of talking.

Prudence felt her forehead. 'Coo blimey, you're as hot as a furnace. Look, I'm gonna light the fire for you, then make you some nourishing bread and milk. Could you eat it?'

'I'll try.' Emily hadn't expected her to, but Prudence got the fire going at her first attempt. She even heated some milk without it boiling over, broke up a piece of stale bread, poured on the hot milk and sprinkled it with sugar.

'Feed a cold and starve a fever, that's what my old gran used to say, so sit up and get this down you,' Prudence ordered, and began spooning the pap into Emily's mouth as if she were a helpless infant.

Although it looked disgusting, it didn't taste as bad as she'd imagined and at least it slid easily down her swollen throat. She also found it comforting in a childish, sickroom sort of way.

When she had finished Emily lay down again and Prudence tucked the blankets in around her in a motherly fashion. 'Have a sleep, don't worry about a thing. I'll keep popping in to check yer all right and to make sure the fire hasn't gone out.'

'I've been thinking, Prudence, I won't get better while this fog lasts, so I'm going home.'

'When?'

'Tomorrow.'

'But you're not in a fit state to travel.'

'If you pack a few things for me and come with me to the station, I'll be all right once I'm on the train.'

'We ... ll, I don't know.'

'I shall go anyway, whether you help me or not.'

'Let's see how you are in the morning,' suggested Prudence, trying to humour her.

'All right.' Emily turned over in the bed and closed her eyes. She drifted in and out of feverish sleep for the rest of the day, but from time to time she was aware of

Prudence standing over her and the rattle of coal as it was tipped on to the fire.

The following morning, because she managed to stagger downstairs to the privy then remained standing long enough to have a wash, Emily convinced herself she was well enough to make the journey back to Leicester. For by now she had one idea fixed in her head, and that was to get home, to slide between fresh, lavender scented sheets in her small bedroom, and be nursed back to health by her mother. Unfortunately, Prudence wasn't an early riser. Deciding she wasn't going to wait until she surfaced, Emily started to pack. She'd had very little ill-health in her life and she found it irksome that she had to keep pausing to rest. Dressing was even more exhausting, but finally she was ready. 'All I need now is Prudence to help me get to the station,' she said to the four walls and sat down on her bed, trying to curb her impatience as the minutes ticked away.

It was gone ten by the time Prudence shoved her head round the door. She looked rather amazed to find Emily dressed and ready to go. 'Do you think yer being sensible, Em, with that cough? Yer chest is real bad and going off on a long journey could make it worse.'

'No, it won't. Once I'm back home, I'll start feeling better, I know it. So can you go and call a cab, please, Prudence?'

There was a rattling sound in Emily's throat when she spoke and Prudence shook her head worriedly at her obstinacy. 'Determined madam ain't you?' she observed but she could see Emily's mind was made up, so she went off to find a cab. Within five minutes she was back. 'Right, I've got one waitin' outside. Give me yer bag and take hold of me arm, I don't want you having a funny turn and goin' arse over tip down the stairs.'

When they arrived at Euston, Emily found there was a train due to leave in about a quarter of an hour and as they walked along the platform Prudence peered into the carriage windows. 'Do you know I've never bin on a train.'

'And I've never seen the sea.'

'When you come back, why don't we take an excursion to Brighton, then?'

'It would be better to wait until the Spring.'

'All right, so that's a promise, then?'

Emily nodded, stepped into the carriage and Prudence handed her the bag. Her voice had nearly gone but she managed to croak her thanks. 'I don't know when I'll be back but the rent is paid on my room. If Edmund starts his nasty tricks again, you have my permission to use it.'

'Thanks, Em.' The train started to move

off, and over the noise of wheels and steam, Prudence blew a kiss and called, 'See you take care of yerself, and come back soon.'

By now Emily felt as limp as a rag doll and she sank gratefully into the seat. She had the carriage to herself and, relieved she wouldn't have to make small talk, she leaned back and slept. She was woken by the porter shouting, 'Rugby, change here for Leicester,' and staggered off one train and on to another.

By the time she reached Leicester she had lost all coordination and when she fell half delirious into a fly outside the station, the driver had to repeat twice, 'Where to, madam?'

Emily's brain was so addled, she couldn't recall her address at first, and when she finally stumbled out, 'Hi ... High Cross Street, please, Fairfax's bookshop,' the driver gave her a funny look and enquired, 'Are you intoxicated, madam?'

Emily couldn't even find the energy to take offence. 'No, ill.'

'That's all right, then, 'cos I don't take drunks,' he informed her, turned the horse round and set off up Granby Street.

Maybe it was the tip or perhaps he discovered a little compassion in his flinty heart, because when they reached the bookshop, the driver did assist Emily down from the fly and hold open the door for her.

'Hello, Mama.' Emily stood swaying in the middle of the shop, aware of her mother's astonished expression, then her legs finally gave way and she sank unconscious to the floor. She came round to the smell of lavender and clean sheets and her mother's anxious face leaning over her.

'Thank goodness,' Rachel murmured, when her daughter's eyes flickered open.

'Sorry, Mama,' Emily croaked. 'Did I frighten you?'

'You scared the living daylights out of me.'

'I had to come home.'

'You did the right thing, dear. I'll take care of you.'

'I knew you would.' Emily smiled and closed her eyes. She was in her own bed and with her mother's gentle nursing, she would be fully recovered in no time.

'I sent Natalie for the apothecary right away. That sounds like them now,' her mother said as footsteps could be heard thumping up the stairs. She briefly left the room and came back accompanied by Mr Blythe, who attended those people who couldn't afford the higher fees doctors charged. Emily had known him since she was a child, so he greeted her by her Christian name.

'Now, Emily, what have you been catching down in that unholy city of London?' he asked jovially.

'A severe chill, and my throat hurts.'

'You don't faint with a chill, and she's very feverish, Mr Blythe,' Rachel put in.

'Let's have a look at you then,' Mr Blythe said to the patient and, holding her wrist, took her pulse. He then gave her a thorough examination, peering down her throat, listening to her chest and tapping her back with his fingers, while every now and then he gave a thoughtful, 'Huh-huh.' Finally, he sat back in the chair.

'Well, my diagnosis it that you have the grippe. I'm not surprised your throat hurts because your tonsils are enlarged. But it's your lungs I'm worried about. They are congested and we don't want it developing into anything nasty, so I shall keep an eye on them. You are under strict orders not to move from that bed until I say so and I'll visit you again the day after tomorrow. I'll make a some medicine up for you, which you are to take twice a day, so tell Natalie to come round and collect it in about an hour. In the meantime, you can enjoy the luxury of being pampered by your mama.'

Rachel saw the apothecary out, and from the other side of the door Natalie's plaintive voice called, 'Mama says I'm mustn't come in and see you while you're ill in case I catch it too.'

'My voice has nearly gone anyway,' Emily apologised in little above a whisper.

'Oh dear, you do sound awful, I'll go and get your medicine for you right away, and maybe you'll soon be better.'

Natalie moved away from the door, Emily dozed, and some time later her mother came in with a large spoon and a bottle. She poured some vile stuff down her daughter's throat, then no matter how much Emily protested, she insisted on rubbing her chest with goose grease. 'Mr Blythe is worried about your lungs,' Rachel said, as she slapped it on, 'and I don't want you getting chest trouble.' But in spite of the greasy concoction, Emily did have the best night's sleep for a long time and her throat was definitely less swollen in the morning.

Mr Blythe called every other day for a week, until he finally pronounced that the congestion in Emily's lungs was clearing. 'I'm going allow you to get up as long you promise me you won't exert yourself?'

Emily enjoyed convalescing, sitting around the fire reading, being tempted with such delicacies as junket by her mother. She was surprised how fragile she felt, and it was several days before she could summon up the energy to write to Mrs Haig. She explained that she'd come home to escape the fog, apologised for any inconvenience she might be causing, but that she hoped, with her mother's care, to be well enough to return to London shortly.

A week later Emily received a reply from Mrs Haig, expressing the hope that Emily was well on the road to recovery. She told her not to worry about hurrying back, because she had decided to have a break from writing over the Christmas period and devote some time to her children. She also explained that the whole family was going to the country and would return to London in the New Year.

When she had finished reading it, Emily handed the letter to her mother. 'Good,' said Rachel, 'that means I can concentrate on building you up with some proper home cooking.' She folded the letter then continued in a thoughtful tone, 'You'll probably tell me I'm prying into something that's none of my business, but Rory's absence is becoming rather noticeable, and I find it difficult to believe that he left you to stagger up to Leicester on your own when you were so ill. So, is he still in Ireland?'

'He was never in Ireland. I lied. He's in America.'

'In America? What on earth is he doing there?' Rachel asked incredulously.

'He was offered work as a journalist in New York after he lost his job in England. Ticket paid for and everything.'

'He left you, just like that?'

'He did promise to send for me as soon as he had saved the fare. But that job fell through as well and the last I heard he was on his way to join the Californian gold rush.'

Rachel shook her head in disbelief. 'This story gets more bizarre by the minute.'

'Oh, there's more. He's promised to come back rich and build me a fine house in Stoneygate.' Emily laughed at the notion.

'Why didn't you tell me before? You shouldn't have had to cope with it on your own.'

'I didn't want to bother you. With Papa so ill it would have just added to your worries. And they'd always been such good friends, I knew Papa would have been disappointed.'

'Your father did feel that Rory lacked the qualities that make a good husband. But because he'd already prevented you from marrying Adam, he kept his doubts to himself. But do you think you'll ever see Rory again?'

Emily shrugged. 'Who knows. Rory's never been the most predictable of men.'

'Do you miss him?'

'At first, desperately. But I love my job and I've got used to living on my own.'

'I don't know what to say.'

'You could ask me why I make such bad choices in men. It's one I've asked myself often enough. Perhaps in future I'll steer clear of them.'

'Well, they have certainly brought you

more sorrow than joy. All I've ever wanted is for you to find someone who can make you as happy as your father did me.'

'Your marriage was exceptional. I don't know too many happy ones. Look at Lily and Septimus.'

'They rub along in a peculiar sort of way.'

'And Christopher and Clare are a devoted couple. Which reminds me, while I'm home, I'd like to go and visit Clare. Why don't we all go? You, me and Natalie? We could hire a gig from the Stag and Pheasant.'

Rachel looked doubtful. 'I don't know. I've always tried to avoid Halby because of Matilda. Any time I visited, she made sure I didn't forget I was once her maidservant.'

'We'll drive in with our heads held high. And that toffee-nosed madam can think what she likes,' Emily decided for them.

'You're quite right. Why should I care what Matilda thinks?'

'I'll drop Clare a note first. She's not in the best of health and visitors might tire her.'

'Yes, I'm worried about this pregnancy, it isn't going well and apparently she spends a lot of time in bed. It would be such a tragedy if she lost the baby. You might find Christopher doesn't want us there.'

'I'll word the note carefully,' Emily promised.

But from Clare's reply it was obvious she

303

was desperate for company.

'Yes, please do, do come and see me. I am not allowed to lift a finger and I can't tell you how bored I am ...'

So, a week later, on a dry but cold December day, and bundled up in plenty of warm clothing, the three of them set off for Halby. Rachel took the reins and after being confined to the house for so long, the stark winter landscape, the leafless trees looked beautiful to Emily and she greedily gulped in mouthfuls of unpolluted air.

Rachel found it a strange sensation to be driving along Main Street. Across the Green she could see Susan and Robert's cottage, where she'd spent some happy Sundays. And now here was St Philips, where they lay buried with their daughter, Polly. Natalie, who couldn't hide her excitement at being back in Halby, was pointing at a red brick building in the process of being erected. 'That's the new school,' she informed them knowledgeably, 'and see, they've got the roof on already. Uncle Christopher must be pleased. And there are the stables where I was learning to ride.'

'Ah yes, Jane Dobbs, Matilda's friend. She had a soft spot for George. The only person in the world, apart from his mother, who could ever see any good in him.'

'Who was George?' asked Natalie.

'Matilda's brother,' Rachel answered, regretting she'd ever mentioned the hated name. Blackthorn Lane was still as rutted as Rachel could remember from her youth, but today the ridges had frozen so hard they bounced their way up to Thatcher's Mount. She took one look at the house and felt so overwhelmed by the past and its ghosts, she wanted to turn the horse round and head straight back to Leicester.

But Christopher and a small dog were already waiting to open the gate for them, and as they drove through, Natalie screamed excitedly, 'Jelly!' leapt down from the gig before it had even stopped, picked up the small dog and covered him in kisses. As she watched her daughter, Rachel thought to herself, *Natalie's the only one of us who hasn't any ambivalent feelings about Halby.*

'Clare apologises for not coming out to meet you, but she has already defied the doctor's orders today and insisted on getting up, so she's waiting for you in the drawing-room,' Christopher explained.

'She's still not well?' said Emily.

'No.' Christopher shook his head worriedly. 'She says she feels fine, but it's to reassure me. Both of us love children and dreamed of having a large family, but I wouldn't put Clare through this again, and

305

I live in dread that something might go wrong.'

'I'm sure nothing will.' Christopher was anxious by nature, so Emily touched his arm to reassure him. 'Clare's young and I hear you've arranged for Doctor Welland to be in attendance when her time is near. He's a very highly regarded physician, so she'll be in safe hands.'

'I've taken every safeguard I can, but I know this, Emily, if anything happened to Clare, I wouldn't want to go on living,' Christopher answered simply.

Touched by his devotion and envious, too, Emily said quietly, 'Christopher, your love will sustain her.'

'Thank you. But come on, we're wasting time out here and Clare is frantic to see you.'

Clare was sitting with her feet up on a chaise longue, dressed in a pretty taffeta gown of blue and green check, her fair hair neatly done, and with a such a smile lighting up her face, at first glance she gave the impression of robust health. It was only when Emily drew nearer and bent to kiss her, that she saw how drawn her features were, how translucent her skin.

'How are you dear?' Emily fought to keep the concern out of her voice.

'I'm fine. It's Christopher who insists on mollycoddling me. By the way, in case you're wondering where Natalie is, she came in to say hello but she's now dashed off with Jelly to see Gabriel, Jane's son.'

'Yes, I seem to recall that name cropping up in conversation quite a lot after she came home,' Rachel smiled.

'Rather a strange young man, but your daughter obviously sees some quality in him that we've missed.'

'Strange?' Rachel asked, looking slightly alarmed.

'Don't worry, he's a bit taciturn, that's all. Prefers horses to humans. But he appears to have made an exception with Natalie. I think it's because she stands up for herself.'

'Well, as long as he's reliable.'

'Oh, he's a gentleman. Rugby School and all that.'

'That's all right then.' Rachel sat back, looking a bit easier and gazed about her. 'Do you know, this room has hardly changed at all.' She stared down at the polished floor. 'And the hours of elbow grease I used on that dratted thing.'

'Well, I've never been in this house before, but you've described it to me so often, Mama, I feel I know every room, every piece of furniture.'

'Would you like Christopher to take you up to your old room?' Clare asked.

Rachel looked doubtful. 'I don't know.'

'Come on, Mama, I want to have a look.'

Emily stood up.

'Oh, all right. Lead the way, Christopher.'

'Will you be all right on your own, my dear?' Christopher leaned over his wife solicitously and she reached up and touched his cheek. Emily was gripped again with envy at their obvious love for each other.

'I'll be fine,' Clare answered, 'and when you come down we'll have luncheon. I told Natalie to be back here by twelve-thirty.'

'We use the room for lumber now,' Christopher explained as they climbed the stairs to the first floor, then groped their way up the dark and narrow attic stairs. He lifted the latch, stood back so that Rachel could enter first and she was a seventeen-year-old again. The few miserable pieces of furniture had gone and there was nothing in the room but cobwebs, battered trunks, ancient books and paintings; all the things a family will never use again but can't bear to throw away. Ignoring the junk, Rachel moved swiftly to the window, looked down at the empty rick-yard and the ghost of a young man, with lanthorn held high and hell-bent on mischief, danced across her vision. Unbidden, the tears came and began to course silently down her cheeks. *Oh Jed, why did you leave me, I miss you so much.*

'Mama, what is it?'

Rachel wiped her eyes. 'Ghosts.'

'Papa?'

Rachel nodded, took her daughter's arm and pulled her away from the window. 'Let's go, it's too painful.'

Christopher, constantly vigilant about his wife, had gone on ahead and they were about to follow him down, when his voice came faintly but urgently from below. 'Rachel, Emily, you must come quickly, something's wrong with Clare.'

'Oh dear, she must have fainted again. But be careful how you come down the stairs, Mama, they're lethal.'

'I know, dear, I've been up and down them thousands of times, although I was a bit more nimble on my feet in those days, I suppose.'

Christopher was waiting for them at the bottom of the stairs, pushing his hands through his hair in a frantic movement. 'What's the matter?' Emily asked.

'Clare's pains have started and the baby isn't due for another month.' There was a look of bleak hopelessness in his eyes.

Rachel touched his arm in a consoling gesture. 'Premature babies often make it, don't worry.'

With a monumental effort, Christopher pulled himself together and began giving instructions. 'Emily, can you go and have a word with Phoebe the maid, explain she's to go down to Trent Hall straight away and ask Adam to bring his mother up here, then he's to ride over to Leicester to fetch Doctor Welland.'

'I'll go myself in the gig, it's quicker,' answered Emily.

'Is there a midwife in the village?' asked Rachel.

'Yes, a Mrs Young. Sixth cottage along.'

'You'd better bring her back with you, too, in case the doctor doesn't make it in time,' Rachel called to her daughter as she went out of the door. 'In the meantime I'll go and organise hot water and clean sheets then come and see what I can do to help.'

As Emily rattled down Blackthorn Lane in the gig, she was in such a panic over Clare she didn't pause to consider how Adam would react to finding her on his front step. She pulled the bell, gave the footman her name, said that it was most urgent that she speak with Mr Bennett, and he invited her to step into the hall. A moment later Adam was hurrying towards her looking deeply puzzled. 'Emily? Is it really you? I thought you'd gone to America.'

'Change of plans. I'm going later,' Emily lied.

'So what brings you to my door? To apologise to me for not turning up that day?'

'This isn't about us but something far more urgent. Clare's life and her baby's. We're visiting for the day and Clare's pains

have started early. She hasn't a strong con-
stitution, and Christopher is worried it will
not be a straightforward birth. He sent me
down to say please, please will you hurry
and get Doctor Welland.'

'I'll go right away and hope I get there in
time.'

'First of all, though, you've to take your
mother up to Thatcher's Mount. Christopher wants her there.'

'Can you drive me up to the Dower House
and take her back? It will save time?'

Emily looked doubtful. 'She won't want to
see me.'

'Never mind what she wants, it's Clare
who matters. Come on.'

When Adam walked into his mother's
sitting-room with Emily by his side, it was
like the years rolling back and Matilda rose
from her chair in dismay. Had they somehow gone behind her back and married?

'Mother, you're wanted at Thatcher's
Mount,' said Adam without preamble,
'Clare's pains have started. Emily will drive
you up there, while I go to fetch Doctor
Welland.' Adam made for the door. 'And
pray that I get back in time,' he called over
his shoulder, then ran out of the house and
down the drive, leaving the two women
regarding each other in wary silence.

'Are you ready, Mrs Bennett?' Emily asked
finally.

'Yes, of course.' Matilda answered, remembering the girl was married, to some Irishman, she seemed to recall and was therefore no danger to Adam. 'I'll get my cloak.'

They got in the gig and drove down the village with Emily struggling to find something to say to a woman whom she knew disliked her and who had done a pretty good job of spoiling her life. And then she remembered they had to collect the midwife. 'Christopher wants the midwife in attendance as well, in case Doctor Welland doesn't get here in time. Can you point out which cottage she lives in please, Mrs Bennett?'

'Mrs Young has gone to visit her daughter in Nottingham. I know that for a fact, because she came to pay her rent the day before she left.'

'Who will look after Clare if the baby comes early?' Emily asked in an anxious voice.

Matilda gave Emily a cold look. 'We're women and we will have to deal with it as best we can.' The tone was sarcastic.

Bloody woman, Emily snarled to herself. The last thing she wanted was to appear inept in front of Adam's mother, but never having had a child, she wasn't sure if she could *deal* with it, particularly if there were complications. She also noticed that it had grown a great deal colder and the sky was grey, the clouds ominously heavy with snow. Please God, she prayed, don't let it snow, and bring Clare through her confinement safely.

Matilda didn't waste time when they reached Thatcher's Mount. She stepped down from the gig and without thanking Emily or waiting for her, hurried indoors. She didn't see herself as clairvoyant, but right from the start she'd had a curious dread about this pregnancy, was convinced the baby would be deformed or not right in the head. Not once, though, had she considered the possibility of Clare dying and the idea struck terror in Matilda's heart, for Clare was much more than a niece to her and she loved her like a daughter. But she wouldn't die, not while she was around, Matilda, decided. She had come to take control. Throwing off her cloak, she hurried upstairs, opened the bedroom door, and found Rachel Fairfax, of all people, leaning over Clare, wiping her brow.

'What on earth are you doing here?' Matilda demanded imperiously.

'Clare and I invited Mrs Fairfax for the day, along with her two daughters,' Christopher explained. 'She kindly agreed to sit with Clare until you came.'

'Well, I'm here now to look after my niece, so we won't detain you any longer, Mrs

Fairfax.' Matilda moved to the bed and began fussing with Clare's pillows.

'Her waters have already broken, and the pains are coming at regular intervals,' Rachel explained and rose to leave. But Clare lifted her head feebly, 'You're not to go, Rachel, I want you here. And Christopher's to stay as well.'

'Clare, you can't have a man in the room at this time, it would be indecent.'

'I'm not moving until Doctor Welland arrives,' Christopher put in with unusual firmness.

To convey her displeasure Matilda's eyebrows rose a fraction. 'Have it your way, Christopher, but it is highly irregular.' Making herself ready, she rolled up her sleeves, washed her hands, sat down and silently urged the doctor to hurry up, for she knew he would settle the matter by throwing everyone out of the room except her.

'Squeeze my hand when you feel pain, it helps,' Rachel suggested and when Clare forced a brave smile, Rachel tried not to think of poor Mrs Brewin and the long agonising labour that produced a stillborn baby and had eventually killed her.

But the sight of his beloved wife in pain was too much for Christopher. Distressed he cried, 'Oh dear, where are they?' and raced to the window, only to back away again and exclaim, 'It's snowing, they'll never get here.'

Watching her niece struggling to conceal her pain so as not to worry her husband, Matilda's patience snapped. Keeping her voice low she said, 'Christopher, you are only adding to Clare's distress, so if you insist on staying, you must calm yourself down.'

'Sorry. But where's the midwife? She was supposed to be here.'

'I'm afraid she won't be coming. She's gone to Nottingham and won't be back for a week.'

Christopher lifted his eyes to the ceiling. 'Why is everything against us?' As he spoke, Clare let out a wild protesting yell. Rushing to her side, he fell upon the bed, declaring, 'I'm here, darling, I'm here.'

Matilda and Rachel exchanged exasperated glances, but when Clare squeaked out, 'Auntie, I ... I think something's happening,' Matilda brushed him aside.

'Out of the way, Christopher,' she ordered and threw back the sheet.

'Oh! Oh!' Clare cried out.

'Breathe and push, breathe and push,' Rachel urged calmly while Matilda exclaimed triumphantly,

'I can see its head! Don't give up, Clare! One more push,' she adjured, then leaning over, she eased the baby out into a harsh, cruel world.

The infant gave a thin wailing cry of protest, and Clare lifted her head and asked weakly, 'What is it?'

'A lovely little girl, with ten fingers and ten toes.' Grinning from ear to ear, Christopher kissed his exhausted wife soundly. Rachel quickly cleaned the baby up, cut the umbilical cord, removed the mucus from her mouth and eyes, then Matilda had the honour of wrapping her in a blanket and handing her to mother.

'Your daughter.'

Clare smiled tiredly and took her baby in her arms and kissed the crumpled little face. 'Our very own baby, I never thought the day would come. Thank you both,' she said and Matilda and Rachel, for the first time in their lives, smiled at one another.

'Have you chosen a name for her?' asked Rachel.

'Annabel.' Clare thought for a moment, 'Or to give her her full title, Annabel, Matilda, Rachel Harcourt.'

Again Matilda and Rachel smiled at each other.

Fifteen

After Matilda and Rachel had washed Clare, they helped her change into a clean nightgown, then she sank back on the pillows and slept. Christopher placed his daughter in her cradle and stood gazing down at her reverently for several minutes. 'Our little miracle. She's beautiful, isn't she?' he smiled.

Matilda, who couldn't shake off her fears, studied the baby carefully, searching for any peculiarities. But Annabel's face had the screwed up look of any other newborn baby; in fact she looked so normal, Matilda felt able to smile and say with absolute honesty, 'She's perfect, Christopher.'

'I'll go and tell Emily, Natalie and Phoebe the baby's arrived,' he said, 'and have some tea sent up for you, it could be a long time before Adam and the doctor get here.'

Silently pleased with themselves at successfully helping to bring a new life into the world, Matilda and Rachel drank the tea gratefully when it was brought up. They didn't move from the room, Matilda re-plenished the fire, the snow crept up the window ledge, and it was another hour before Adam and Doctor Welland arrived, ploughing through the deepening drifts.

'Count yourselves lucky we got here,' said the doctor, shaking the snow from his heavy coat. 'It's not too bad on the turnpike but once we turned off, it was hell. I must warm my hands before I touch the patient and I'd also be glad of a little light refreshment. A tot of whisky will do.'

'I'll get it for you right away,' said Christopher and rushed to the whisky decanter. 'Thank you for turning out on such a terrible night, doctor, and I must apologise, because I'm afraid you've had a bit of a wasted journey. You see, the baby wouldn't wait. She arrived over an hour ago, with the able assistance of Mrs Bennett and Mrs Fairfax here.'

'Is that so? And how is Mrs Harcourt?'

Matilda smiled at him. 'Mother and baby are doing very well, doctor, and both of them are sleeping, so why don't you sit down by the fire and drink your whisky first?' she suggested.

'I'd rather go and check on my patient,' said the doctor, who quickly poured the whisky down his throat and picked up his bag. 'Now, Mr Harcourt, if you'd like to show me the way?'

When he came back down again, Doctor Welland congratulated Matilda and Rachel on their midwifery skills, then they all adjourned to the drawing-room to wet the baby's head.

Since they were locked in by the snow, arrangements had to be made to accommodate everyone for the night. Doctor Welland, it went without saying, would remain at Thatcher's Mount and Matilda decided she would stay as well.

'And you and your daughters, Mrs Fairfax, will of course be my guests for the night at Trent Hall,' said Adam.

The snow had stopped by the time they set off and as they drove down Blackthorn Lane, the only sound was the rattle of the harness and the crunch of wheels on frozen snow. The cold bit at their cheeks, but the clouds had cleared and Rachel stared up at the black, star-studded heavens and thought to herself, well, it hasn't turned out to be quite the day we imagined when we set off this morning. Still, in spite of everyone's unspoken fear, Clare and Christopher have the baby they've always longed for, and I'm going to stay as a guest for the night at Trent Hall. A younger self would have found that impossible to imagine all those years ago, she mused.

Adam seemed equally pleased to be paying host to them all and he ushered them into the drawing-room where a huge fire burned, then disappeared to order refreshment from the kitchen. Watching Natalie taking in the luxury of it all, Rachel said to her younger daughter, 'It wasn't always like this, you know. I can remember a time when the house was falling down around old Squire Bennett's ears. It was Matilda who brought it back to its former glory and built up the estate to what it is now. The Squire was a drunk and when he died, he left her with nothing but unpaid bills. Yes, you've got to hand it to her, she's a good business-woman, I admire her for that.'

'Go steady, Mama, or you'll be saying you like her in a minute,' Emily laughed.

'Well, we worked in harmony while the baby was being born. It was a worrying time. I know I've had three children, but I was terrified something might go wrong.'

'You were brilliant, Mrs Fairfax, and I'm sure Christopher and Clare will be eternally grateful to you,' said Adam, returning from the kitchen and sinking into a chair. 'I've ordered ham sandwiches and coffee, and that will be along soon. In the meantime, if you'd like to follow me, I'll show you where you'll be sleeping.'

They'd been allotted a bedroom each and as she glanced in, Rachel saw that fires had already been lit, the lamps trimmed and the beds turned down, and she thought of the invisible army of servants that made the smooth running of the household possible. And no doubt shortly, a maidservant would struggle up with a warming pan full of hot coals to heat the beds. No wonder life runs on oiled wheels for these people. It was inequalities such as these that had always got Jed's goat.

When they went back down to the drawing-room, the refreshments had been laid out on a side table and Adam suggested they help themselves. When Natalie gave an uninhibited yawn, he said with a laugh, 'You look as if you're ready for bed, young lady.'

'And that's where she's going as soon as she's finished eating,' Rachel said in a tone that would brook no argument. 'I won't be far behind.'

'Me neither, it's been a long day,' said Emily finishing her coffee.

But I don't want to go to bed, thought Natalie mutinously. I want to sit in this grand room, beside this roaring fire and pretend I'm lady of the manor. She'd been watching Adam, noticed how he kept glancing at Emily and she wondered if he still loved her. Natalie sighed. It was so sad and yet so romantic and if things had been different, all this could have been Emily's home and she could have visited whenever she liked.

As she ate, Rachel also observed Adam. He still loved Emily, of course he did, it was evident in every look he gave her. And she could trust her daughter not to break her

321

marriage vows, such as they were. Maybe it was a bit unorthodox, but what was the harm in them spending a little time alone together? She finished her coffee and stood up. 'Come along, Natalie. Bed.'

Adam rose and wished them good-night, and Natalie dragged reluctantly after her mother, muttering that it was still early. Emily went to follow, but Adam put a hand out to delay her. 'Emily, please stay a while.'

'I don't think I should,' she said doubtfully. 'You know how servants like to gossip.'

'I've dismissed them for the night. And we don't often get an opportunity to talk.'

Emily sat down again. 'All right, what do you want to talk about?'

'A couple of things. One: why aren't you in America? Two: if you cast your mind back, we arranged a day out together, only you never turned up. I'd like to know why.'

'I intended to come, truly. In fact, I was looking forward to it, but I got involved in a domestic dispute. Prudence, who lives upstairs from me, got beaten up by her boyfriend, a nasty piece of work. She was so terrified, I let her spend the night with me. Then he had another go at her in the morning, so I didn't dare leave her and the time rather passed. As for America, all I know is, Rory's somewhere in the wilds of California digging for gold and I'm promised untold wealth. Personally, I doubt whether I'll ever see him again, which leaves me in some sort of limbo.'

Adam moved nearer to Emily and took her hand. 'Do you still love him?'

Emily sighed. 'I don't know. We were very happy at first. And he is still my husband, but I feel humiliated by the way he's treated me. I do make bad choices in men, don't I?' She looked straight at Adam, but he didn't answer.

'Have you thought about divorce?'

'Good heavens, no! You know it's almost impossible for a woman to divorce her husband. Besides, where would I find the money to pay for it?'

'The money side of it needn't concern you, I have plenty.'

'I have no grounds.'

'You would after seven years, for desertion.'

'That seems a long time to wait. And I don't know why we're even discussing it, Adam, it's impossible.' Emily rubbed her forehead wearily. 'It's been an eventful day and a long one and I'm grateful to you for putting us up, but now I'm going to bed.'

'Not before I've kissed you,' Adam answered and drew her to her feet. She didn't argue and his mouth on hers was gentle at first but grew more insistent, and she responded with a hunger that matched his, until the little voice of reason whispered in her head, 'Don't be a fool! Remember how he's turned your world upside down before!' and she pulled away angrily.

'Stop it! You seem to forget I'm married.'

Ruffled, Adam answered, 'Rory appears to have forgotten he is, too.'

'That was cruel. Good-night, I'm going to bed.'

'Who would we be hurting?' Adam called after her.

'If history is anything to go by, probably myself in the end. I'm sorry, Adam, but I'm not cut out for infidelity.' She walked to the door. 'I'll see you in the morning.'

As always, Emily had slipped from his grasp and Adam was grateful, in a way he'd never been before, that he had the Christmas festivities to take his mind off her. Judith always returned to England for Christmas, and she, Olivia and their father had come over to Halby, like the three wise men, bearing gifts for the new infant. To celebrate Annabel's birth, it was open house at Thatcher's Mount and friends and neighbours had been invited to pop in to be introduced to her and to congratulate the proud and happy parents.

The house was bedecked with greenery. Hot punch and mince pies were on tap for the guests and Adam was helping himself, when he noticed the schoolmaster, John

Brown, enter the room and look around him. 'Hell, don't come over here,' Adam muttered and kept his head lowered to avoid catching his eye. He wasn't sure what the man was up to with Hattie, although he could make a good guess, and he'd feel uncomfortable standing making small talk with him. It was irrational of him, he knew, minding what Hattie did with other men, but she was the mother of his children and he still felt he had first claim on her. And now the Bellamys were arriving with Grace. Oh God, he would never be able to look at that girl again without there leaping into his mind's eye the sight of her in the barley, stretched out naked on the ground with her legs wrapped around her servant and moaning with pleasure.

It was difficult to avoid people on an occasion like this without appearing rude, but as Adam gulped down his punch, he looked around for a means of escape. Thank heavens, there was Judith beckoning to him. Adam helped himself to more punch, strolled over and sat down. 'And how's the revolution in Paris?' he asked, biting into a mince pie.

'Over, I hope. Louis Napoleon has been elected President and everyone is confident that we're in for a time of stability.' Judith rested her hand on Adam's arm. 'I've been wanting to have a word because I have some grave news about Isabelle. I thought about writing but then I decided to wait until I could tell you personally.'

'Grave news? What's Isabelle been up to now? Has the law finally caught up with her?'

'No, worse than that, I'm afraid. You'd better prepare yourself, she's dead.'

'Dead?' He repeated, not quite taking it in.

'Yes, and it was a rather nasty end, she was murdered.'

Shaken, Adam paled visibly. 'Murdered? How?'

'I wasn't in France at the time so I only know what I've been told, but it was during the June days when the barricades went up in Paris and the fighting was ferocious. She was trying to get out of the city with her money and jewellery and was held up by a band of vagrants. When she wouldn't hand over her valuables they strangled her with her own scarf.'

Adam shuddered. 'My God, what an awful way to die. But just like Isabelle to value jewels more than her life.'

'If it's any consolation, they caught her murderers. Apparently, they stripped her of her clothes too, and one of the women was wearing them. But they paid the price for their crime. Subsequently, all of them went to the guillotine.'

'Where is she buried?'

'In Paris.'

'When you go back, could you arrange for a stone to be put on her grave with her name on it. I'll pay for it, of course.'

'I'll see to it immediately I return.'

'Does Olivia know Isabelle is dead? She considered her a close friend at one time.'

'Like everyone else, she felt terribly betrayed by her, particularly in the way Isabelle hoodwinked Sir Austin Beauchamp. But I don't want to spoil her Christmas, so I'll wait until later to tell her.' Lowering her voice, Judith went on, 'I see your friend, Miss Graceless, is here.'

'Yes, and that young lady is flouting convention in a very dangerous way.'

'Why, what's she up to?'

Adam glanced over his shoulder to make sure nobody could overhear them, but the noise levels were such that he realised there was little chance of that. 'You remember that Indian servant of the Bellamys, Anil?'

'The handsome young man who came riding with us? Yes.'

'Well, it's rather an indelicate subject, so I don't exactly know how to find the appropriate words without offending your ears.'

'I live in Paris and I do consider myself a woman of the world, Adam. Not a lot can surprise me, so I doubt if I'll be offended,' Judith smiled.

'Well let me put it this way, I caught them lying together naked in a field not long ago.'

'Yo-you ... mean copulating?' Judith stuttered.

'Yes, she and Anil are lovers.'

'I eat my words, you have surprised me. Astonished me, in fact. Although come to think of it, that day we all went riding, it crossed my mind then that their relationship was a little unusual. It was the way she spoke to him.' But although their affair would be judged as highly irregular by most people, Judith couldn't bring herself to condemn the young couple. Her own raw pain, her attempted suicide because of her unrequited love for Clare was still too real for her not to sympathise with them. 'I hope you're not going to tell her parents?'

'Of course not. I'm frightened for them though, because eventually they'll be caught by someone less discreet than me and it will cause the most enormous scandal. I dread to think what the consequences will be, and I can see it all ending in tragedy, particularly for Anil. Grace will be whisked away until the dust settles, or the Bellamys will move, but what will happen to him?'

'Perhaps they'll send him back to India.'

'Hush, she's coming over,' Judith said quickly, and as Adam rose to greet her, Grace gave him a bold stare.

'How are you Mr Bennett? And you, Miss

Bennett? It's strange how you both have the same name.'

'There is a family connection,' Judith explained.

'And Lady Collins is your sister and Mrs Harcourt is Mr Bennett's cousin. Why, the whole village seems to be connected.'

'That is often the way in small places.'

'Yes, I hate small villages, small towns, small countries. I'm trying to talk my parents into sending me back to India. I've already written to my brothers.'

'I hope your wish is granted, Miss Bellamy,' Adam replied.

'Grace, come along dear, we're going,' Mrs Bellamy called.

'Coming, Mama. We must go riding again, Mr Bennett.'

'Yes, we must,' Adam answered gallantly, thinking to himself, not on your life, Miss Bellamy, not on your life.

Sixteen

Emily had a fairly quiet Christmas, but a traditional one. It snowed, they decorated the small living-room with mistletoe and holly, Emily went with her mother to hear Handel's *Messiah*, the Waites played carols around the streets and somehow they managed to keep up the pretence that it was just like past years. But when they sat down for a Christmas dinner of prime roast beef followed by one of Rachel's rich and spicy plum puddings, all three of them were so aware of Jed's empty chair that the joy went out of the day.

Although she didn't say so, Emily knew her mother would have liked her to remain in Leicester permanently, but although a part of her did want to stay, now that she was again in glowing good health, she also felt the pull of London. In spite of its disadvantages, it did offer variety and there was a danger and uncertainty about living there that she responded to. She wrote to Mrs Haig telling her she would be back at work on the second day of January and travelled down on New Year's Day.

When Emily came out of the station the

footways were deep in dirty, half-melted snow. She caught an omnibus and by the time she was within sight of Franklin Street, she was shivering with the cold, her boots were leaking and the hem of her dress was wet and dirty. Never mind, Emily thought, she'd be home and out of them in a minute and once the fire was going everything would quickly dry. She had no worries about food either; her mother had packed enough for an army: slices of cold beef, pork pie, mince pies, plum cake. She had so much, in fact, she might as well give a bang on Prudence's door and invite her down to share it. It would be rather nice, having a cosy picnic round the fire and catching up on each other's news, Emily decided.

Although it was only the middle of the afternoon, with the leaden sky and black smoke pouring from factory chimney-stacks, night seemed already to be drawing in and Emily had to feel her way up the stairs to her room. She thought she heard a slight movement from the other side of the door, and wondering if it was Prudence, she tried the handle and it gave way immediately to her touch. The fire was lit and glowed on to the two naked bodies on the bed. Too shocked to speak, Emily stood motionless and watched them, Prudence astride Rory, his hands cupping her breasts, while she moved slowly on top of him, eyes closed, neck arched. There was complete silence except for the rocking of the bed, and Prudence's small sighing moans of pleasure. The sight of them, their betrayal, filled her head, her mind, her heart, her body with such a pulsating hatred, Emily screamed, 'Stop it!' and whammed her heavy bag with such force against Prudence's head, she screeched,

'Christ almighty,' and slid off Rory onto the floor.

Rory sat up slowly, his pupils dilated and blinking with confusion. 'Em ... Emily, wha-what are you doing here?' he stuttered.

'Well, that's a question I clearly don't have to ask either of you.' Her voice was strident with anger and, hellbent on revenge, Emily swung the bag again. It caught Rory full in the face, he let out a yell of pain and blood spurted from his nose on to the sheets.

Crouched on the other side of the bed, her big black eyes and wild, frizzy hair just visible, Prudence whimpered, 'I'm sorry, Em.'

'Sorry? You will be sorry by the time I've finished with you, because I'm going to kill you!' Emily strode round the bed, raised the bag to take another swipe at Prudence, but seeing it coming, she scrambled under the bed out of harm's way. 'I thought you were my friend.' Emily's voice was high and hysterical with grief at Prudence's betrayal.

'Ooh, I am. But I always envied you, with yer pretty face and nice way of talking,' Prudence sobbed, as if this excused her behaviour.

'Edmund's right, you're nothing but a whore, now get out of here.'

'Don't 'it me,' Prudence pleaded and crawled cautiously from under the bed. She reached out to grab her clothes lying on the floor, but Emily quickly put out a foot to stop her.

'You're not having them. Go and explain to your boyfriend what you've been up to with my husband, you dirty little tart. Go on, go, go, *go!*' Emily moved in on Prudence, forcing her out of the door and, stark naked and snivelling noisily, the girl scuttled out of the room and up the stairs.

Rory, who had made no attempt to defend his lady-love, was still nursing his bloody nose with the sheet. Emily turned her bile on him now. 'And you get out, too, you tom-cat,' she ordered. 'This is *my* room. You haven't paid for it, you deserted me and as a wife, I owe you *nothing!*'

'Emily, let me explain.'

'Explain how you came to be lying on my bed having sex with that slut? Don't bother! Just get out of here before I stick a knife through what passes for your heart. And here, take these.' She threw his clothes and his bags after him. 'Our marriage is over and

I never want to set eyes on you again.'

Rory paused at the door. 'I'm sorry, but Prudence is to blame, not me.'

'Don't give me that tired old Adam and Eve story, about her tempting you. You didn't really want to have sex with Prudence, but she seduced you, is that it?' Emily sneered.

'You should have had a letter from me saying I was on my way home. But when I got here yesterday, she spun me this yarn about you absolutely hating me for going off to America, and said you'd gone back to Leicester and never wanted to set eyes on me again.'

'That Judas cow! But I notice you didn't have to be asked twice to leap into bed with her.'

'She was all over me and I was sort of ... lonely.' Rory gave an apologetic shrug.

'Don't try and excuse your behaviour to me. You're my husband, in case it's slipped your mind, which makes your betrayal a hundred times worse. And Prudence is quite right about one thing, I do loathe and despise you, utterly.'

'I love you, Emily.'

'Stop your lies!' Emily grabbed an ornament of a flower girl and hurled it at him. But Rory had the wit to use the door as a shield, and it smashed against the wood before shattering into a hundred pieces on the floor.

'Emily! It was just a lapse. Please, can't you forgive me?'

'Forgive you?' Emily shrieked, beside herself with fury. 'Put your head round that door and I'll show you just how much I've forgiven you.' Her hand reached to the mantelpiece for a large plaster dog.

'All right, you've made your feelings quite clear, I'm going,' Rory said huffily. 'And you've seen the last of me.' He made it sound like a threat.

'Good, because I never want to see you again,' Emily shouted back. She heard him shuffling around getting into his clothes, then he hurried off down the stairs and the door slammed on him for the last time. Like a hurricane, Rory had swept through her life and out again, leaving a trail of destruction and Emily stood in the middle of the room with her head bent in defeat, her whole body shaking as if she had St Vitus Dance. But she had to sit down or she'd collapse. Grabbing the end of the bed for support, she eased herself down on the bed. It smelt of their sex. Disgusted, she stood up again. Tears dripped down her cheeks and her sense of desolation reached deep into her soul. She couldn't spend the night here or ever sleep in that bed again. Although barely capable of thinking rationally, Emily began stuffing the rest of her belongings into a bag: books, a few ornaments and the rest of her clothes. She was on her way out when she saw Rory's letter, obviously telling her of his return to England. Without reading it, she picked it up and tossed it on the fire. Another chapter of my life going up in flames, she thought, as she watched it burn.

Emily didn't look back and, leaving the door swinging, she dragged her goods and chattels after her, bumping them down the stairs. They were heavy so she needed frequent pauses to rest her aching arms, but she finally reached Broadwick Street. As she banged the knocker, she intoned to herself, 'Please let Mrs Haig be home, please.'

The maid, Dorcas, answered Emily's knock, and looked slightly taken aback to find her standing on the step. Seeing herself through the girl's eyes, Emily could sympathise, for she knew she resembled a rather bedraggled street urchin. A distressed one at that. 'Good-evening, Mrs Aherne,' the maid managed finally.

'Is Mrs Haig at home, Dorcas?" Emily blurted out.

'Yes, come in.' The maid leaned forward and took one of Emily's bags from her. 'I'll go and tell Mrs Haig you're here.'

She disappeared, Emily heard the faint murmur of voices, then a moment later her employer came hurrying into the hall. She took one look at Emily's ravaged features and the bags at her feet, and enquired in a concerned voice, 'My dear, whatever is the matter?'

'Can I speak to you privately?'

'Of course, come into the study.' She opened the door so that Emily could pass through, 'And come and sit by the fire, you look frozen.'

Warming her hands, Emily asked, 'You received my letter to say I would be back at work tomorrow?'

'Yes, I did.'

Trying to keep control of herself, Emily spoke slowly. 'Something so sordid has happened, Mrs Haig, I hardly know how to tell you.'

'Sordid?' Mrs Haig repeated.

Emily drew in a small shuddering breath. 'When I got back to my room this afternoon I found ... Rory ... and...' An image of them together, flashed before her eyes and Emily couldn't go on. Having reached the limits of her endurance, she covered her face with her hands and began to weep unrestrainedly.

'My dear!' Mrs Haig exclaimed and rushed to her side. 'Would a drop of brandy help?'

Emily shook her head, wiped her eyes and struggled to calm herself. 'My life is in ruins, Mrs Haig. I've been doubly betrayed, by Rory, my husband and by Prudence, someone who I thought was a friend. I caught them in my room, in my bed, *doing it.*'

'You mean having sex ... together?'

Emily nodded.

'Animals!' Mrs Haig spat out.

'I still can't believe that they would do such a thing to me.'

'It's utterly contemptible. I thought your husband was in America?'

'So did I. The marriage, it goes without saying, is over, and I never want to set eyes on him again, which means I shall be leaving London, for good.'

'In other words, because of that stupid man, I'm going to lose an excellent secretary. People really should try to control their baser instincts, it causes so much unnecessary trouble,' Mrs Haig observed irritably.

'I've really loved working for you, and I shall be sad to go, but I haven't any choice.'

'Yes, I can understand that. There would always be the chance that you might bump into him. I just wish the wretched man had stayed in America.'

'So do I. It would have spared me this humiliation.'

'When do you plan to return to Leicester?'

'Tomorrow.'

'Oh dear, so soon. But you're obviously going to need a bed for the night?'

Emily nodded.

'Wait here, I'll go and see that a bed is made up and a fire lit for you in one of the bedrooms.'

'Thank you, Mrs Haig.' Emily smiled tiredly.

'And I'll have something sent up on a tray. You won't feel up to company this evening.'

This is it, I'm home for good, Emily thought, as she came out of Campbell Street station. She paused and looked about her at the familiar landmarks, and suddenly Leicester seemed very cramped and provincial. *In less than two years I'm back where I started, without a husband and destined to spend the rest of my life behind the counter of the bookshop.* It was hardly what she'd envisaged for herself when she'd married Rory. And worst of all, she now had to go home and explain to her mother that she'd failed in yet one more area of her life. Emily gave a depressed sigh and called for a cab.

Seventeen

A few days into the New Year, Adam was in his office trying to get his paperwork organised when the young kitchen-maid, Nell, scuttled in and pushed a note across the desk. She curtsied then said quickly, 'It's from that Hattie Bonner, sir. She said I wa' to be sure and give it to you an' no one else. I did right, didn't I?' She glanced nervously over her shoulder, because the main house was out of bounds to a girl in her lowly position and if Cook caught her there'd be all hell to pay.

Adam smiled and slipped the girl a shilling. 'Of course you did and thank you, Nell.' It must be urgent he decided, as he unfolded the note, because as far as he could recall, Hattie had never written to him before. Usually, if she had anything to say, she shouted it to him across the street to cause him the maximum embarrassment. He scanned the words, which were terse and to the point:

'*Adam, please could you come down to the cottage as soon as possible, the babies are very poorly and need a doctor, Hattie*'

340

Nudged by guilt at his neglect of his sons, Adam stuffed the accounts into a drawer and set off with long urgent strides towards the cottage. Here he found a frantic Hattie trying to pacify two screaming babies, both of whom were covered in an unpleasant-looking rash, but to his relief, not dying as he'd imagined.

'Here, you take one,' Hattie said and shoved a squalling infant into Adam's arms. His little face was blotchy and screwed up in distress, but Adam knew without asking that it was Luke because of the child's amazing likeness to him. It was an unfamiliar experience, nursing his own child, and feeling large and clumsy, Adam began to rock him to and fro. Strangely, Luke stopped screaming and gazing down at the small being who shared his features, his blood and most likely many of his characteristics, Adam was troubled by a strange emotion, a feeling akin to tenderness, a need to protect him.

'What do you think is wrong with them?' Hattie asked worriedly. 'They won't stop crying and I'm at the end of my tether.'

'Well, I'm no expert but from the look of them and the rash, I would say they've caught some childish infection.' Adam laid Luke back in his cradle. 'I'll go right away and get one of the servants to fetch the doctor. Try not to worry, Hattie.'

'It's easy for you to say, don't worry, because you never have. If they died it would solve your problems nicely, wouldn't it?' she lashed out.

Adam was aghast. 'How could you even think such a thing, never mind say it?'

'Because it's true.' Tearful and exhausted, Hattie started to cry.

'Hattie, please, it isn't true, I swear it.' To show he wasn't entirely without a heart, Adam put an arm round her shoulder and she clung to him, warm and feminine and he felt his body stir in response. He knew he could have lifted up her skirts and had her, as he'd always done, without preamble, here in the small parlour. But he smothered the urge. He had sick children who needed a doctor's attention. Extricating himself before his common sense deserted him he said, 'I'll go now, but I'll be right back.'

Adam instructed the servant to bring the doctor back with him. However, he returned with the news that the doctor was out on his rounds, but that his wife would give her husband the message as soon as he returned.

This news made Hattie even more agitated, and when the doctor eventually found his way to the cottage, she was pacing back and forth in the small parlour, convinced her babies were at death's door.

'Chickenpox,' the doctor immediately

diagnosed. 'Quite a bad attack for the poor little fellows, that's why they are so fractious. They will feel poorly for a few days, but keep them indoors and make sure they have plenty of liquid. A bonny pair like this will soon be back to full health. I'll leave you some Godfrey's Mixture, that will help them sleep.'

'There you are,' said Adam after he'd paid the doctor and seen him out. 'Has that put your mind at rest, Hattie?'

'I suppose so,' Hattie answered grudgingly. She'd already given both of them a spoonful of the medicine and was leaning over them, rocking their cradle and trying to calm them to sleep. 'You've handed over some money, so I suppose you feel that you've done your duty as far as your sons are concerned?'

'No.'

Hattie turned. 'They're pulling themselves up and trying to walk now, but when was the last time you bothered to ask after them or even visit?'

'I did call one evening to see them, if you remember, and you wouldn't let me in.'

'It wasn't convenient, I had a visitor.'

'So I gathered.' There was a knowing edge to Adam's voice.

'Don't use that tone of voice. I can guess the way your mind's working but it wasn't a man. I was altering a riding habit for young

Natalie and she'd come to collect it. You thought it was the schoolmaster, didn't you?' Hattie challenged.

'Ah ... um...' Adam stumbled.

'Well, let me tell you this. Mr Brown is an extremely honourable gentleman who respects me and never once has he tried to take advantage of my situation.'

'I have never suggested that he might.'

'I bet you've thought it.'

'Never,' Adam lied. 'What you do with your life is your business, Hattie, and I certainly have no right to interfere in it.'

'You're quite right, you haven't.'

Adam stood up. 'I'd better be on my way, but I'll call in again tomorrow to see the boys, I promise.' Adam let himself out and as he passed the schoolmaster's cottage he had a strong sense that he was being watched. Adam believed Hattie when she said that John Brown treated her with respect, but he also paid her a lot of attention, so what was his motive, if it wasn't to get her into bed? Although Adam couldn't quite say why, the man irritated him, and if there was going to be a contest, he had too much pride to lose out to a mere teacher. So, from tomorrow he would become a model father and visit his sons every evening and see how things developed with Hattie from there.

But fate horrifically and tragically intervened in Adam's plans.

On Plough Monday when ploughboys, with their soot-blackened faces, ribbons and outlandish costumes, were going from house to house blackmailing householders with their rattling money-boxes, Grace and Anil went out into the stables and shot themselves through the heart with two pistols belonging to Mr Bellamy.

The scandal, like the shots, reverberated around the village, particularly when word got out that Grace had been pregnant. Adam had been as shocked as anyone by the tragedy, but ever since that day he'd come across them in the barley field, it had been plain to him that theirs was a doomed love and so there was a certain inevitability about their deaths. But guilt always follows death and Adam found himself searching his conscience and wondering whether, if he'd done more, maybe spoken to them, he could have prevented the tragedy. He knew though, that society and prejudice were at the heart of their violent and desperate act, not him personally, and there was nothing he could have done to stop their suicide. Shortly after this, the Bellamys sold Chenies Manor and moved to another part of the country and the tragic eruption passed into part of the village folklore.

In the meantime, though, caught up in the calamitous events, and the need to help the bewildered grieving parents, a week had passed before Adam realised, with a jolt of guilt, that he hadn't been to see how his ailing sons were. Expecting an earful from Hattie on his shortcomings as a father, he stood outside the cottage door, rather like an errant husband, already planning his excuses.

'I'm sorry, Hattie,' he apologised, when she answered his knock. 'I know I should have been down to see how the twins were before this, but there was this terrible business with Grace and Anil, the police to deal with, then an inquest, and the least I could do was offer the Bellamys my support.'

'Don't worry,' Hattie surprised him by saying, 'the rash has turned into lots of little scabs and they're almost better.'

It soon became obvious that, like everyone else, it was the suicide Hattie wanted to talk about and after she'd brought Adam a glass of her parsnip wine, she sat down opposite him. 'I knew about Miss Grace and her servant, you know.'

Adam's eyebrow rose a fraction. 'Oh, did you?'

'I saw them more than once in the woods, holding hands, kissing. They really seemed to love each other.' Hattie gave a wistful sigh. 'It seemed so sad that they had to kill themselves. Why couldn't they marry? Why do people care so much about differences?'

346

Adam knew that this question was aimed at him personally and he took several gulps of the wine to hide his acute embarrassment. What could he say to Hattie? 'Apart from the fact that I don't love you, I can't marry you because you're slightly uncouth, uneducated and don't speak properly, and I'd feel ashamed to be seen with you in society.' Because that was the brutal truth. Fudging it, he said instead, 'Anil was of a different race ... a different class,' he dared to add. 'Marriage was out of the question; they would have spent their lives as social outcasts and a burden like that soon kills love. Although she flouted convention, Grace understood these distinctions.'

Hattie refilled his glass and moved closer. It was getting dark in the room, the only light was from the fire and its glow softened her features. After a couple more glasses of wine, Hattie looked even prettier, and Adam noticed that the top buttons on her dress had mysteriously become unfastened. The temptation was too powerful and he reached out and touched her breasts.

Without a word, Hattie manoeuvred herself on to his lap, and he was fumbling to undo the remaining buttons on her dress, when there was an almighty thump on the door.

'Bloody 'ell, who's that?' Hattie cursed, leapt off Adam's lap, buttoned her dress, hissed to him, 'Light the lamp,' and walked calmly to the door. Before opening it, she paused to collect herself and smooth her hair, then with a bright welcoming smile, exclaimed, 'Oh, hello, John!'

'Have I come at an inconvenient time?' John Brown asked, peering into the parlour.

'No, come in. Mr Bennett was passing so he looked in to see how the twins were after their illness.' Having got over her fright, Hattie was enjoying herself. Men had never fought over her before. 'But you were just leaving, weren't you?' she smiled at Adam.

'I am.' Adam stood up and as the men passed each other on the threshold, they faced up to each other like two stags, ready to lock antlers. Adam strode home in a state of sexual frustration and umbrage, planning his next move. That schoolmaster would not outwit him.

Eighteen

To trail home once again, to have to admit to her mother that she had a faithless husband, to describe the unsavoury details; the scene in that room, on that bed, had been one of the difficult tasks of Emily's life. To her it was an admittance that she hadn't measured up as a wife. But she'd been determined not to flinch from it; there would be no fudging, no more covering up for Rory. Her mother would hear the un-varnished truth.

Not unnaturally, Rachel's reaction had been one of appalled disgust. 'I have never heard anything like it before in my life. You must apply for a separation at once,' she urged.

'No, I shan't bother.'

'Then, as your husband, Rory could force you to go back to him.'

'I doubt if he would do that. A wife is a nuisance and he'd be obliged to start supporting me. He's always had a casual attitude towards money, but do you know, I've not had a penny from him since he went to America? And to cap it all, I even gave *him* some of my savings before he left, and

349

yet for all he cared I could have been starving in the gutter.'

'I wonder why he bothered to come back?'

'Another failed enterprise, I imagine. He was supposed to be going to California to make his fortune, but obviously he didn't.'

The following weeks were hard for Emily. Her self-esteem hit rock bottom and life struck her as pretty pointless. January and February were dark grim months with heavy rainfall, and it wasn't until March, when the days began to lengthen and the golden daffodils trumpeted that spring was on its way, that Emily woke one morning, saw that the sun was shining, stretched and thought, I must stop raking through the ashes of my failed marriage. From now on I'll take each day as it comes, accept that no man can be trusted and get on with my life.

Of course, nothing much could be hidden from Lily, who was deeply curious about her return. She'd grown used to Emily's comings and goings, her excuses about Rory's whereabouts but when, after two months, Emily was still working behind the counter, she asked outright one day, 'Are you home for good?'

Emily gave an evasive shrug, and hurried away to serve another customer. Lily had always lent an ear, involved herself in the many ups and downs of Emily's love life, taken risks on her behalf, and Emily knew she was hurt that she was no longer her confidante. But she felt too shamed and tainted by the memory of that first disbelieving second when she'd stood in the doorway and her eyes had tried to unscramble what they saw: Rory enjoying sex with another woman as much as he did with her. But to have to keep dredging it up was painful, so Emily became quite adept at deflecting Lily's more blatant questions.

But Lily wasn't a girl to give up and one morning she came into the shop, slapped her library books down on the counter and said, 'Why don't you come round for tea, this afternoon, Emily?'

'Oh, I don't know,' Emily dithered, guessing her motive – a womanly heart to heart.

'She'll come, Lily,' said Rachel, deciding for her daughter. 'She's been cooped up in this shop long enough. It will do her good to get out.'

'Good, that's settled then, I'll see you at three o'clock,' said Lily, picking up her new library books and hurrying out of the shop before Emily could change her mind.

In a perverse sort of way, Emily was glad in the end that her mother had forced the decision upon her. It was a pleasant stroll up New Walk and on past the tollgate at the top of London Road, for Lily had finally achieved her ambition and now resided amongst the toffs in Stoneygate. The villa Septimus had purchased for his family was broad and solid like him and Lily had spent freely on curtains and furnishings. Her indulgent husband had also bought her a pianoforte and as Bertha let her in, Emily could hear her thrumming away on the keys.

Lily stopped playing when Emily entered the room. 'Well, what do you think? Am I any good?' she asked.

'It's early days yet, you'll improve,' answered Emily, with the honesty of a friend.

'The children are both better than me already, Helen in particular.'

Emily looked quickly round. Lord, she wasn't going to have to spend the afternoon in the company of Lily's ghastly daughter, was she? That really would give her indigestion.

Reading her mind, Lily laughed. 'Don't worry, my darling daughter is at school, probably trying her teachers to their limit. Now, sit down by the fire, while I go and have a word with Bertha about tea.'

She returned a few minutes later with Bertha waddling behind carrying a tray loaded down with fruit loaf, sponge cake, biscuits and small sandwiches.

'That sponge cake looks so delicious you must have made it, Lily?'

'I did. Septimus likes my cakes so I still do my own baking. Tuck in,' Lily invited and handed her a plate. 'You've no idea how much I missed you when you left Leicester, Emily, but this is like old times.'

'And I'm back for good,' Emily replied, deciding to get it out in the open. 'Rory and I have separated and it's permanent, after less than two years of marriage.'

Lily, who was pouring the tea, put down the teapot and sat back. 'I always knew he wasn't the right man for you, but that's still quick. What happened?'

'He couldn't keep his trousers on. He was having an affair with a girl I thought was my friend. That hurt as much as anything, her betrayal.'

'The beast! How could he?' Lily expostulated, forgetting her own infidelities.

'Rather easily, it appears. But I don't support the view that wives should be long-suffering and forgiving, so I left. Maybe I didn't love him enough. He swore he still loved me, though. Aren't men the limit?'

'Does Adam know?'

Emily shook her head. 'It wouldn't serve any purpose if he did. I'm not free.'

'That needn't stop you seeing each other. You could meet here. This house is so large, you could get lost in it and we've got umpteen bedrooms. I've always been discreet, and no one need know.'

'It's kind of you to offer. But I'm not ready for the complications of an affair. Anyway, I think my heart has turned to stone.'

'You can't live the rest of your life as a nun.'

'I might have to and when word gets round that I've left my husband, there will be some scandalised Leicester matrons. They'll be keeping their beady eyes on the Jezebel in their midst, ready to stone me if I step out of line.'

Emily was finishing her second cup of tea, when she heard the children returning, then Helen burst in the room and grabbed the last sandwiches on the plate.

'You pigs, you've eaten everything!' she accused and glared at Emily. Outraged by the girl's insolence, Emily's hand itched to slap her hard across the face and she had to hold it down to stop herself. 'Please don't call me a pig, Helen,' she said tightly.

'Go to your room, this minute,' her mother ordered.

'No.' Helen poked out her tongue and ran for the door.

Lily sighed. 'I really don't know what to do about Helen, she grows more difficult by the day.'

'You're not firm enough with her, Lily.'

Lily bridled. 'Why do you say that?'

'Well, you've ordered her to her room, and she's ignored you.'

'She wouldn't stay there for five minutes.'

'Lock her in.'

'It seems a trifle harsh.'

'Well, she's your child, you must make the decisions, but she's going to be the dominant one in this family soon if you don't exercise a little discipline.' Emily picked up her bag, 'And now I must go.'

'Oh don't, not yet,' Lily wailed. 'It's because of the wretched child isn't it?'

'No, it's not,' Emily answered, lying a little. 'I know I came with her blessing, but I feel guilty if I leave my mother on her own in the shop for too long.'

'But you'll come again soon, won't you?' Lily pleaded. 'In the evening when Helen's in bed. Come round for a game of whist and supper. You need to meet people socially, Septimus doesn't like playing very much, but Marigold and her husband are very keen on card games.'

'All right, let me know the date.' Emily thanked her friend for the tea, kissed her goodbye, but walking home, she couldn't help comparing her life in London with the one she had here. To think that, next to church, an evening playing whist with Lily's sister, Marigold, and her dull husband was the most exciting event in her social calendar. She wasn't looking for a good time, just an aim in her life. She had failed with Mary, but there were still plenty of children that needed rescuing from ignorance, and there must be some who were longing to be taught to read and write. Or maybe she would take up Lily's offer and lead a life of sin. Her friend was right, she hadn't taken a vow of chastity and she needn't feel any guilt about breaking her marriage vows, because Rory had already beaten her to it. But she wasn't sure her bruised spirit was quite ready for the emotional turmoil of an illicit affair. And what was the hurry anyway? she asked herself, because she only had to say the word and Adam would come running.

Nineteen

It was muck-spreading time and the smell pervaded the whole village. Most villagers thought manure a good healthy odour but the more delicate-nosed twitched their nostrils disdainfully and made sure they kept their windows firmly shut while the oozing carts trundled down Main Street.

To fill in time while she waited for Nell to come and pick up the twins, Hattie had stopped to gather catkins and sticky buds. Thinking how nice they would look in a jar in her window, she was balanced on the edge of the ditch, stretching up to a branch just out of reach, when Adam happened by.

'Here, let me do that,' he offered, snapped off a branch of willow, and with a gallant flourish, handed it to her.

'Why, thank you.' Hattie expected him to pass on. Instead, he leaned over and tickled both his sons under the chin.

'They seem to be coming on in leaps and bounds,' he observed, as they gurgled at each other in their incomprehensible baby language. 'Sounds as if they're trying to talk, too.'

Hattie studied Adam. He didn't normally

show this much interest in his children, so what was he after? Her, she sensed and continued picking catkins with a sense of triumph. She'd held back from John Brown in the hope that Adam would come crawling in the end. She'd also grown wiser of late and there'd be a price this time or he'd get nothing.

'Are you waiting for Nell to pick them up?' asked Adam casually.

Hattie gazed at him, all girlish innocence. 'Yes, she'll be here in a minute.'

He edged nearer and lowered his voice. 'Do you remember the hayloft, Hattie?'

'With two sons, I'm hardly likely to forget it.'

'There's nobody about this afternoon, they're all up the in fields. Could you meet me up there in a quarter of an hour?' He moved even closer so that their bodies almost touched, then lifted his hand and gently touched her breasts.

By now Hattie was so agitated she could only nod her assent.

'Good.' Adam smiled, then quickly backed away as Nell emerged from the drive.

'Sir looks in a mighty hurry,' Nell observed as Adam strode off. 'And you look a bit peculiar, too, Hattie Bonner. Yer face and neck 'ave gone all red and blotchy. What you bin up to?' Nell, who was a sharp-eyed little madam, peered into Hattie's face.

'I haven't been up to anything, apart from discussing the boys' health. And you're late, so instead of poking your nose into other people's business, get on with what you're supposed to be doing, or you'll be in trouble with Mrs Bennett,' Hattie shot back. 'And see you don't bump them over the pot-holes in the drive, it's not good for their little bodies.'

'Don't give me orders, Hattie Bonner, you don't pay me.' Nell answered with a toss of the head, then very deliberately dragged the wagon over the deepest pot-hole she could find.

'Cow!' Hattie muttered, gave her five minutes then, keeping well into the under-growth, followed the maid up the drive, making her plans as she went. Adam needn't think he was going to have his way with her, then cast her aside like he'd done in the past. But the main trouble was herself. Just anticipating their snatched time together in the hayloft had put her in such a high state of arousal, she knew when Adam touched her she would ignite. But you mustn't let him beguile you, Hattie lectured herself, you must stay in control, hold out until he's ready to promise you the moon.

Full of resolve, and with these points in the forefront of her mind, Hattie negotiated the last part of the drive. When she reached the yard, she paused and looked about her.

She didn't want prying folk asking what her business was, so she was relieved to see that Adam had obviously made plans for her visit well in advance and dispatched his workers to the four corners of the estate. 'Right, this is the day you have the chance to change your fortunes, so see you don't muck it up, Hattie Bonner,' she muttered to herself as she scuttled across the deserted yard, hitched up her skirts, and climbed the ladder to the hayloft.

'Hattie, over here,' Adam called softly. He was casually dressed in shirt and trousers and when she reached him, he took her hand and pulled her down beside him in the hay. When he began caressing her breasts, she wanted to surrender to him immediately and she had to call upon all her strength of will to squirm from his embrace.

'Just a minute,' Hattie said, sat up, untied the ribbons of her bonnet and laid it aside. Next she lifted her skirt and very slowly rolled her stockings down her legs. 'Don't want to spoil them,' she explained, noticing from the corner of her eye that Adam was propped up on his elbow watching her every movement.

'Unfasten my dress,' she ordered, back in control again, and as his hands fumbled with the buttons, she slid both hands along his muscular thighs and up to the fly on his trousers. When they were undone, he quickly pulled them off and when they were both naked Hattie pressed him back in the hay. His skin was as clean and smooth as she remembered and smelt faintly and erotically of carnations. Neither of them spoke and she began to kiss him lightly all over his body and work her fingers on him until he was hard.

'Oh, Hattie, that is wonderful,' Adam groaned, but he had been without a woman for a long time and was impatient. Rolling over on top of her, he went to enter her. But this was her moment. Clamping her legs together like scissors, Hattie stared up at him.

'You could have this every day of your life, if you had a mind.'

'Hattie, stop this torture.'

'Would you like it every day?' she repeated.

'Of course I would.'

'Marry me then.'

Adam, who had being trying to edge her legs apart, paused. 'Hattie, I can't.'

'Why not? You could do a lot worse.'

'We're different, you and me.'

'You mean I'm not good enough for you except here in the hay,' she challenged. 'Right, find yourself some frigid-faced young madam of your own class and see if I care.' She pushed him off, sat up and started searching around for her drawers and stockings.

'Hattie, what are you doing?' Adam tried to grab the clothes out of her hand.

'I'm going.' There was a tussle then a tearing sound as one of her stockings ripped in two. 'Now look what you've done,' Hattie accused.

'I'll buy you more but please, you can't leave me like this!' Adam implored.

'Just watch me. And if you think yer such a toff, go and ask yer mam who yer father was, for it certainly weren't the Squire,' she spat at him.

Adam suddenly went very still. 'What are you talking about?'

'Yer mam. With all her airs and graces, she weren't no better than me, just lucky to get some old fool to marry her when she were in the family way, or you'd have bin a bastard like your sons.' Hattie's voice was strident and in her anger she forgot herself and reverted to her old common way of speaking. She stood up, stepped into her dress, then buttoned it. 'If you don't believe me, go and ask her. And now I'm going. Goodbye.'

His stomach turning over sickly, Adam stood and watched Hattie disappear down the ladder. Was she speaking the truth? If so, who *was* his father? Shock had extinguished all thoughts of sex and he quickly dressed. He had to find out the truth.

His mother was in the garden with the

twins when Adam arrived, and she looked up with a smile as he crossed the lawn towards them. 'Luke grows more like you every day, don't you think?' Matilda asked. 'And it's true what they say, children do bring their love with them.' She picked each one up in turn and kissed them soundly.

'Did I bring my love with me?'

'What a strange question. Of course you did.'

'But I wasn't particularly wanted.'

'Adam, what are you going on about?'

'You were pregnant with me before you married, weren't you?'

'Ah ... yes.'

'But Francis Bennett wasn't my father?'

'Who told you that?'

'Never mind. Was he or wasn't he?'

'No.' Matilda's lip began to quiver.

'Who was then?'

'Harry.'

'Do you mean Olivia and Judith's father?'

'Yes.'

'But why didn't he marry you?'

'Harry never loved me in the same way that I did him. He was a soldier, it was the time of Waterloo and I thought he was dead. Instead, he'd met Charlotte, a wealthy heiress, in Brussels and became engaged to her. I loathed the Squire, he was old, dirty and disgusting, but I had no choice but to marry him. My father forced me into it. As simple as that. And you should thank me, at least you're not labelled a bastard, you've got the estate and Francis always accepted you as his son.'

'But why have you never told me before?'

'Because Harry treated me so badly. He never knew for certain that you were his child. I felt very bitter towards him so decided to leave him guessing as a punishment. For years, we never spoke, but when he went to fetch you back after you ran away with that Fairfax girl, he demanded to know the truth. Then you went off to America, and when you came back married I decided to let sleeping dogs lie.'

Adam began striding up and down on the grass. 'I've got a father, two half sisters and yet you kept it from me all these years?' He paused. 'In fact, I'm so angry, I'm not sure I want anything further to do with you.'

Matilda clutched his arm. 'Adam, please don't speak like that. There's no one I love more than you. I had no choice but to marry Francis. Imagine the shame.'

'You had enough to say about Hattie. Called her for everything. Refused to have her in the house. She's not even allowed to bring her own sons up here in case she contaminates you. Talk about hypocritical! But I know what I'll do, I'll marry her, give my sons a name and see how you like that!'

Matilda stared at him aghast. 'Adam, you

can't. It would be a terrible tragedy. She's not the girl for you.'

Adam had begun to stride off, but he stopped and stared at Matilda with hatred in his eyes. 'You stopped me marrying once, but you won't this time.'

Adam heard his mother's sobs, but there was such a hard knot of anger in his stomach at her deceit, he couldn't think rationally and still wearing nothing more than shirt and trousers, he marched down to the village. He would grant Hattie her wish and even though he was adding to the catalogue of disasters he'd already made, at least he would be making one person happy.

'Adam.' He turned when he heard his name and saw Clare and Christopher emerging from the now completed school. He didn't want to be delayed, because that would give him the chance to have second thoughts, but by now they had reached him.

'The new desks for the school have arrived today, and blackboards and maps,' Christopher said excitedly. 'We'll almost certainly be able to open immediately after Easter.'

'Oh good,' said Adam absently.

'Adam, you look pale. Are you all right?' Clare asked, searching his face.

'I'm fine,' he lied and watched John Brown come out of what was going to be called Bennett School, close the door and walk across the Green.

'One misfortune, though, is that we're about to lose Mr Brown,' said Christopher following his gaze. 'He's been offered a more senior post in a school in Nottingham and has decided to take it. He's an excellent teacher who will be hard to replace. I never expected him to stay long, but he has chosen an awkward time to leave.'

'You mustn't worry, Christopher. I'll help until you find another teacher,' said Clare.

'But your health—'

'I'm as fit as a fiddle.'

Adam left them arguing amiably. He had to get this done, he thought grimly and set off across the Green with a determined set to his jaw.

'What do you want?' Hattie's expression was less than friendly when she opened the door to his knock.

'I want to ask you something, but I'd prefer not to do it on the step.'

'You'd better come in then.' She stood back, Adam stepped inside and when his eyes adjusted to the light, he noticed John Brown sitting in a chair by the fire.

'Good-afternoon, Mr Bennett.' He stood up as Adam entered.

'Good-afternoon,' Adam growled, thinking, what the hell is he doing here?

Hattie went and got some glasses down from the dresser, opened a bottle of parsnip wine and started pouring. 'We were about to drink a toast. You might as well join us.'

'Oh, what's the toast to?' Adam enquired, lifting his glass.

Hattie had a self-satisfied look on her face. 'John will tell you.'

'I have just asked Hattie to be my wife and she has accepted.'

'You're marrying her?' Adam was so stunned the wine slopped all over his hand.

'Yes, very shortly at St Philip's. You see, I have a new post to go to, with better wages. I will be quite able to support Hattie and the twins, whom I intend to bring up as my own. So, if you don't mind, I would prefer it if you had no further contact with them, Mr Bennett.'

'What do you mean, no further contact?' Adam asked sourly. 'They are my sons and they have a grandmother who is devoted to them.'

'You've never bothered about them that much,' Hattie interrupted. 'And you've got no legal rights. My name is on their birth certificate, so don't start being difficult, Adam.'

To get one over on the schoolmaster, for a moment Adam was tempted to blurt out his own offer, but he stopped himself. By the skin of his teeth he'd been saved from another disastrous marriage and this man was ideal for Hattie. He was stable, ambitious and hard-working. Socially she would be rising in the world and she would make the perfect schoolmaster's wife.

'I'm not as cold-hearted as you make out, Hattie, so I would like you to write to me occasionally and let me know how my sons are getting on. I don't know how my mother will take this, she was devoted to her grandsons.'

'You must provide her with some more,' Hattie answered practically. 'By the way, what did you want to see me about?'

'Er ... it was a question about the boys, but it doesn't matter now,' he lied. Adam lifted his glass. 'Anyway, congratulations to you both. I hope you have a long and happy marriage.' He drank the glass dry, put it down on the table, wished the newly betrothed couple good-afternoon, then, sweating with relief, let himself out. Feeling generous after his lucky escape, as he walked back up to Trent Hall, Adam resolved to give Hattie and her fiancé a generous sum of money as a wedding present. Even though he knew he hadn't been the most attentive of fathers, Adam felt strangely bereft at the thought of losing his sons. Even more painful would be the task of breaking the news to his mother. She adored her grandsons and he knew she would be heartbroken, and he prayed that the fact that he wasn't marrying Hattie might go some way to alleviating her distress.

Twenty

'Letter for you, looks like London.' The letter carrier scrutinised the envelope closely before dropping it on the counter in front of Emily. 'Don't recognise the handwriting, though.'

'I'm sorry about that,' Emily answered tartly, and stuffed the letter in her pocket. Unfortunately, sarcasm was lost on him, because his interest in letters extended not only to knowing who they were from, but their contents as well.

'Well, must be on my way,' the man said at last, realising that Emily probably wasn't going to oblige him and tear open the envelope.

'Good-morning to you.' To make sure he didn't linger any longer, Emily went round the counter and held open the door. She waited until he'd trundled next door to the greengrocers, then took the letter from her pocket and opened it. She didn't recognise the handwriting either and when she checked the signature at the end she was astonished to see it was from Edmund, the last person on earth she would expect to hear from.

'*Dear Emily,*

Please prepare yourself, because this letter contains very grave news. Prudence has died. You might have read that cholera has moved over from France and it's reached epidemic proportions in London and dozens of people are now dying every day from this scourge. It strikes them down in a few hours and I can't tell you how terrible the symptoms are, sickness, agonising cramps, diarrhoea. Prudence was in full possession of her health but suddenly became sick on the Sunday morning and by the time she got medical assistance it was too late and I lost my treasure the following day and I am heartbroken. And now equally bad news for you, because I have to tell you that Rory, too, has succumbed to the disease and is in the Fever Hospital. He has asked for you and I think you should come. Don't lose hope, cholera isn't always fatal, and he is a big strong man. However, I suggest that you go straight to the hospital, which is in Liverpool Road...'

With her hand pressed to her thumping heart and stunned by its bleak message, Emily read the letter twice, then again. Prudence dead. Rory mortally ill. But perhaps not if she could get there in time. Impelled to do something before it was too late, Emily rushed to the bottom of the stairs. 'Mama, can you come down please?'

Rachel saw Emily's stricken features and the letter clutched in her hand and without a word, took it from her and read it. 'This is dreadful news, what are you going to do?'

Emily ran her fingers along the counter in an agitated manner. 'Catch the next train to London and try and see him. It's my fault, Rory wouldn't have got ill like this if I hadn't left him. And if he gets better, I swear to God I'll go back to him and be a loyal wife.'

'Emily you can't hold yourself responsible for Rory's illness. London's an open sewer. Besides, if you go down there you'll be putting your own life at risk,' Rachel protested, but she could see from her daughter's abstracted expression that she wasn't listening.

'I'll go and put a few things in a bag,' Emily said by way of an answer and disappeared upstairs. When she returned, she was dressed for a journey and carrying a small valise.

'You'll need money, take this.' Her mother pressed several sovereigns into her hand. 'And try not to imagine the worst. Cholera isn't always fatal and Rory might be on the mend by now.'

It was late afternoon by the time Emily arrived at Euston, and raining. 'Can you take me to the Fever Hospital, please?' she called to the first driver on the cab rank, and went to jump in.

But the man shook his head sorrowfully, 'Sorry, madam, but I ain't goin' nowhere near that Fever 'Orspital, you never know what you'll catch in them places.'

Exasperated, Emily slammed the door shut and moved on to the next cab. But it was the same story here, and the one after. Emily was beginning to think she'd have to find her way there on foot and in the rain, when the last driver on the row called, 'I'll take you, but it'll be double fare, madam, I'm afraid.'

The rain was pelting down now and Emily knew she was in no position to bargain. 'All right,' she said and jumped in.

'Grim-looking place, ain't it?' the driver observed as they drew up outside the hospital. 'But there are worse places. The authorities are turning old warehouses and army barracks into isolation hospitals and dumping the sick in them.' He cocked his head as he pocketed the money. 'Someone close to you in there?'

'Yes, my husband.'

'Well, I wish you the best, but I'm glad it ain't one of mine they're looking after.'

Hardly comforted by his words, Emily turned, took a deep breath, then bracing herself, she pushed in through the doors. There was very little light and the place had a strange, unpleasant smell. Of death may-be? A terror seized Emily and she wanted to run, but she forced herself to move forward. The place seemed deserted and she was wondering what she should do when, through the gloom, she saw a nurse. However, there was nothing about the woman to reassure her, because as she approached, Emily could see that she was a rough-looking creature, obviously the worse for drink. 'I'm looking for my husband, a Mr Rory Aherne,' she said.

The woman eyed Emily up and down. 'Cholera, is it?'

'Y...es.'

'If yer lucky he'll be in Ward Two. Straight along the corridor.'

Emily could hear the groans and cries of the sick now and her heart stirred with pity. To think that Rory, her husband, was lying in this dismal place. But not for much longer. As soon as she could, she would get him out, she decided and pulled open the ward door. Here Emily found her way blocked by a hefty-looking nurse

'You can't come in 'ere.' The nurse folded her arms across her chest.

'I want to see my husband, he's a patient here.'

'Name?' the nurse barked.

'Mr Rory Aherne.'

She went to a desk and ran her fingers down a list. 'Sorry, deceased.'

'Dead?' Emily hung on to the door for

support. 'But when?'

She again referred to the list. 'Day before yesterday.'

'But what about the body...?'

'We don't keep 'em. The corpses of cholera victims have to be buried within twelve hours, in special pits.'

'In pits?' Emily repeated in an appalled voice.

'Them's the rules.'

'Is there no funeral service?'

'I expect the priest says a few words. You people don't know what we've got to deal with 'ere. It's like a plague, this. People are dying like flies, and we're doin' the best we can.' The nurse's voice had become defensive.

'Of course you are. Did my husband by any chance mention me before he died?'

The nurse held out her hand, Emily placed a sovereign in it, and as the woman's fingers curled around the money, she became suddenly maudlin and wiped a non-existent tear from her eye with her apron. 'Full of praise for you he was. Said he'd married a saint...'

'My husband said that?'

'Oh yes.' In full flow the woman went on. 'Said how much he loved you, and what a wonderful mother you were to his children–'

'Children? But we never had any,' Emily interrupted.

'Oh sorry, must 'ave got you muddled up.'

'You lying beastly woman! You vulture! How could you take advantage of my grief?' Emily screamed, grabbed the nurse's hand and tried prise the sovereign from her fingers. 'Give me my money back, this minute!'

'No fear.' The nurse gave Emily a shove that sent her reeling, then she tore off to the end of the ward where she was surrounded by other nurses, who all glared balefully at Emily.

Her body sagging with defeat, Emily turned and left the place of sickness and death. But as she walked out of the hospital, she realised that she hadn't got one thing to remind her of Rory. No last words, not even a letter, and she regretted now the ones she'd thrown unopened on to the fire during the past months. But hardest of all was knowing her husband lay in a pit, with not even a headstone to mark his passing.

Emily reached the end of the street then turned and took a final look at the dreary hospital. What she must do was try and hold on to the good times, the early days of their marriage, before it all turned sour and she'd stopped loving Rory. And as she walked on Emily made a pledge with herself; she would not allow herself to be weighed down with the guilt and recriminations that a death brings. Rory had led the life he wanted, and it had ended early. And with his attitude to religion, of all the people she knew, Rory was the last person who would expect her to grieve for him.

The sheepshearers had arrived and Adam was on his way up to the pens with them, when he heard a crunch of gravel and Clare came trotting up in a gig. She drew to a halt in front of the house and called, 'Have you got a moment, Adam?'

'Give me five minutes to sort out these chaps,' he answered and when he returned, Clare was waiting for him in the office and from her expression, bursting to tell him something.

'I've got some news for you.'

'I rather gathered that,' Adam laughed.

'Christopher and I were in Leicester yesterday buying books and discovered that Emily's back home.'

'Yes, she's got an unreliable husband, so she does comes and go rather.'

'Actually, her husband is dead.'

Adam was so shocked he leapt to his feet. 'You mean Rory? Are you certain?'

'I heard it from Emily's own mouth. It's very tragic, he died in London about a month ago of cholera. The disease is spreading like wildfire, and it's being said that people are catching it from the drinking water. Oh, Adam, it won't come here, will it?'

'Londoners get their water from the Thames, which is filthy. We've got good clean spring water here in Halby, so God willing, we'll be spared,' Adam replied, his thoughts on Emily. 'But how is she taking it?'

'Much as one would expect. Subdued, a trifle pale, but putting on a brave face.'

'Do you think it would be all right to go and see her?'

'I'm sure it would. But Adam, I beg of you, please go slowly. I know you are both free now, but don't start making demands. She has lost a husband and a father within a year of each other, so she must be feeling pretty bruised.'

'On my oath, I won't say one word that will upset her.'

In spite of his promise, after Clare left, Adam's instinct had been to rush into Leicester and ask Emily to marry him, but the more he thought about it the more he knew Clare was talking sensibly. He mustn't act like a bull in a china shop. He'd made enough mistakes, but this time he had to get it right, so to start with he would go and see his mother and on his way, decide what he was going to say to her. He and his mother were back on reasonably good terms again, and he'd got over the shock of the revelations of his birth. Harry had gladly acknowledged him as a son and Olivia and Judith appeared as delighted to have a brother as he did two sisters.

Matilda was sitting sewing when Adam arrived and she greeted him with a melancholy smile. Hattie was now a respectable schoolmaster's wife in Nottingham, her cottage stood empty and this lay at the heart of his mother's unhappiness. The loss of the twins had been a tremendous blow, and the card Adam intended to play was the promise of legitimate grandchildren.

Adam sat down beside her. 'Mother, I want to talk to you seriously.'

'Go ahead, dear.'

'Clare has been to tell me that Emily is back in Leicester, and also that she was recently widowed.'

Matilda eyed him warily. 'So?'

'I intend to ask her to marry me.'

Matilda laid down her sewing. 'It would be highly improper for Emily to remarry when her husband is hardly cold. There has to be an appropriate period of mourning.'

'We've waited twelve years. A few more months are unlikely to matter. What I want is your assurance that, if she does agree to marry me, you will make her welcome here.'

'Why, of all the other suitable girls in Leicestershire, you have to choose her, I can't imagine.'

'You can't seem to get this into your head, Mother, so I'll repeat it. Because I love her.

Only this time I don't intend to let some stupid family feud stand in our way. And I'll make this quite clear: if, because of your attitude, she refuses me, I will remain single for the rest of my days. So you'd better decide, do you want more grandchildren or not? A legitimate heir to the estate?'

A picture appeared in Matilda's head of several little plump replicas of Adam playing on her lawn and relented. And Adam was right, it was time to forget old enmities, they achieved nothing but unhappiness. 'You know I do.' She kissed her son. 'And I'll make Emily and her mother and sister welcome, I give you my word.'

'Right, I will go into Leicester tomorrow, ask Emily to marry me, then I want you to arrange a small party for her family and ours. Will you do that?'

'Gladly.'

Adam stood up. 'Thank you, Mother. And who knows, before long, you could be a grandmother.'

'Oh, I do hope so,' Matilda replied, and for the first time in a long while she smiled.

Savouring the moment, Adam watched Emily through the shop window, then pushed open the door. Removing his hat, he said formally, 'Good morning Emily, Mrs Fairfax.'

'Hello, Adam.' Standing side by side,

mother and daughter smiled at him then, as if she'd been expecting him, Rachel hurried round the counter and turned the sign to closed. 'I'm going to do some shopping, and afterwards I will call on Lily. I expect to be gone for sometime, so if you don't want to be disturbed, I suggest you lock the door after me,' she called, then with a knowing smile, was gone.

'While I'm at it, I think I'll pull down the blinds as well,' Adam said, then in the dimness of the shop, moved forward with his arms outstretched. 'Emily, my love, come here,' he murmured, and almost shyly, she walked towards him. Sensing a hesitancy in her, he kept his emotions firmly in check and he kissed her with a gentle tenderness: her hair, her lips, her cheeks, her neck. 'Oh Emily, my sweet one, I do love you. Do you love me?'

She linked her arms around his neck. 'Yes,' she answered simply.

'So, will you marry me?'

'I will. But we'll have to be patient or it will cause a scandal.'

Adam held her away from him. 'I've had a brilliant idea, let's really scandalise the town, finish what we started and run away to Gretna Green together.'

Emily giggled. 'Dare we?'

'Why not? We're free, we're adults and no one can come and haul us back this time.'

Drawn along by Adam's wild scheme, Emily clapped her hands excitedly. 'When shall we go?'

'Why not be completely mad and go this minute.'

'Without packing?'

'I have plenty of money. We can buy all the clothes we want on the way. And you shall have a splendid gown to be married in, and afterwards we will tour Scotland,' Adam promised.

'It would be a great adventure, something to tell our grandchildren.' Her eyes and cheeks glowing, Emily reached up and kissed him. 'Let's be on our way, then.'

'Just one thing, we mustn't forget your mother.' Adam searched around, found a pen and a piece of paper, then printed across it in large letters: 'GONE TO GRETNA GREEN. SEE YOU IN TWO WEEKS. LOVE ADAM AND EMILY.'

Suddenly aware of his responsibilities Adam gazed at Emily intently. 'Are you quite certain about this?'

'Absolutely.'

'Right, we'll sneak out the back way.' Adam held out his hand, Emily grasped it, then laughing and carefree as a pair of seventeen-year-olds, they ran down the street towards their future.

The publishers hope that this book has given you enjoyable reading. Large Print Books are especially designed to be as easy to see and hold as possible. If you wish a complete list of our books please ask at your local library or write directly to:

Magna Large Print Books
Magna House, Long Preston,
Skipton, North Yorkshire.
BD23 4ND

This Large Print Book for the partially sighted, who cannot read normal print, is published under the auspices of

THE ULVERSCROFT FOUNDATION